DEATH IN
THE RAIN

DEATH IN
THE RAIN

A NOVEL

Ruth Almog

Translated by Dalya Bilu

R·E·D
CRANE
BOOKS

SANTA FE

1993

Copyright © 1982 Keter Publishing House, Jerusalem.

Originally published in Hebrew as *Mavet ba-geshem* by Keter Publishing House, 1982.

Translation copyright © 1987. The Institute for the Translation of Hebrew Literature, Tel Aviv.

First English language edition, 1993, Red Crane Books.

Library of Congress Cataloging in Publication Data
Almog, Ruth.
   [Mavet ba-geshem. English]
   Death in the Rain : a novel / Ruth Almog : translated by Dalya Bilu.
     p.   cm.
   Translation of: Mavet ba-geshem
   ISBN 1-878610-09-0 (pbk.)
   I. Title
   PJ5054.A4972M313   1993   91-61530
   892.4'36—dc20   CIP

Cover design and painting and text design by Paulette Livers Lambert

Printed in the United States of America

Red Crane Books
826 Camino de Monte Rey
Santa Fe, New Mexico 87501

CONTENTS

PART ONE

Happy Are They That Sow

LICHT

Someone's ringing the doorbell. He won't go away. He keeps ringing the bell and yelling: Professor Licht! Please open the door! Please open up!

I don't know what to do. It must be panic, I suppose. With an effort I go to the door and ask who's there. My voice sounds strange in my own ears. I haven't heard it for a long time, and now it sounds like someone else's voice. But the voice on the other side of the door is a familiar one, and I feel somewhat reassured. Nevertheless I hesitate, as if I am about to commit some crucial, fateful act. The man urges me, he pleads with me, and I know that I won't be able to withstand his pleas. It's clear to me that I'm going to open that door. Even if I hesitate a second or two longer, to put the decision off, I'll open the door in the end. I'll open it because I want to open it, not because anyone's twisting my arm. After all, the man on the other side of the door isn't about to break it down and force his way in.

It's the neighborhood mailman. I've known him for years. For a moment it even seems to me that I've known him since we were both children, that we grew up together, along with all the ugly buildings that have grown up in this street which was once so quiet, with all the little houses that have gradually been demolished.

I remember, Noa was already a big girl (how old was she when we came to live here, ten or eleven?), and when we passed him in

3

the street he would stop and speak to her. Pull faces to make her laugh, as if she were a baby. He always had a packet of sour sweets in his pocket for the children, and they would run after him begging for another and another. Funny, it makes me think of the way we used to run after the ice cart, catching the splinters of ice that flew when the iceman chopped pieces off the block with his pick. And the way we used to suck and suck . . .

Forgive me for disturbing you, Professor Licht, he says, but things can't go on like this. Please understand. Your mailbox is already full. There's no more room. You have to open it and see what's inside it. Maybe there's something you should see, something important.

I am a tall man and the mailman is small and fat and there's something obsequious about the way he talks. His friendliness is forced. I think: he wasn't born that way. Humility is an acquired not an inherited characteristic. He must have acquired it during the war. Taking into account the fact that he survived. For all his affability, he must be a dangerous man. Anyone who came out of there alive has to know how to fight. I don't trust them, the ones who stayed alive. At the same time I realize that he's trying not to upset me. Maybe he's afraid of some kind of outburst. On the other hand, I say to myself, it's precisely his past that makes it easier for him than for anyone else to come knocking at my locked door. As if he and I now have something in common.

I've always treated him with kid gloves, not having any desire to drag myself to the post office every day. And now, for God's sake, I'm thinking of myself and this man, whom I loathe, as if we had something in common. But even as the thought occurs to me I realize I can't even guess at what he's been through.

When I don't answer, he recovers himself, as if drawing strength from my weakness, and orders me in a firm, even commanding tone to go fetch the key to the mailbox.

And I do as he asks, curiously eager to obey. As if this is what I've been waiting for all this time: for someone to come and tell me what to do, so that I can find a justification for doing something it might not really be right for me to do. Perhaps he, too, once found excuses in his own passivity and helplessness for doing things he shouldn't really have done.

I know it's ugly of me to suspect him. I know I have no right to judge him. It's my own self-doubt, my suspicions about my own morality, which lead me to find fault with others. You're a shit, Professor Licht, I say to myself. An unadulterated shit. And I snigger to myself at the thought that it's been years since I addressed myself by my first name, as if the Avigdor I once was is dead. And I say to myself, what a hypocrite you are. You always tried to be buddies with your students, but woe to anyone who dared address you without your academic title. You didn't waste any time putting him back in his place. And you weren't squeamish about the means you used to do it, either.

I follow the mailman downstairs and suddenly he stops and turns around and lays his hand on my arm in a friendly gesture. I shrink from his touch and pull my arm away. He says to me, Listen, you can't go on like this. Do you understand? It's impossible. He tries to smile at me, but only his mouth twists in a smile. His eyes are stern and hard. I know what it's like, he says, I've been through it myself, and worse. Of course you can't forget, but you have to go on. I say nothing and he shrugs his shoulders and turns back to the stairs. I say to myself: Who says you have to? If you don't want to, you know what to do about it, like my Noa. She didn't think there was any "have to" about it. . . .

The blinds in my apartment are down and the strong light that suddenly greets my eyes in the lobby dazzles me. There in the lobby, fixed to the wall, is my mailbox. Set apart from all the others, large, green, and bursting. I get a lot of mail, mainly professional. I have surprisingly few friends. No, there's nothing surprising about it. . . . I subscribe to journals from different countries, I am a member of various committees, organizations, I have colleagues and acquaintances all over the world who write to me from time to time. Which is why I need a particularly large mailbox. I open it and the letters drop into my hands, some of them fall onto the floor. Brown envelopes, large- and medium-sized—journals and invitations, letters from professional colleagues all over the world, perhaps from my brother who has wandered far afield, and a few postcards and bills. The mailman picks up a few letters, hands them to me and says good-bye. Before leaving he shakes my hand solemnly and says: Remember what I said. I'm talking from experi-

ence. You have to go on. That's all there is to it. And then he adds:
All the best. Just as usual. Just as if nothing has happened.

As with many lonely people who obtain their contact with
others through external events, the mail has always been a source of
comfort to me, and sorting and opening it was one of my pleasures.
Even at work I never allowed my secretary to deal with the mail,
reserving that pleasure for myself.

I return to the apartment and put the bundle down on the kitch-
en table. The yellow Formica surface is clean. I've always wanted to
change that table. I can't stand yellow. Yellow is the color of
madness. All Van Gogh's madness came out in yellow. But my wife
Leah liked this table which we bought when we moved into this
apartment. To her it was a symbol of the comforts we had done
without for so many years. After the war, she said, "Why don't you
stay in the army so we can save and get established?" But I wasn't
having any of that. "You find yourself a job in Jerusalem," I said,
"and I'll go back to school." And so for a few years we all lived on
her meager earnings.

In our rented room in Mishkenoth-Israel, our landlady looked
after Noa. It wasn't easy living under those conditions, with a
baby, too. Leah hated her job and agonized over the fact that she
was unable to devote herself to her baby as she longed to do. The
truth is that there was nothing good about our lives then, except
for my academic success and the marvelous, tall hollyhocks which
grew, in the spring, I think, in an empty lot at the edge of the
quarter. Later there was Oxford, and then Harvard, where Leah
wasn't happy either. No, she was never happy anywhere, the tem-
porariness frightened her. It was only here, in this apartment,
where we settled down at last after she persuaded me to come back
to Israel, that she was happy. And even though she was a woman of
some sophistication, it was Formica, not pine nor mahogany—
Formica of all things—that symbolized affluence for her. And why
not? It isn't really so surprising. She had seen plenty of wood where
she came from. Her childhood, her youth, had been passed among
heavy, old furniture. Formica stood for the new, the modern, the
different. Wood was something, perhaps, that she wanted to turn
her back on and deny, in order not to seem old-fashioned in her
own eyes. Yes, my wife Leah wanted to be a modern woman.

The table is clean. I eat little and keep things scrupulously clean. All this time I haven't had a bit of bread, although I've polished off all the rusks and other baked goods in the house. The painted tins where Leah kept the cookies and candies are empty. So are the jam and honey jars. All that's left are a couple of tins of sardines.

A siren wails in the street, a fire engine or ambulance. Maybe the police. I can't stand those sirens. My heart always skips a beat when I hear them. I feel a kind of panic and that shames me. When I was a young man I was fearless; we mourned the dead less then, too. There were so many dead, I don't think there have ever been so many dead. But we took it differently. Of course people grieved, but nevertheless it was different: this delicate, gnawing sadness—we ran away from it. But in recent years, so it seems to me, perhaps because I'm getting older, because I don't actually fight any more—and precisely now, after our great, unprecedented victory in the Six Days War—I've grown nervous, like everyone else. Perhaps it's because the nightmare has gone on too long. A kind of cumulative effect. And maybe it's since Noa went into the army. Hardly a day passes without its dead. The contractors make money and the young go to their deaths.

I hate sardines. I left them to the last. Because there's no bread and no crumbs there aren't any ants either. I know there are cockroaches, I can see them scurrying about here at night, big ones and little ones, harmless but disgusting. Sometimes I manage to kill a few of them, heroically overcoming my revulsion, but it doesn't do any good. There's nothing for it, I'll have to spray even though I can't stand the smell. Leah never sprayed when I was at home, but sometimes when I got back the house was still full of the stifling nauseating smell. My irritation then was uncomfortable and Leah didn't know how to appease me. She was obsessed with cleanliness and D.D.T. was her ally.

I'll have to get someone to fumigate the apartment. I'll have to go out and do the shopping. The supplies of food my daughter, Noa, shopped for have run out. Perhaps I'm trying to starve myself to death, like Gogol in his insanity? But I'm not mad, nor am I a genius, although I liked to think so once, and used that as a ploy in my seductions. All I really am is an old magpie, a moldy bookworm. And I don't want to die. I've had plenty of time to think about it, and I'm incapable of condemning myself to death. I can't even do that. Even now I'm still capable of thinking about young girls. . . . An old lecher, that just about hits the nail on the head. No, not yet old. Only aging. An aging lecher who decided for his sins to sit down and write a book. . . .

No bills, water, electricity and telephone bills. The municipality apparently has forgotten me. Or perhaps Noa paid for the whole year in advance. A few statements from the bank. Invitations to exhibitions which perhaps, which certainly, have already closed. Nothing interesting. An invitation to an international congress. An invitation to deliver a series of lectures in Rome. Oh, to meet a pretty girl in Rome, a pretty girl carrying a heavy suitcase in the street in Rome. I offer to help. A mild flirtation ensues, nothing serious, no commitments. . . . Am I really still capable of thinking such thoughts? A letter from my brother in Australia: Happy are they that sow and do not reap, for they will wander far. He lost both his sons and left the country. He couldn't stay here. I understand him, I've always understood him. Scientific publications, a few journals, and a letter from Greece. And a notice from the post office to come and collect a parcel. Also from Greece.

When Leah died a lot of people came to offer sympathy, and we sat, my daughter Noa and I, all day long in the living room on improvised stools. People came and went, they spoke to us and we answered them. Sometimes we even smiled. Acquaintances of mine, colleagues, relatives, even distant ones who suddenly remembered our existence, neighbors, friends of Noa's. Even the mailman came and said, May the Lord comfort you. He sat for a few minutes, taking a packet of sour sweets out of his pocket and offering them to Noa as if she were a little girl. He didn't offer them to me. Grownups don't need sweets. In the evening we would lock the door, Noa or I, pull down the blinds each in our own room and go to sleep.

Noa prepared our meals. One of her friends did the shopping and almost every day the supermarket would deliver a crate full of cans, bottles of juice and oil, eggs, cookies, and chocolate, as if war was about to break out. (I was surprised, but I never asked Noa what she thought she was doing.) Noa dusted the furniture and the pictures every day and swept a feather duster over the books. She showered faithfully every morning and her scent invaded the rooms of the house like some intruder. Whenever I went abroad I used to bring her a bottle of scent, the best and most expensive. She collected the bottles like a child and displayed them on the shelf above her bed. In the summer she used the light, slightly sharp scents by Weil, and in autumn she preferred the Dior. Winter and spring, she used the heavy, dominant scents of Guerlain.

I noticed that every day the garbage can was full of her old exercise books and torn up pages of writing. She was throwing out things that were precious to her, too, things from her childhood that until now she had refused to be parted from. Even the yellow teddy bear I brought her from England, the one she used to take to bed with her. Noa, who found it so difficult to part with her possessions, was ridding herself of all her treasures. Every year before the Pesach spring-cleaning, there used to be violent arguments, with Leah insisting that she throw out some of her rubbish and Noa refusing. One day I said to her, When your mother was alive you kept all this junk to annoy her, now you don't want it any more. What a fool I was. What an ignorant fool. On the seventh day after my wife died, I went back to work. Later we put up a gravestone and everything seemed to return to normal. And one morning, a few months after Leah left us, I found her dead on her bed. My daughter, Noa.

ELISHEVA

"All the lonely people. Where do they all come from. Where do they all belong. . . ." A gentle song, capable of piercing the heart and melting some melancholy there. I like this song and other Beatles' songs, too. But at full volume, in a closed bus? What's happened to everybody? Are they all deaf? How can they stand the noise?

And if you complain to the driver you'll get nothing but rudeness for your pains, abuse and insults in front of everybody. God save us from these drivers. I'll never forget how the driver once shut the door on my elbow when I was getting on the bus. There was no

queue and the bus wasn't full. I was the only passenger waiting at
that stop. But he parked the bus in the middle of the street, yards
from the stop, and I had to run after it. He must have been in a
hurry, perhaps he had a girl waiting for him at the end of the line.

The loud, blaring music, suddenly shocking my ears, the
elegiac "Eleanor Rigby"—a song which should be played softly—
shook me, and detached me from the vague, painful pictures which
had been passing through my mind on the journey, like distant
flashes of lightning. One after the other I pushed them away, yet
they kept coming back. And then came the music that stopped the
tears which had welled up despite my efforts to suppress them, and
I saw that we had arrived in Tel Aviv. Black holes gaped at me like
monstrous jaws from the entrances of the buildings, their broken
windows displayed against their sooty walls like a memorial to some
holocaust, their facades rotting and the plaster falling from their
balconies to expose the rusty pipes beneath: a shameless striptease
in broad daylight. And the wrought iron balcony railings—a
popular art form, these vestiges of past beauty—now crooked and
rusty, here and there half torn from their foundations.

In the midday sun, the heat of the winter's day, the harsh light
underlined the ugliness. The driver's radio pounded in my
temples: "Eleanor Rigby waits at the window, no one comes near."

I took an aspirin from my bag and swallowed it dry. I would
have climbed off the bus right there and found something to drink
at a kiosk, but I was far from home and my feet were swollen with
weariness.

Why are my countrymen so callous and inconsiderate of
others? Is it the climate, or a secret legacy from the Turkish Sultan? I
don't dare to think the Diaspora is the cause. Nowadays such a
thought smacks of sacrilege.

Why did I go there? To meet what need? Why did he pretend
not to recognize me? Or perhaps he really didn't? Perhaps his
eyesight has deteriorated. He's grown older, too. Perhaps it was the
changes which have taken place in me. . . .

On the outskirts of Tel Aviv the images left me and the nagging
questions took their place. I didn't want to answer them. As I
always do, I escaped from them into the landscape, into the now, to
distract myself from the past, and the future.

Yanis once drew my attention to this. He said: "You didn't

choose to be a landscape architect by chance. An architect who builds houses can't afford to think only about external things, he has to pay attention to human needs. But you—you escape into the outside world. You say you like being an observer. And I believe you, of course. But your interpretation is wrong. You're simply escaping from yourself."

How could I explain to him that it was the wounds which refused to heal that forced me to escape into the world outside?

There was a traffic jam in Chlenov Street, but a motorbike managed to cleave its way through the rows of cars inching forward and hooting helplessly. When you're alone you can race full speed ahead.

The driver leaned back and waited patiently. It was always the same here, almost every day at this hour. He was accustomed to it, but I felt my impatience rise. The car in front of us spurted ahead and then braked. The bus driver waited indifferently, the music blasting. What must it be like to be assaulted every day by engine noise and screeching brakes? Life grinds us to dust, I thought, one way or another.

No. I don't understand why I went there. What for. Yesterday, out of the blue, P. passed me in the street. He didn't even greet me. He didn't recognize me. Or maybe he was pretending. I wanted to run after him, say something to him. How my heart trembled. But I went on walking, memories whirling. Why didn't I stop, why didn't I follow him? He would have stroked my hair and said, Your hair's hard, you're still using the same shampoo, you're still as flirtatious as ever. The way he used to. And as he spoke to me, in this chance, unwished-for encounter, I would have been able to remember the rough, hard hand which had once stroked my hair, filling my body with an inexpressible serenity.

But I didn't follow him, and all the way home I was accompanied by heavy, burning, even insulting thoughts. And when I got home I opened this diary and read it. For years it's been gathering dust, in this drawer, in others. I used to take it with me everywhere, read it rarely, write in it sometimes. Sometimes I would sit on a bench in the avenue and write, or in a café, or even in a bus. On every page the handwriting is different, but the pathos everywhere repels me, and when I come back to it I read the end and not the beginning. I feel ashamed. I was so young when I began to write there, I no longer remember why. . . . All those appeals to the man I called Pierre: Your eyes are narrow as slits, my dear. I see them laughing at me and I lower my eyes to your lips—rather pale lips, flat and broad. . . . An accurate description, but I feel nothing but emptiness as I read: I don't kiss them, only touch them with my lips. Breathe in the air you breathe out, the smell of tobacco and the dry, gingerish taste of your skin, and I know an unimaginable sweetness, the sweetness of oblivion, the joy of a yearning streaming towards extinction. And you can't understand. A man with a lust for life.

The things I wrote have become as foreign to me as if they were written by another woman, and it seems to me as I read, that today I am closer to him in a number of ways, that I share the indifference and bemusement that the young girl I was then gave rise to in him. Nevertheless, I went there today. What for? To meet what need? To put flowers on a white stone with a name and initials I never bothered to decipher. I walked and walked and walked, yellow sand as far as the eye could see. Rows and rows of white stones. And I walked down the paths between the stones, seeking for a place to lay my flowers. Flowers. What for? To meet what need?

Why did I respond to that futile, foolish impulse? Why have I resumed writing in this old copybook? Filling page after page, writing like Yanis, who is dying. Alone. Sitting shut up in his house in Kefissia, looking out of the window perhaps. And writing, writing. And like Alexander, writing letters, like Alexander who lost everything. Yanis once said to me: "It's an obsession with him. He's an obsessed man. Has he really lost everything? I don't know. Perhaps he kept his rage. And his rage feeds him like the air feeds the flames. . . ."

Because of the traffic jam, and my wish to escape, I took pen and paper out of my bag—I always keep notepaper in my bag. It's an old bag, full of papers, candy wrappers, receipts, notes. I'm so disorganized, always putting things off. Yanis bought me this bag in Florence; it lost its shape over the years, but I like the feel of its soft leather, its shabbiness, its creases. I wrote rapidly for the rest of the journey, recording everything I saw through the window, keeping my thoughts at bay.

♦

Yesterday I saw P. in the street and today I didn't go to work. I called and said that I was sick, and I lay in bed for another hour. Then I got dressed and went out. At the flower stall on the corner I bought a few narcissi, and with a compulsiveness I cannot understand I got on the bus and went to the cemetery. I didn't give myself a reason for what I was doing, and now, too, I can't explain why I went there. I don't think about Michael much. I've put away his pictures and I've almost forgotten what he looked like. I forbade myself to sink into mourning and I locked his memory away in the dark, dim little room and never opened the door again. When I arrived there I didn't even know how I would find the place. After burying him, I never went back. And the truth is that even now I don't really want to think about him. Better to think about Leon, who died sometime this week, or about old Mr. Kleinman.

My neighbor, old Mr. Kleinman the tailor, whose little workshop has a concrete floor and whose sewing machine is forty years old, loses his temper when he sees a lavatory seat abandoned in the street. The veins on his thick neck swell under the transparent skin hanging raggedly there, and he says through clenched teeth: "Elisheva, Elisheva, everyone's gone mad here. When they came to this country they worked the land and wore blue shirts or khakis, and now they throw into the street whole bedroom suites they bought a year or two ago. They haven't learned to read, they don't know the Torah, but they're all experts at stealing. Tell me, Elisheva where does all the money come from if not from stealing? They steal as much as they can, from the income tax or the poor. You tell me, is this what we dreamed of, this? . . ." When he calms down he pulls out from somewhere in a pile of rags—the remnants left over when he cuts the cloth—a collection box for charity, in the name of Rabbi Kalonymus the Miracle Worker, or Rabbi Shimon Bar Yochai, and he holds it out to me and says: Drop a few pennies in the slot and God will bring you luck, so you'll find a husband at last. And hesitantly he adds: I know someone, a widower, a good man, he earns a good living, perhaps. . . .

When I pass his little workshop I stop to ask him how he is and he always asks me tactfully: Perhaps you're short of money, perhaps you need something. Don't be shy, you can return it next week. And sometimes I really do need money, and when he gives it to me and I thank him he says: Don't thank me, that smacks of interest. Give it back when you can. For me it's a *mitzva*.

This morning I saw a notice of Leon Dantes' death in the paper. Yes, Dantes, like the hero of the Count of Monte Cristo, an adventure story for the young. And Leon was a hero in his own way, his life an adventure story the details of which I shall never know. In life, he was far from my heart. And now I think of him with affection and longing.

Leon died in a distant land, alone, in a rented room, among strangers. He probably never managed to call for help and he suffocated slowly, stumbling astounded about his room, his lungs too constricted to give birth to a cry. I think I'll go and see his mother. . . .

ALEXANDER

Dear Yanis,

This is Alexander writing to you. I'm sure you'll be glad to hear that I've been better lately. I'm already allowed out from time to time. I'm sitting in a café in Dizengoff Street in Tel Aviv and writing to you. You may be surprised to hear that I'm writing to you from a café of all places, but you have to understand that I'm not used to coming into contact with people yet. Sitting in a café without doing anything embarrasses me a bit. So I hide in this writing paper. It shields me from my surroundings. Perhaps I'm not explaining myself too well. I confess that I've already forgotten how to write a letter. Actually, I never knew. It was never my strong point. Who knows better than you. Before, when I was sick, I wrote to you often, but I destroyed everything I wrote. This time I intend on putting the letter in an envelope, stamping it, and sending it to you. Some people I know are sitting at the table next to me and I'm listening to their conversation. I like being here, in this café, where I can listen to conversations and never be really lonely. Someone always turns up, alone like me, and sits down and starts talking, and in that way contacts are created. Tenuous contacts, but

I don't need any more. Since I began coming here I've made a few friends. One called Carmela, for instance, quite a nice girl. She even invited me round to her place. Next week, she said, on Monday, it's her birthday and she's having a dinner party. And I'm invited. Encouraging, don't you think?

It's crowded here. A warm winter's day with the sun shining, and everybody comes out to sit here and warm themselves, rub shoulders with one another. So it's crowded today. The people at the next table are talking about someone called Leon Dantes, who just died. In Athens, apparently. Did you know him? They say that for the past year he was living in Athens and making a living by giving guitar lessons and teaching English. They snicker as they talk about him, and there's something obscene about that. He didn't know how to play the guitar, someone says and laughs. He didn't know English, someone else says. And they split their sides laughing. When they recover someone says, He didn't know anything. And they all laugh again. It's beginning to annoy me. The man's dead and they aren't ashamed to laugh at him.

The name, Leon Dantes, sounds familiar to me, but I can't remember where I heard it. It seems to me that he was an acquaintance of your Elisheva's. Listen, there's a chap at that table who doesn't stop cursing and bad-mouthing the country. I'd like to go over there and punch his ugly mug. But I can't afford to be violent. My freedom is too precious to me. That stupid creature is announcing to his pals that there's no respect for culture and the theater here, that a serious artist hasn't got a chance. But France, on the other hand, is an enlightened country where you can succeed. He says that the only people who prosper here are building contractors, and culture hasn't got a hope. I have to say that he himself doesn't make a particularly cultured impression. I think about all the people who never stop complaining about this country and its lack of culture, about how provincial they are themselves. About how all their complaints are rooted in their provinciality. What do you think? I'd be interested to know if it's the same in Athens, if people there carry on all the time about the inferiority of their own city in comparison to Paris, London, New York, or if they know how to respect the place they come from. You know, Yanis, that I'm not against criticism. And don't misunderstand me. I look at him, and I can see how angry he is. Maybe he's drunk. Somehow he gives rise to more pity than anger in me. Small people always look elsewhere for what they're never going to find anywhere anyway. There's something very strange about him, a phenomenon I'd like to research, it really tempts me. Have you ever seen hands where the ball of the thumb is red, blood red? But only the ball of the thumb, on the palm, not at the back of the hand. It's almost the color of raw liver, bright red. It's interesting. Must be something genetic. Maybe the capillaries are too close to the skin. Maybe the pores are abnormal, maybe it's a symptom of some disease.

Yes, Yanis, things of that nature still interest me. Next to the possessor of the red palms is quite a young man with a little body and a huge head. That's an interesting phenomenon, too. Typical of Germans, not Jews. In general, the Northern peoples have big heads, whereas the Mediterranean people's heads are relatively small. Like me, for example, and you, too.

And you, Yanis, what are you doing with yourself nowadays? Have you found a job? When we parted you said that you wanted to teach, you'd had enough of laboratories, you said. I suppose that people with your knowledge are needed in your country. And so—are you teaching?

There's an actor sitting there, too. I can't remember his name but you know him, making propaganda for Transcendental Meditation. He's trying to infect them with his enthusiasm, but no one's paying any attention to him. He's offering them salvation, a refuge from all the agonies of the soul. But they don't care. It always amuses me the way people never despair of salvation. A few years ago everyone was into yoga, or Feldenkreis, or the Alexander method. Now there's a new fashion. I've read about it, of course. Believe me, it's all nonsense.

Yanis, have I ever told you about my Chinese garden? A few years ago, when Henrietta was still alive, I had a Chinese garden. I planted miniature paper flowers in it, flowers I made myself out of colored crepe paper. You know what? They couldn't stand my Chinese garden on the kibbutz, and they destroyed it. And today the place that was once so pretty is desolate, and the wind blows over it day and night. But I shouldn't be thinking about it. In the institution they put a lot of effort into making me forget my garden, and they almost succeeded. (They don't use Pentothal, thank God. They've got different methods. No less violent, actually.) There are times when I don't remember it at all. And when I do remember, I can think about its loss quite calmly. But now I feel sorry. Perhaps because of the talk about Leon Dantes at the table next to me. The way they talked about him, a sneering kind of way, reminded me of the attitude of the people on the kibbutz. The same tone. But I don't want to think about it now. It's no good for me to look back. It's dangerous for me. So I'll stop now, and maybe tomorrow when I come and sit here again I'll write and tell you about it without sorrow, and it will be alright. Write to me. I want to know how you are and what you're doing. Good-bye.

Yours,
Alexander

LICHT

When my daughter Noa died only a few people came. Even the mailman didn't come. And when the phone rang it always turned out to be a wrong number. They stayed away because of the embarrassment and the difficulty, I suppose. In fact, I'm sure of it, it's a well-known fact. People aren't afraid of the leper, they ostracize him because he is inconsolable. And since there is no way to console him, his distress gives rise to feelings of guilt in the hearts of his fellows, as if they were in some way responsible for his condition. And if you like, they really are responsible. Because if everyone had leprosy, the leper would be no different from anybody else. After all, it is the nonleper who identifies the leper as such. I know that this is all very theoretical, and I also know that what I'm saying is an oversimplification. But there is no profundity about these things. They're simple. The simplest things, the most uncomplicated, disconnected things, are the ones that it's impossible to talk about. There's nothing to say about them, just as there's nothing to say about a dot.

But you can talk about a line or a combination of dots, like in Seurat's paintings, for example. There's plenty to say about Seurat, you can devote a chapter in a book to him. But if someone comes along and puts a dot, never mind what color, as long as it's visible, on an empty canvas, he'll be doing something problematic. It will be possible to talk about his action and explain its problematic nature, but about the dot itself? What is there to say about a dot? People professionally involved in the field, like me, will have a lot to say about the whole affair, and most of what they say will be completely arbitrary, however serious and even portentous it sounds. They'll construct an entire philosophy on the act of placing a dot on a blank surface and its meaning. Okay, I can live with that, but I must stress once more that about the dot itself there is nothing to say. In art, ironically enough, an act of this kind takes us back to the primeval state, when man attributed far more significance to the scratching of an animal picture on the wall of a cave than to the picture itself. The act was a magic act, an act of invocation, and that was the crucial thing.

In any case, there was no need to go out anymore, and gradually it became clear to me that the sucking mud of the soul, a mud I spent so much time wallowing in, has no depth. Like the dot. In itself it has no meaning. Only the wallowing in it has a certain meaning. In vain I cast net after net and came up with nothing.

At night, memory died. Astonishingly enough, I slept well. No bad dreams came to haunt me. And in the bedroom where I slept, in the Formica wall closet (another status symbol from other years, which we may later have been ashamed of, except for the fact that nobody came into our bedroom), summer dresses and winter dresses hung next to coats and skirts and silk lace blouses. There was one drawer full of shoes and high-heeled sandals from Italy (I bought them for her, she had small, narrow, well-manicured feet) another full of elegant leather bags (she relied completely on my taste), and jewel cases with cultured pearls and glass beads and scarfs and kid gloves, white and black and brown (I liked her to be quietly elegant). . . . She had class, my wife Leah. She dressed well, went to the hairdresser (not one of the most expensive ones) once a week to have her hair and nails done, kept fit (every morning she went to swim in the pool), and smeared her face with all kinds of creams, although her makeup was very discreet, nothing exaggerated. A handsome, cold woman. She never changed her perfumes like my daughter Noa. She had one perfume for all the seasons of the year, sweet and heavy, Madame Rochas, and in a certain sense it suited her, although she was an outdoor type, the kind of woman who liked wearing well-cut suits and tailored coats, and a light, fresh scent would have suited her better. But the scent she chose was more compatible with her philosophy of life than with her appearance—a serious, puritanical woman, and at the same time secretly, perhaps unconsciously, provocative. Men would turn their heads to look at her, but I doubt whether any of them ever tried to make it with her. No, it's inconceivable that she ever had a lover. . . . And in the room next door, in the closet covered with posters and brightly colored wallpaper, more dresses, summer dresses and winter dresses. Did Noa ever actually wear dresses? Very rarely. She usually wore jeans and embroidered Arab kaftans, which became fashionable after the occupation and looked like rags, and flowered blouses and t-shirts, and Indian blouses and flat shoes and sandals and Swedish clogs and bags made out of woven fabrics, or canvas, big and shabby, and socks, and oriental jewelry, and lots of woolen and silk scarves. Noa's taste was youthful, a little loud, too bohemian for my liking. . . .

Bank statements, electricity and water and telephone bills, invitations to exhibitions, journals and scientific publications, and a letter from my brother in America—"Happy are they that sow and do not reap, for they will wander far. . . ." (Why do I keep coming back to this bitter verse?) I understand him and I feel sorry for him, but I don't love him. There's a roughness and a crudeness about him that I can't stand. Saul, my first born brother, all our lives you were the first, and for all my successes I never succeeded in usurping you. And unlike the case of Rebekah, our mother preferred you to me, even though I was the gifted, successful, brilliant one, and perhaps precisely for that reason.

And a letter from Greece too, according to the stamp. And a notice about a parcel, also from Greece. The address on the airmail envelope is written in a fair, clear hand with a fountain pen, in blue ink, a neat, hard hand, but definitely feminine. I don't know the handwriting, at least I can't remember it. A letter from Greece without a return address. Who could be writing to me from there? Sending a parcel? I don't know anyone in Greece. I rack my brains.

No, I definitely don't know anyone in Greece.

Now there's a big mess on the table. I collect the empty envelopes and the obsolete invitations and throw them in the overflowing garbage pail. An appalling smell rises from it. Hastily I close the cupboard door. In a little while I'll go downstairs and empty the pail. Then I'll go to the grocery store and buy a loaf of bread, butter, and a bottle of milk. Is there anything I fancy in particular? Bitter green olives, perhaps. Why bitter green olives of all things? How banal to say that these crushed, bitter olives, broken and wounded, more than anything else, symbolize Israel. Bitter, hard, and nevertheless appetizing and tasty, if you're used to them. It's connected to my childhood, of course. The cosmopolitan Professor Licht, at home in the wide world, but still a lousy *sabra*. All I have to do is open my mouth to give myself away, despite my almost perfect English accent. You can't get rid of the roughness, even if you polish it up in Oxford or Harvard. Which is the reason, one of the reasons, that I can't stand my brother Saul. I see my own image reflected in him and I don't like it. It's disagreeable to think that all my sophistication hasn't helped me much. I was and I remain a lousy *sabra*, a bitter, green olive.

In this sense Leah was very different, which is why I was so attracted to her. In her house, a house which was always full of Arabs, where all the members of the family spoke fluent Arabic, there was a kind of European atmosphere, that quality which I so envied and yearned for as a boy and a young man. They spoke Arabic, but also French. They knew the Arabs intimately, and visited the surrounding sheiks as Levantine "notables" in their own right, but they studied in France. They absorbed something there, and passed it on from father to son. They went on playing the role of the Baron de Rothschild's agents long after the "Palestine Jewish Colonization Association" was a dead letter. And there was nothing artificial or theatrical about it. It was in their blood. They respected themselves and their own past, although they were hated and rejected, and they continued to employ Arab labor in the teeth of the indignation of their neighbors. As for my father, he wouldn't even allow the Arabs to pick our olives. At the end of summer they would come down from the hills, whole families would come and invade the colony's yards to shake the branches of the olive trees and gather the fruit. But my father would never let them into our yard. We gathered the olives from our trees ourselves, and my mother would pickle them in tins, just like they did. Later we would sell them to the grocery stores. The profit was small—olives weren't a big deal in those days, not like today, when we pay a lot of money for olives, and prefer the imported kind—the big olives from Greece. Nobody picks the olives that grow in their yards anymore and the trees that grow on the edges of the pavements shed their fruit on the asphalt, or on the big concrete paving stones for passersby to trample on. Who would have guessed that a day would come when we would think of olives as something that made a mess on the pavements? What did the early artists of Eretz Israel paint but olive trees? Olive trees and more olive trees.

I need my head examined, I do—escaping to thoughts of olives and olive trees, of an Eretz Israel which no longer exists. I wish that I was really crazy, crazy about olives. I would walk the streets shouting: Olives, olives, preserve the olive trees! A harmless lunatic with the capacity to escape from his own head. Like that woman in Jerusalem who used to walk the streets with a little flag crying: Connect to the One! She did no harm to anyone and she was at peace with herself.

Sorting the mail, I leave the letter from Greece to one side. I don't feel like opening it. What I really feel like doing is driving up to the Galilee, to some small, out of the way place, a place where they still gather the olives from the trees. Is there anywhere like that still left in Israel? I doubt it. But if there is, I would like to see how people live there. It's years since I drove around the country. I was too busy with my travels abroad, advancing my career. Most of the people in this country are divorced from the natural landscape. They live in the cities and suffocate.

Things have changed, my son, my father would say to me at the end of his life, watching a new landscape grow up around our house, strange and alien to him. He refused to sell. But we, Saul and I, sold it as soon as he was dead. There was no point in hanging on to the land, the house. The place which was once ours was wiped off the map. The place which formed me disappeared, and I myself grew remote from the country landscapes. I forgot the blue mountains on the horizon, the olive groves. . . .

Nowadays people sit cooped up in the cities and suffocate. On holidays they go out to the forests and have picnics. They take charcoal and tripods and spits and look at the landscape through the haze of smoke from their campfires. When they go home they leave their litter behind them. Truly, there's nothing to wonder at in what's happening today. When people lose their ties to the land they grow corrupt. Inevitably, they grow corrupt.

I steal a glance at the envelope I set on one side. A neat, clean handwriting. It reminds me a little of my Noa's handwriting. She left a letter, but she didn't honor me with an explanation. She claimed the right to do what she liked with her own life, she apologized, she said that I was a strong person and that I would get over it without any difficulty, since the only thing I'm really interested in is my work, or rather, the main thing—apart from girls of her age. . . . How did she know? Why should she have cared? What did it have to do with her? She was my daughter, not my wife. Did I ever question her about her boyfriends? And when I didn't like them, did I ever interfere? Did I even say one word? Ah, the girls, the girls! So many, and not even one love. Yes, she wished me success, and hoped I would write a lot of books, and she expressed no regrets or contrition.

Take the Formica, for example. I despised Leah for liking Formica, but now I think that there was a kind of inner logic in it. A solid kind of logic. This new material is light, washable, clean—a metaphor for comfort and progress. No, it's got nothing to do with provincialism. I needed to see it that way to prove my superiority over my wife, whose family's home had been furnished with oak, full of style and so very French. I had to prove my superiority, after she had supported me for so many years, after I had already lost all interest in her, because she came from an aristocratic family and I was the son of poor people.

No, I was never really interested in her, in her inner life, not really. Now, too late, I realize it. I was never close to either of them. I was too busy with the publications I churned out one after the other: the relationship between the architecture of popular housing and Op-art; the Gothic influence in the painting of El Greco; the emotional life as a key to formal perception; the Spanish ele-

ment in Picasso and Dali; the trauma of birth in modern painting. . . . To be brilliant! To shine!

And my wife and daughter were almost strangers, a convenient
background for me to shine against—passive, obedient, quiet. For
both of them were very quiet women, my wife Leah and my
daughter Noa. Like Jacob, however, I loved not Leah but Rachel.
All my life I've loved Rachel, the legendary, inaccessible Rachel, a
woman seen in a dream, the woman I've never met.

What a banal man I am, like all the others who love no one but
themselves—for what is the meaning of these longings for the inaccessible, the impossible, if not a disguise for self-love, for the narcissism which prevents you from loving anything outside yourself?
This Rachel, instead of whom you were given Leah, what is she but
a figment of your imagination, something taken from your own
flesh and bone? And not taken out either, surgically removed like
Adam's rib, but left inside you forever, inseparable and undifferen-
tiated from the rest of you.

Perhaps this is the correct interpretation of the myth of
Orpheus's descent into the underworld—a narcissistic descent into
the depths of the self, in order to find there the Eurydice he really
wanted to lose in the first place. An idea worth developing. Yes,
definitely an interesting idea. I should make a note of it. It could be
the point of departure for a whole new view of art, showing how it
grows from purely narcissistic sources and leading to a better
understanding of the artist.

Fantastic! You're a genius, Professor Licht! And, on the other
hand, we have the androgynous creatures cut in two, who are the
rest of humanity. Did Noa die because she never found her second
half? I don't know. I don't know anything about my daughter
Noa. True, I sometimes noticed that she seemed depressed, and I
even asked her why. But I was always satisfied with meaningless,
evasive answers, because I've never had the patience to listen to
others. I'm insulted when people don't give me their full attention, and I like talking myself, but I haven't got the patience to
listen. Actually, I hardly ever have conversations with people,
listening to them is such an effort. I listened to the clever ones, of
course, because I could profit by it. Yes, I always knew how to
extract the maximum enjoyment or profit from others. But the

moment they came too close, I shook them off.

I never sensed any dangerous chasms in Noa, nor did I feel the least curiosity at the sight of mother and daughter solemnly discussing God knows what. In my eyes Noa always remained the cute little girl I occasionally took for a walk in the park, pushed on the swing, fetched home from kindergarten once or twice when my wife was sick. I'm a conservative man. Or, to be more precise, an egoist, and I always believed that the care of children is the woman's task. A point of view, of course, which stems from the egoism of the male. But Leah took the same view, maybe because she didn't have a choice. My career came first, and it was her job to assist me as best she could. She effaced herself, at first for love, and later, perhaps, because she vicariously shared my ambition and prestige. There's no denying that she enjoyed entertaining important people in our home and clinging to her important husband's arm when she made her entrance into a room full of people. Besides, I was often away from home: travels abroad, courses, reserve duty in the army.

As I've said, Leah was an aristocrat, heiress to an aristocratic family. Rare tropical trees grow in their garden, planted there by the founder of the family, the agronomist. You won't find anything like them anywhere else in the country. And if I keep harping on this subject, the reason is simply that this is the way I always think of her. Her forebears were estate owners, presented with their estate by the Baron, and French was their mother tongue. They sent their children to study in France. As for us—poverty stricken peasants, earning our bread by the sweat of our brows—the language we spoke at home was Hebrew, and we never hired an Arab worker in our lives, or a Bedouin washerwoman either. My father was a tight-fisted man who picked his own olives—how many olive trees did we have in the yard altogether? Four in all—and he made his living mainly working as an overseer on an orange grove, our plot being too small to support us. One of the last of the Second Aliya*, he was only a lad when he arrived in the country, and he used to speak reverently of Brenner and Gordon whom he met here in his youth.

---

* Second Aliya was the second wave of Zionist immigration to Eretz Israel, 1904-1920. The writer Brenner and philosopher A.D. Gordon were among the leading figures of the Second Aliya.

He hated the established middle-class farmers with a profound hatred. . . .

A few tomatoes to sell in the market in the summer, a few cucumbers, a few eggplants, a few chickens, a few eggs. A hard, bitter man, not to say savage, like the olives, like me, like my brother Saul. He planted olive pits in us with a blow of his fist, with a humiliating slap in the face. And my mother hoed the yard and planted vegetables, and did the laundry in giant black tubs, and baked bread in the clay oven my father built her in the yard. We lived like Arabs, and how could I ever have escaped from that god-forsaken place, a place which has been wiped off the map of the country, and made it to Oxford, to Harvard, but for the fact that my wife supported me and spurred me on.

But that's a lie too, of course. I'm the most ambitious man I know, single-minded and driven. It was my ambition that made me marry her in the first place, because she came from a rich family, a family it was an honor to marry into, an old family, a founding family, representatives of the Baron de Rothschild. What a load of crap! What importance does all this have today? My mother would always say (when my father wasn't listening): Marry into the rich, notable families, and benefit from their privileges. Then your lives will be better than ours.

Privileges! Once, when Leah's father was visiting an Arab sheik, one of the local notables, he was appalled when they served him his food in a white enamel chamber pot. In answer to his question, the sheik explained that they wanted to show him a mark of special respect: they all ate from a common dish but they wanted to serve him separately, according to the customs of the Jews, and so they had bought these new dishes in his honor. A chamber pot! Some honor! Some privilege!

I'm no different from my father. True, I read more books in a year than he read in his whole life, ignorant peasant that he was. But the essence is the same: the same egocentricity, the same single-mindedness, the same stinginess, the same values. He didn't know how to listen either. He never talked to us, he always gave orders, always preached. And of course he always knew better than anyone else. And although he himself never achieved anything, he always despised his fellows, found fault, sought out weak points.

And, in his eyes, the most important things were prominence, prestige, and riches—although he would never have admitted it, because he was an idealist, one of those who scorned possessions. And I resembled him in everything; I treated my own family exactly the same way that he treated us, tyrannically, humiliatingly. Yes, when I was at home I would shut myself up in my room. And Leah would see to it that Noa never disturbed me, God forbid, at my work. How irritable I was. I never had any patience with the screaming, bad-tempered little girl that she was then, and she learned to shut herself off from me.

My father was never aware of that fact that he took no interest in us. He was sure, like most fathers and mothers, that he fulfilled his role as a parent very well, and he really did work hard to support us. After all, you need a certain amount of subtlety in order to reach self-awareness.

And I didn't realize either, until recently, that I too am not really interested in people, not even in those close to me. I never realized that I exploited them, made use of them; I never admitted that the subjects of my research were far more important to me than the people really close to me. But I used them, I exploited them, too, without loving them. I admired some and wished to be like them, but it was really envy. Henrietta would sometimes say to me: "You lack all self-awareness." And I would be angry and offended. So young and yet bold enough to criticize me. "You've got a nerve," I used to say to her, "a little girl still wet behind the ears, what do you know about self-awareness?" And then she would laugh and throw me out. "Come back when you're capable of listening to what others have to say," she would tell me. But she was the one who would come back. Now that it's too late, it's absolutely clear to me that she was right. I hardened my heart against her, I didn't want to hear. But, really, what good could her words have done me? I wasn't ready.

I speak of the people who were really close to me. What does it mean, "really close to me"? Was I ever really close to anyone in my life? I'm not capable of closeness to others, of intimacy. I married Leah for reasons which had nothing to do with intimacy. When I was younger I believed that I loved her, and I honestly think that what I felt for her was the maximum I'm capable of feeling for anyone. And is it really possible to say that I didn't love Noa? I loved her in my own detached, uninvolved way. But she rejected me. She didn't want my love—in any case she never demanded it. Aren't I exaggerating here? Aren't I seeing things now in this light because I need to see them in this way, in order to torment myself, because only suffering, as it were, will atone? And in order for the suffering to be really severe you have to cultivate the guilt, nourish and cherish it like a baby, so that in the end, when it grows up and loses all its charms, you'll be able to rid yourself of it forever. . . . Isn't it all an elaborate game?

Why don't I open the letter from Greece? Don't I really know who wrote it? Can't I guess? Perhaps I can, but I'm afraid of the disappointment. It can't be possible that she's remembered me after all these years. It's simply wishful thinking. But it's definitely a woman's handwriting. And I know one woman who might conceivably write to me from Greece. Can it be she, the girl I once almost loved? I'm afraid that I'm falling back on romanticism in my despair. It simply doesn't make sense. It was only a short affair, it hardly meant a thing. I met her in the street a year ago and I ignored her, pretended not to recognize her, not to remember. . . . The truth is, I refused to remember. She'd grown old, lost her freshness. I didn't have the patience to stop, be friendly, smile, ask meaningless questions.

Like most people out for quick success, I usually made do with the kind of information that can be rapidly assimilated; historical processes seemed far more interesting to me than this or that individual life. A human life is complicated, understanding it demands painstaking labor, sensitivity, and, of course, involvement of an order I was never prepared to invest. When it comes to impersonal processes, it's easy to seem brilliant and make an impression. You can invent new terminology, like Sartre, for instance. All his innovations, in the end, are merely terminology. If you want to succeed you have to know how to make complicated statements about simple things; you have to know a little about a lot, and I was always an expert at that game. What does all my genius amount to, in fact, the genius I was always so proud of? You'll have to think again, Professor Licht, revise your attitude, experience love. Self-abandonment. Giving. Am I capable of devoting myself to another? Is it really possible to say that I didn't love my wife, my daughter, or even, for a short time, Elisheva—my first, gay, light-hearted affair with a girl who seemed to me the very incarnation of spring, of a blooming, angelic innocence—Botticelli's Flora? What a fool I've been! I think that I loved them in my own way, the way I loved all the girls who came after them. Selfishly, casually, without commitment. I loved them in the selfish, limited and uninvolved way of the egoist, of a man interested mainly in himself, and my wife indulged me and admired me, and so did Elisheva and so did all the girls who came after her. And the ones who showed no inclination to indulge and admire didn't interest me in the least. And when the love of others became oppressive, serious and deep, I shook it off without any compunction at all.

ELISHEVA

Carmela called. She's having a birthday party next week. She said, Do come, I'm making dinner, I've asked someone for you too. She laughed shrilly, a little hysterically. I met him at Kassit, she said. Quite handsome. A pipe-smoker. A bit too quiet for my taste. His name's Alexander. I'm sure you'll like him. He's just your type.

I think: Alexander. Alexander and Yanis and Henrietta and Pierre, whom I see before me now with exceptional clarity, wearing a white Irish sweater. A big, bearded man, a slightly ginger beard, sitting opposite me in a café, smiling at me with narrowed eyes, then bursting into loud, mocking laughter. I saw him yesterday in the street and he didn't recognize me. The pain, the gnawing pain.

I think I'll go and see Leon's mother. Leon grew up in an old part of Tel Aviv. What an open-hearted man he was. Whenever he returned from his wanderings he would come to visit me and talk without stopping, stammering, hurrying, swallowing his words. Delicate-limbed, sickly, his eyes black and burning, he seemed to me like a Spanish prince. He grew up not far from here, in a quarter which was suddenly, perhaps prematurely, stricken with old age. But he never felt at home here, and all his life he wandered from country to country with scribbled paper in his bag, with great dreams conceived by the restlessness in his frail, inconstant heart. I'm writing a novel, he would announce as soon as he arrived, pulling out of his haversack as proof a few crumpled pages, a child's exercise book or a tattered notebook. And the last time he was here he showed up with a guitar, the guitar he had learned to play late in life with fingers whose joints were already stiff, and which he believed would be his salvation. He bought it in Spain, and there he learned to play *fandangos* and *bulerías* and *alegrías* and *soleares*, trying to find expression for the gypsy soul seething in his breast—a soul confused with vague visions, incoherent, half-baked thoughts. He brought me a record of Rafael Farina's, "El Rey Gitano," and explained *flamenco* to me.

Leon Dantes was not close to my heart. I was glad when he came and glad when he left. I found it hard to listen to him: the persistent self-pity, the egocentricity, and mainly, perhaps, the confused thoughts always going round in circles. I have always preferred clear thinkers, without melodrama, people who shun the kind of dreams that are inherently vague and undefined. I was repelled by the tortuousness of Leon's thought: his hands were always damp as if from some inner fever; his speech was rapid, indistinct; he spoke from a boiling heart and infected his listeners with his own restlessness.

Leon was not really close to my heart. Then why am I thinking of him now? How can I explain this affection, this nostalgia? Is it because he kept his youth, his innocence? Yes, he really was ageless, and his face hardly changed as time went by, unlike the face of this town slowly being eaten away, the lovely poincianas in its avenues covered with soot and dust.

Leon Dantes had suffered from asthma ever since he was a child. He needed a different air, which he never found anywhere. When he was a child, the boulevards I drove through this morning swarmed with children, at night lovers sat on the benches, and boys and girls going home from youth movement activities would kick up a racket and disturb them. Now beggars sleep on the benches at night and the fine old houses are empty. Instead of people they house tills and safes and files ranged on metal shelves or in metal cupboards, full of insurance certificates and receipts. Nobody plays hide-and-seek in the deserted courtyards anymore. Once there was a piano in every salon here, and Viennese waltzes and Russian songs would burst out of the windows and invade the boulevards, strains of Chopin, of Schubert, of Mendelssohn. And in the evening you sometimes heard a mother singing her child a lullaby. The jacarandas shed their pale blue flowers and the wisteria climbed the walls of the houses, giving off intoxicating scents. If they dug a tunnel for a subway underneath the boulevards, then the lovers would be able to come back here, and with the offices gone, the children would come to play, and the fine old houses would fulfill their proper function again.

But instead of this, now insurance offices, and agencies for razor-blades, venetian blinds, sliding asbestos balcony shutters (a booming business), a laboratory for amateur photographers, a land registration office, lawyers, a gynecologist, an old cinema which never got around to putting in air conditioning and whose customers have gradually dropped away. It will probably be pulled down soon and replaced by a skyscraper, another bank, another insurance agency, offices, and a garage where that nice florist shop stands now.

I think about the old housing project for workers a little farther down the road and how it marks a moment of light in our history. The grass is still growing wild in the spacious yards, the trees are tall and green, jacarandas, brachychitons, kalistemons, grevilleas. A few flowers grow at the bottom of the crumbling limestone walls, and in one of these little houses there once lived an extraordinary woman called Devorah Baron, a sickly woman who enslaved her family to an illness which may have been imaginary. A writer whose books nobody reads anymore. Flaubert survived and Devorah Baron died. The French are faithful to themselves and we—what are we?

Leon Dantes did not live in this well-to-do neighborhood. He spent most of his childhood and youth in his father's little tobacco shop, not far from where they lived south of the boulevards, reading the books he borrowed from the school library or the municipal library in Montefiore Street, and serving the customers. He knew all the brands of tobacco and cigarettes and cigars, and he loved the aromas which filled the seedy little shop, where his father, an invalid, a dreamer, used to tell him about the magnificent villa of his youth in Spain, and the vast fortune he had left behind him in Salonika. Sometimes he would stroll with his mother along the boulevards, dying and blackened with soot, which I drove down today, and a breath of aristocracy in the air would stir his imagination and join the pictures he had woven from his books and his father's stories, and he would dream of his inheritance in Spain and Greece, the inheritance his father had promised him would be his one day.

With my head still aching from the Swingle Singers' Bach thundering against the metal walls of the bus, the memory of the sweet sounds Leon Dantes produced from his Spanish guitar echoes in my ears, the sound of sweet, strangled weeping and taut, vibrating strings. Once I went to pay him a visit and found several people sitting in his room, among them an aging Spanish dancer with a clown's face, his puffy, flabby cheeks pink as if they had been rouged and his eyebrows thick and black as if they had been painted on. And Leon took his guitar out of his case and plucked its strings with a heartrending sound, and the Spanish dancer with the weeping clown's face stood up to dance, and his steps were slow and noble, and his movements very proud, and his back very straight, and he danced before us, with his eyes closed, a dance he had once danced many years ago, long before he had gone into exile, in a little café where Lorca and his friends used to meet. I remember that I couldn't bear the sadness emanating from his body moving silently and slowly with small, barely perceptible steps, and I went away weeping. And afterwards, when Leon was no longer a child, after the soot had already eaten away the leaves of the trees like leprosy, and after he had already abandoned the dream of the brotherhood of the working class—for Leon in his youth was a fervent member of the Young Communist League—and after he had abandoned, if not entirely, the dream of his inheritance in Spain and Greece, and the dream of the novel which he never finished, and after he succeeded in escaping the clutches of his wife—a British aristocrat whose father turned him into a servant, forcing him to wash his car and guide the tourists, upon whom they depended for a living, around their stately home. . . . Then he took off on his travels again and left his now-widowed mother behind in the little tobacco shop, her eyes red with weeping, with weariness and age, his mother who yearned for grandchildren, and who never stopped sending him as much money as she could afford.

◆

Some cities age quickly, like women whose faces are always exposed to the sun. Here the damp sea air ages, disintegrates, wrinkles. In Greece they overcome this problem with whitewash, creating a cleanliness and a kind of beauty, too, by virtue of their rooted and aesthetic instincts. But we are nomads and our habitations show it.

Yanis has asked me to come to him, and I'll go. There is nothing to keep me here any longer. Maybe that's the answer to my question. The reason why I went there today. To say good-bye, to lay a few flowers on a stone and say good-bye. Yanis has sent me a ticket and there are no problems. If I knew Leon's address, I would go to his landlords and ask them how he died: a young man suffocating slowly. Tomorrow I'll go to the travel agent and make the necessary arrangements.

ALEXANDER

Dear Yanis,

Every day I sit here in this café and write to you. I suppress the wish to write about my Chinese garden, and when I finish the letter and realize that I've written things I shouldn't have, I tear it up and throw it away. I want to write about neutral things, things happening around me that have nothing to do with me, but once I start writing my pen pulls in a different direction. The truth is that the only thing I really want to write about is the Chinese garden. Today I can't restrain myself any longer, and I'm not only going to tell you about it but I've made up my mind to send you the letter, even though I know how dangerous it is.

I'll begin by saying that a few years ago, when my beloved, your beloved, Henrietta was still alive I had a little Chinese garden. I planted in it little paper flowers. I know that you were lovers. I always knew. The thought tormented me and it still does. What a fool I was to believe you. She never admitted it, of course. She swore that she'd never gone to bed with you. But I never believed it. She wasn't a virgin when I married her. I think she treated me disgracefully, that she deceived me. Before we got married, when I was courting her, she refused me, she evaded me, she never gave way. I wouldn't have been angry if she'd been honest with me, but she went on lying and you conspired with her to deceive me. I ask myself how you could have treated me so. After all, you were my best friend.

The place where I planted the garden is exposed today to every passing wind. By day the wind comes from the west, stealthily, with restlessness invisible to the naked eye. This west wind is cunning, like the frenzy that sometimes descends on the inmates of the institution where I have spent a number of years. Cunning like you, Greek that you are. Admit it, you made love to Henrietta behind my back. But at night the wind blows from the south, aggressive and undisguised, and the shifting of the sands is clearly visible. In this way, the dust of the earth has hidden my Chinese garden without leaving a trace, and in the same way, with the passing of time, the sand will cover Henrietta's grave far away from here, on the edge of the wilderness of Paren, and she will be forgotten. But we, you and I, will never be able to forget. The treachery stands between us and we won't be able to forget. I don't understand. If she loved you, why did she marry me? There must have been something perverse in her to do such a thing. Sometimes it seems to me that I can understand her despair, and I am able for a few moments, truly moments of grace, to forgive her. But I can't find the same forgiveness for you. A woman has needs and drives that we can't understand. But you're a man, and you were my best friend.

My garden. In imagination I often stand before this expanse of yellow sand. My eyes scan the desolate plain, but there is no sign to tell me where in days gone by I left many little plants made with my own hands; many paths marked by pebbles I gathered in the wadi beds; a number of central squares and a complex system of pipes which fed water to the fountains. My eyes encounter a little mound erupting from the plain, carpeted with soft waves of yellow sand. I draw nearer, kneel down, and carefully begin to clear the sand away. - I wonder if I really will find the remains of my garden here.

This hope stirs longings in me, which I try to ignore. But, although years have passed, I can still see my beloved Henrietta's bare feet sinking into the sand. I look at her, standing a little way off, watching me at work. Her voice reaches me, scolding me for concerning myself with trifles, and there is a note of hidden hostility in her voice. I reject her reproaches, turning my gaze away from her white feet standing in the sand, and my heart fills with resistance. Why can't she understand me? Nevertheless, I finally crawl towards her and cover her feet with the reddish-yellow sand, like a child playing on the beach, and I say, "Admit it, admit that you went to bed with him. Admit that he was your lover." Henrietta laughs, then she cries, the tears pour from her wonderful black eyes. But I don't soften. "Admit it, I say, admit that you went to bed with him." She says: "It's true that Yanis loved me. It's true that he came to visit us once a week. But he always slept in the kitchen, on the floor, on the bed I made for him on a mattress there. Ask Elisheva, she'll tell you everything." "Liar," I yell. "You and your girlfriend, too. She'd do anything to cover up for you. And maybe she doesn't even know, maybe you hid it from her. At night he slept on the kitchen floor, and what about the day, when Elisheva wasn't at home?"

What nuisances people are! Even when they're dead they keep on pestering you. So I hold my tongue. I refuse to argue with Henrietta. Her objections to my Chinese garden are incomprehensible to me, the childish caprice of a woman who is remote and hostile now, denying me her love on account of trifles.

I go on digging. All day and every day I dig. The sand is warm and rough on my fingers and it soothes me. I am careful of my nails, I hate it when dirt accumulates under them. At the institution they were always very understanding about my revulsion from dirt, and they let me wash several times a day. When we lived on the kibbutz it was impossible because of the water shortage, and I suffered dreadfully. I always felt the filth on my fingers. Always the same unsatisfied need. Every time I dug into her I felt the filth. And I thought, somebody has been digging here before me. My good friend Yanis Stefanides. And so it didn't worry me at all that she was dry as sand and screaming with pain.

But in my garden, when I dig in the sand, my mind is empty. I spend hours there and I never feel the time passing. Every now and then my hand encounters a little stone and my heart fills with hope. Then I pause a moment and postpone the joy. I drop the stone into a little bag I keep specially for this purpose. One day, when I reconstruct the garden, I'll need lots of stones. I'll need tiny sticks of wood, colored paper, delicate strips of cloth, silk and muslin, fine wire. From these things I'll make the flowers for the garden, the rockeries and the paths, there in the heart of the wilderness.

It doesn't matter what you do, as long as you do it with complete concentration. You taught me that secret. That way you'll find peace, you said. And so, I dig. On either side of me, mounds of earth rise slowly. From time to time, when I pause to rest, the suspicion that I am wasting my time reawakens in me. So I stop less often, and whenever I feel my knees beginning to hurt I shift my position. If this turns out not to be the place I'm looking for, I'll try my luck with another hillock. I have to find the remains of the garden. Perhaps I'll be able to restore it. Serenity comes to you when you're engaged in work of this kind, work which demands all your attention, complete concentration. And this, Yanis, is how I spend most of my time, absorbed in fantasies. No, I don't delude myself. I know they're fantasies. I try to make contact with people, I do all kinds of things, but I'm detached from them, they're quite external. Sometimes I feel detached from my own body, floating somewhere at a great distance from it, among the shifting sands, or in the institution, or in our room in Jerusalem. Don't misunderstand me, Yanis, I'm not talking about memories. I'm talking about life itself. For example, I'm sitting here now, in a café in Dizengoff Street in Tel Aviv, and I know exactly where I am, and still a clear voice comes to me, as if from vast distances a clear voice comes to me, like the sound of a bell breaking into the walls of an empty, abandoned house; like the church bells of a deserted village sounding over a vast snow-covered plain where a man walks in silence. A dull, metallic sound, like the announcement of the coming of expected guests, of fire, of death, of a great defeat or victory. The ringing reminds me of. . . . Here he comes, the man with the blood-red palms. He amuses me. He's drunk. I'll change my table now. I'll move closer to them and listen to their conversation. That's all for now. Good-bye.

Yours,
Alexander

PART
TWO

The Lucky
Flower

Magnolia: An ornamental tree of the Manoliaceae family, with large white flowers and hard leaves. Common in the temperate regions of eastern Asia, North America and southern Australia.

ELISHEVA

My manuscript is thick by now, because I bind the copybooks together. Soon morning will come. There's a dull milky light in the sky, the birds are singing, and I haven't slept yet. I came home at midnight. I was at Carmela's, and I told her about Leon. She remembered him vaguely, but the news didn't move her. When I came home I couldn't fall asleep. I tried to read and couldn't, and in the end I got up. The copybook was lying on the table. I leafed through it, and now I'm writing in it. I'd like to write a story. But it's all so personal, it's impossible for me to be objective, I'm still too involved. Perhaps in a few years' time. Nevertheless, I try for style and precision; and so my writing is no longer typical of a diary, which is more or less spontaneous. At the beginning I wrote freely, without design. Now I write with the thought that maybe one day these notes will serve as the foundation for some more solid structure. I'm well aware of the lie at the bottom of this kind of writing, which leaves some things out and invents others. The impulse is very strong, and so is the fear. I relive the events as I write, and, as I relive them, I interpret and mold them to my heart's desire.

On the way to Carmela's, in the lane I use as a short cut, suddenly I saw Henrietta's face before me. She smiled at me, a gentle, tender smile. It shone out of the depths of the silence of her white face, the stillness of her cheeks, transparent as twilight—a smile like a rosebud just opened to the sun.

I remembered Henrietta because of the magnolia tree growing at the end of the lane behind a high fence. Her wonderful black hair

39

piled all around, smooth and fine as a halo. One day Henrietta looked at me with her frank, unhesitating look. She said: "You've changed, Elisheva. You've lost your sweet doll face. I'm glad, that sweetness didn't suit your character. You used to look like a doll, but you were never in the least like that."

I ask myself why I should have attributed malice to Henrietta. But perhaps I misunderstood. She wasn't bad, she never made fun of people, but nevertheless she said those things to me. And afterwards, when she saw my embarrassment (we hadn't met for a long time and she had come especially from the kibbutz to see me), she said: "Elisheva, Elisheva, who was it who used to call you Flora?"

There was no doubt that she was trying to hurt me. And now I say to her, "Don't you know, Henrietta? You should know." And then she laughs and says: "No one could call you that anymore. You haven't been Flora for a long time now."

It's quite clear to me now that Henrietta has a need to hurt me. I can't understand why. Perhaps it's her way of protecting herself. There's a new bitterness in her. A bitterness I never saw in her before. But what is she protecting herself from? I'm not blaming her. I've never reproached her by so much as a single word.

The first time I went to visit her at the children's home twenty years ago or more, she smiled at me from underneath a beautiful magnolia tree growing in the garden there. And pressed close to her chest she had a huge white flower which gave off a sourish smell, a lemony scent. I asked her the name of the flower and she didn't know. The leader of her youth group didn't know either, nor did the principal. But not long ago I was walking down the street parallel to the lane. It was evening and there was a light in the window of the little florist shop which was usually closed by then. Through the window, I could see a vase with three magnolia flowers in it. I went into the shop and in an agitated voice I asked the woman sitting there knitting if the flowers were for sale. And she said, "Yes, five pounds each." "What are they called?" I asked. And she said: "Magnolias." And I stood looking in amazement from the flowers to the faded little woman who went on knitting calmly, and I couldn't control myself and I asked her: "Where do they come from?" Then she raised her eyes from the knitting, with a dull, empty look, and said: "I have a tree in the garden and when it blooms I open the shop and sell a few flowers.''

I bought them, of course, even though they were so expensive, and gave one to Carmela. And I brought the other two home to my flat.

Henrietta arrived at our school in the middle of the year. She didn't know much Hebrew and she was years older than we were. Like the other refugee children who lived in the Home and attended our school, she too was quiet and withdrawn. The other girls in the class bullied her. We were in the sixth grade, and they would pounce on her and feel her back to see if she was wearing a bra. In the seventh grade she was already one of the best pupils in the class. And in the eighth grade she was elected president of the Health League.

Once, after a drawing lesson in the eighth grade, she suddenly said to me: You draw very well. Come and visit me on Saturday at the Home. Come in the afternoon.

And when I came she greeted me with an enormous flower in her hand, clasped to her chest, casting a white glow on her face. Henrietta was the prettiest girl in the class. She was the prettiest girl I had ever met. But I wasn't jealous of her, because she was modest and retiring. And on that Saturday when I went to visit her for the first time, I saw a magnolia tree in bloom for the first time in my life. Magnolia—the lucky flower. Any connection between good fortune and the magnolia flower is, of course, the fruit of my own invention.

And I ask myself if that's how I see the connection between us, as a lucky one. And if so, why? What luck did Henrietta bring me? When I think about it, I have to admit that there was never anyone closer to me than Henrietta, and that the kind of friendship we had was as rare as the magnolia tree is in our country. A single tree in the whole of Tel Aviv. It's true that in the years before her death we drifted apart. Many things came between us, but the love I felt for her never disappeared, in spite of everything that happened.

The Home where the refugee children stayed was a blue, two-storied building with a row of large, arched columns in front. A long avenue of shady grevillea trees led up to the building, their leaves silver where the rays of the sun fell on them. Among the tall trees it was always cool, even in the height of summer, and the loose earth of the path was always carpeted with fallen leaves. The columns on the veranda were covered with bougainvillea, and rose bushes and raspberries grew wild in the front garden.

The children had hiding places in the garden, and little huts with benches and tables made out of rough planks of wood. We sat in one of these little huts and spoke about God. Henrietta asked me if I really believed in God and if I said the prayers seriously. When I answered her questions in the affirmative, she laughed and told me that none of the children in the Home believed in God, not even the smallest. And that if the principal hadn't made them pray, none of them would have done so.

"When all the girls in the class pray," she said, "I think about other things. But I move my lips so the teacher won't be suspicious."

"What do you think about?" I asked curiously.

"About my youth movement leader," she said, without going into details.

When I parted from her at the end of that first visit, she suggested that we ask the teacher to let us share a desk at school.

The teacher had no objections. And in the mornings, when we said the morning prayer, I was able to observe her as she pretended to pray and thought about her youth movement leader. We sat at the back, and when the teacher wasn't looking we drew pictures: roses, baskets of flowers, hearts with red arrows running through them.

I still have one of those pictures here, between the pages of my copybook. It's a picture of angels with baby faces and on the back of the page in a round, rather childish handwriting, the words: To Elisheva, from Henrietta, with love.

That year I went to the Home every Saturday to visit Henrietta. And it was there that I first became acquainted with the secrets of love. One day when we were sitting in the hut in the garden, a boy of about fifteen, one of the children from the Home with ugly pimples all over his face and lanky limbs, began to pester us.

"Why don't you introduce me to your pretty friend, Henrietta?" he said, with a provocative, impertinent smile on his lips.

"Stop bothering us," said Henrietta sternly, but the boy said:

"I want to get to know your pretty friend. She's cute. I want to kiss her."

"Go away, you idiot," she scolded. And the boy went away, looking a little ashamed of himself. And then Henrietta confessed to me that the boy was in love with her, and that he had once broken into her room and kissed her again and again. "The youth leader loves me too," she said with an open, shining face. "When I grow up I'm going to marry him. That's why I let him kiss me every night before I go to bed."

In the summer vacation Henrietta went to stay with her aunt in Jaffa, and all summer long I wrote her love letters, full of longing. At the end of the summer she did not return. Her aunt had decided to send her to a boarding school in Jerusalem. After that we saw each other only rarely. To this day I often wonder how she was saved, and what happened to her parents. She never spoke about that, but once she told me that she had spent the whole of the war hiding in a cellar, and when the day of liberation came at last, and the Russians entered the town, she was afraid to leave her hiding place because their nailed boots made a frightening noise and everything seemed even worse than before.

The lane I walked down this evening, some twenty years after that time, was paved with rough stones. But there were grevillea trees at its entrance, with delicate orange-gold blossoms and leaves which turned silver in the rays of the sun. The Home no longer exists. The blue building with its arched columns, which stood in a different lane in another place and time, fell into ruins long ago. But whenever I pass this way I see an image of it in my memory: quiet and peaceful in its wild garden, with its secrets spreading stealthily from mouth to ear, bursting out of the stillness.

"The children from the Home are spoiled," the girls in my class would say, "all the refugee children are corrupt. They already know everything about love."

They were different, old before their time, their experience of life too heavy for their years. I was often warned not to go there, for fear that they might corrupt me too.

In the eighth grade the rumor spread that one of the girls from the Home had been seen lying with a boy in the field behind the central bus station. "Whore," the whisper spread, "whore!" And one day a group of girls fell on her with curses and abuse. The refugee girl laughed in their faces. She said: What do you know about love? You're a lot of babies. You don't know what it means to enjoy yourselves. You don't know the first thing about men. After that she was ostracized, and none of the girls in the class would speak to her. But the boys in the school across the road came out in breaks between lessons to try to flirt with her.

That year the class was split and full of conflicts. Some of the girls secretly read forbidden novels, like *A Woman Alone* or *Daughter of Zion*, which described a woman standing naked, examining her body in front of a mirror. And we looked up the rules about menstruating women in the *Shulchan Aruch** and read them in recess, whispering and giggling. The girls who had read the novels felt superior and regarded themselves as grown-up. But the conflicts were mainly political. The Yemenite and Sephardi girls supported the *Irgun** and one Ashkenazi girl, too, who was their leader, because her father was a freedom fighter. The others supported the *Hagana**, and at recess there were constant vociferous arguments, which occasionally erupted into fistfights. The refugee girls took no part in the political arguments, or in the religious arguments either, and everyone turned away from them. Only Henrietta was respected, because she was an outstanding student and the president of the Health League.

When I walk down the lane with the beautiful tall grevillea trees planted at its entrance, I often stop to look at one particular tree growing behind a high wall. I'm not sure what it is called. It has spreading branches and its budding leaves have the same wet gleam as the leaves of the magnolia tree. I'm waiting for the end of spring. If the big white flowers bloom on the tree I'll get in there somehow and pick myself a flower. In a few days' time, on the twenty-second of the month, on the anniversary of her death, I shall receive, as I do every year, a telegram from Yanis: I've sent camellias via Olympic. Put them on her grave.

The first anniversary of Henrietta's death fell when I was with Yanis in Venice. We had arrived there at the beginning of February.

Shulchan Aruch. A book of Jewish Law. *Irgun*. Right-wing fighters against the British Jabotinskij followers. *Hagana*. Left-wing body of fighters. Mainstream at that time.

After having travelled all over the country together, the joy of our meeting had evaporated and we were each alone with ourselves. We were staying in a small, run-down pension, not far from St. Stephen's Cathedral. The owner of the pension, a man with a blank face and faded yellow hair, spent his days in front of the television set, and sometimes, when Yanis went out to wander in the rain alone, I would watch the football games and boxing matches with him. At night we sometimes heard laughter rising from the narrow street beneath our window, as we lay side by side in silence. A dark cloud had settled on us in this town steeped in dampness and wintry desolation, whose crumbling beauty no longer moved us.

Leafing through my copybook, I come to a page written some time ago. I read: Yanis is drifting further and further away from me. All he can think of is Henrietta. He hardly talks. I hate Venice. It's time to go home.

I remember: during the day we used to walk along the canals, or go for a sail on the ferry boat. It rained without stopping. We ate our simple meals in our room: wine, cheese, sausage and salami. And we would try to hold down and conceal from each other our disappointment. The city oppressed us, showing us a reflection of ourselves—people slowly sinking, like Venice. But we were afraid to look into that mirror.

Yanis spent a lot of time writing, and he took his notebook with him everywhere. Perhaps he was writing poems, he didn't tell me. Then, I too, began to take my copybook with me to write things down. Perhaps I was envious.

Yanis withdrew into himself, and sometimes after I had gone to sleep he would leave me and go where his fancy took him. When he came back late, wet through and shivering cold, I would pretend to be asleep. I never asked him where he went.

On the twenty-second of February, after breakfast, Yanis said to me: "Let's go to church. I want to light a candle for Henrietta." I looked at him in astonishment. And with a hollow laugh he said: "I don't understand it myself. Don't look at me like that. That's what I want to do. It's stronger than I am."

We lingered long in the dim silence of St. Stephen's Cathedral, breathing in the mold and incense in uneasy silence. Yanis didn't pray. He sat opposite the altar with the candles burning all around it, staring silently. After a while he suddenly stood up and said: Let's get out of here. The bright light which greeted us when we emerged dazzled our eyes, and Yanis, trying to break the sense of oppression, said: It's idol worship.

We climbed a bridge and, leaning on the railing, looked down at the dirty black water. A black gondola sailed past. It was a fine morning, and there were tourists in the gondola and an Italian boy singing a popular song in a high, pure voice. After a while the gondola disappeared round a bend in the canal and the sound of the boy's voice died away. Yanis said: "Henrietta should have died in the spring, when all the world was blossoming. She should have been buried here, on a very clear day, with the light pouring onto the water and reflecting back from it in showers of radiance. Naked in a gondola, her white body shining in the radiance and her black hair covering her breasts and arms. She had wonderful arms. Her face white in the sun. I never saw her naked. . . . I wouldn't have let the gravediggers close her eyes. With her black open eyes she would illuminate the world. Surrounded by flowers. . . , I'd choose white camellias. I'd float her from canal to canal in a black gondola, display her to the world, astonish them with her beauty. All around other gondolas would be sailing with little boys wearing black jackets and white shirts and black bow ties. They would sing ancient liturgical songs in high, pure voices, and all the people of Venice would come out to her radiant face, to hear the sad song rise into the air. Flooding all the canals, water rising over the magnificent crumbling, vaulted houses, sliding under the Rialto bridge. And from there, on to the splendid royal square. The doves would flutter and coo, keening and lamenting. They would escort Henrietta, making a holy canopy for the ship of the dead beneath the blue sky. . . ."

Then he roused himself and said: "How disgracefully romantic I am. . . ."

I felt hurt and said mockingly: "I didn't know you were a poet."

The magnolia flower makes me feel lucky. I'm sorry that its time has not yet come. When it stands in the vase, its huge velvety white petals in a nest of glossy leaves, I can sit before it and feel at peace. Then the strength of my longings is overcome, guilt hides its face to lie quietly in wait. In the evening I lingered opposite the tree in the little lane, watching the late winter clouds sailing slowly past, hiding the memory of Henrietta's face in their airy pink. Now I hear the thudding wings of the birds warbling outside my window and I push down my longings. I pray for them to fade and go away. I don't intend to become the plaything of my own desires. I can't afford to give way to wild longings that throw my life into confusion. I don't want the bitterness, the sorrow, and the momentary happiness. I need peace of mind, rest. Yanis wrote and told me to come. And I'll go.

Late returns, like meetings out of season, are no good to anyone. As Odysseus the much-enduring has taught us. This is not the time for a renewed confrontation with the bittersweet yearning for extinction, with the single-minded passion of fleshly love. Nevertheless I can think of nothing but my love, my guilt, my happiness, my death: I can only wait for someone who is not now and never was within my grasp. I can only live this bitter, slavish compulsion, and place a few yellowing leaves in my basket of offerings. No summer fruits. No green fruits of spring.

We cannot stay the hour advancing towards the night, shine like the dawn, pray again for a great love.

All my life I've waited for a miracle, an hour of grace bestowed by a stranger, for dead things to rise and live again, for wild imaginings to come true; for the earth and the sky, the trees and birds and people, the whole world to be transformed like a sudden sandstorm, like an unexpected slap in the face.

And the miracle has already happened. I walked past it without noticing that it was there, baffled by its strangeness. And thus it was lost in the oblivion of time without my knowing what it meant.

ALEXANDER

Dear Yanis,

I don't know if I've written to you about Carmela. One day all the tables were occupied, and she came and sat down beside me and ordered whiskey and began to talk. Girls today have no shame.

It's really incredible the way a girl can sit down in a café next to a man she's never seen in her life, and immediately begin to talk about herself without any inhibitions. And this girl said to me, without any preliminaries, In winter I can't be without a man, I'm cold, and I like the look of you. When I didn't answer she asked me if I was shy or something. Afterwards we just chatted about all kinds of things. And when I got up to go she told me that her birthday was the next week and she invited me to dinner. I think I'll buy her some flowers and go. Why not?

In my last letter I told you about the ringing I sometimes hear. It's not an imaginary ringing, it's simply something that happened once. I'm going to describe it to you, because it's important to me to do it, because it concerns you too. I think that everything that happens to me concerns you because, from a certain moment on, everything that's happened to me is overshadowed by your betrayal of me.

I was in the yard of the institution and I heard the phone ringing in the distance. I've got a very sensitive sense of hearing and even the smallest noise can disturb me when I'm trying to concentrate. I was busy digging in the yard and I heard the ringing and I saw a woman coming down the arcade in front of the Arab house at the top of the hill.

Alexander! Telephone! the woman called to me. She was wearing a starched white uniform and she treated me familiarly simply because from time to time I take my trousers down in front of her so that she can give me an injection. She doesn't know that sometimes I feel like strangling her. I hate her. I can't stand it when she calls me by my first name, and I pretend not to hear.

Dr. Segal! Telephone!—she called, her crude voice shattering the still transparent air of the morning. You know, I love this place for its quiet. . . .

Telephone? I asked myself who could be capable of dying on such a fine, clear spring day, one of the loveliest days of the year. Not a suitable day for death. I thought about the way our Lord and Master laughs in our faces. I was sure that this was what it was all about—someone had died and someone else was phoning to tell me about it. I was sure that it was you, Yanis, who had died.

The day that my father was murdered was also a spring day, and

I remember how I hurried home from school. And I didn't give a damn that you had died on a fine spring day too, because in my eyes there's no difference at all between you and him. My father betrayed me too, and to this day I suffer for it. Is that why I became your friend, to create a situation where that betrayal would repeat itself? I believe that men reconstruct their childhood fates as adults. I am convinced that orphans do everything in their power when they grow up to ensure that their children too will be orphans, or at least something resembling orphans. That children of divorced parents will do all they can to make their own children the children of divorced parents too. Anyone who was beaten as a child will be violent towards his own children in one way or another. I know this sounds crazy but I've gone into it and I've always come up with the same results.

On the face of things it sounds illogical, because you would suppose that people who suffered as children would want to compensate with their own children, no? But apparently in matters of psychology it's not logic that operates but compulsiveness.

In any case, I got up and turned towards the house on the hill. You've never been here. We used to go far afield on our trips and hikes but we never came upon this corner. I must describe the house to you. It really is a handsome house. Henrietta would certainly have admired it. The style is a hybrid, colonial and Arab, and it's surrounded by citrus groves and has arcades, pillars, and arches, painted sky blue and white. Once a rich effendi lived here. On the ground floor he received his guests and hatched his plots against his Jewish neighbors; on the second floor he kept his offspring; and on the third his wives. Today this beautiful house is used by the Health Ministry, and in my opinion that's just fine. It suits its purpose.

I approached the woman who was leaning her elbows on the balustrade of the arcade. If you could have seen her! The personification of infuriating impertinence. Square as a man, hard as a stone. Every injection of hers was like a slap in the face. She said to me: A lady wants you on the phone, Dr. Segal. She emphasized the "Dr. Segal" in a derisive way. She knew she had made a mistake when she addressed me by my first name. I can't stand lack of respect. But she mocks me for my formality. They tend to forget here that I have a degree in physics, and that but for what happened

I could have been an associate professor with an international reputation today. In my opinion, they should take this into account. In my opinion, you should put people in their place. I thought to myself, who can this "lady" be? I haven't any lady friends, and no one, male or female, would suddenly phone me up from the kibbutz. At the entrance to the hall the telephone stood on a white table. Everything is white here, they don't use bright colors here, they're afraid they might be upsetting. Red, for example, can provoke anger. I took the white receiver in my hand and put it to my ear. I listened and answered calmly. I heard the strange, distant voice of a woman I had never met—a woman who once was a close friend of Henrietta's. She disappointed my hopes.

I want to tell you something about her voice. I remember it exactly. It was low, and slightly rough and coarse. I could hear her breath rise and fall, thrusting towards me, gathering strength, and I listened to the ebb and flow, the changing rhythm and frequency of the waves, trying to limit what I heard to a mere pattern of sound waves. But, despite myself, I found myself wondering if this woman might be capable of feeling some affection for my Chinese garden. I cursed you, Yanis. Yes, I cursed you aloud. I said to her, I wish he would die, what a nerve he's got telling me to write to him, what a nerve to ask you to give me his regards. It was terrible. Her voice filled me with yearnings and longings which I did not want, which I had worked hard at repressing. And then, suddenly, as by an enemy coming from the great distance of other times, my soul was invaded by sounds of laughter and song, which faded and died away each time she forced me to answer her questions.

I tried to answer indifferently. At first I said, Thank you, and how is he, and where did you meet him. When she spoke about you I heard the happiness in her voice and my gall rose. I had the feeling that she was bubbling over with experiences she wanted to share with me and that she lacked all awareness of my situation. I couldn't answer, and then I began to curse you. I said to her, "Listen, I'm busy with my own affairs, I'm looking for my Chinese garden, I'm digging now, do you understand, and you're disturbing me." And she replied, "Perhaps you would like me to come and help you, perhaps you need something." And I got so angry that they had to drag me away from the phone by force and put me into a cold bath. You understand, that square woman was keeping an eye on me during the whole conversation, and when I began to yell, she grabbed the receiver out of my hand and cut me off.

You can't get away Yanis, I'm going to write you everything, and you'll read it. You'll read and you'll know exactly what you did to me, to Henrietta, maybe to Elisheva, too. And one day, I'm sure that one day, you'll take up a pen and answer me and you'll admit everything. And then, then I'll buy a plane ticket and I'll go there and kill you.

LICHT

I'm holding the letter from Greece in my hand. Despite myself, I smile. The address is written in a fair, clear hand, with a fountain pen, in blue ink. A neat writing, restrained and revealing a certain rigidity, but definitely feminine. I once had a girl who used to write me letters with a fountain pen. But her writing was different, childish, impulsive, reckless. Big round letters, scatterbrained, written in haste, trying to keep up with the speed of her thoughts, every letter a scream. This writing is too deliberate, very rational, calculating, adult. I don't know the writing. I don't know anyone in Greece. No. I certainly don't know anyone in Greece.

I take this letter, about the identity of whose writer I really have no doubts whatsoever, but about whose contents I have not the faintest idea—maybe a letter of condolence—into my study.

I really don't know the handwriting. (Don't you really, Professor Licht?) Nor do I know anybody in Greece likely to write me. But although it's no more than a wild guess, I'm sure.

I haven't been in my study since my daughter Noa died, and when I open the door a graveyard smell overcomes me. The shutter of the window over the desk isn't properly shut, and I can see motes of dust floating in the rays of light coming through the slats and falling slantwise on the desk. The sunbeams are full of movement, almost commotion, the commotion of particles which never for a moment rest, and there's dust on the desk, too, on the books piled there, on the inkwell and the marble pen holder, on the pipe stand, and the typewriter cover, on the shelves and the books, the leather chair in the corner, on the drooping leaves of the philodendron—the earth in the pot is dry, cracked. The plant I tended so devotedly is dying.

With a handkerchief I wipe the dust from a free space in the middle of the desk and move the transistor aside. The last news headlines I heard here surface in my memory for a moment. A successful attack on Sheduwan. Sheduwan. Whoever heard of it before? After that, I heard no more news. I didn't go into this room again, nor into other rooms. What happened in the time that has passed? How many young men have been killed? How many died in road accidents? How many contractors have made a fortune building how many houses? How many immigrants have arrived?

And I cannot hold back any longer. A few minutes past eleven. I turn the knob and the voice of the announcer sounds loud and solemn. The funeral arrangements will be announced later. . . . Who has died? The prime minister? The finance minister? Maybe she'll repeat it at the end. I listen. I wait. Aha! Agnon. At his home in Talpioth, in Jerusalem. And I switch off, indifferent. "A Night Among Others." "The Oath." "The Doctor and His Divorcée." Fine stories.

All this time I've been holding the blue envelope in my hand. Now I take up the paper knife with its carved ivory handle and very sharp blade from the pencil holder. It's long and narrow, narrowing from the hand to the point. I bought it on one of my trips, in Hong Kong, on my way to Australia for a series of lectures at the University of Adelaide. I slip the knife into the corner of the envelope and sweep the blade through. The paper crackles as it cuts, and it seems to me that the friction gives rise to a burning smell. One day Leah was brushing Noa's long, fine, silky hair, still golden then, and the comb made a crackling noise as it went through her hair. Leah said: There's electricity in our hair today, because of the desert wind. And I explained the concept of friction to Noa. . . .

It was Noa who looked after Leah. She was the one who went with her for the radiation treatment. Even that she wouldn't let me share with her. I offered more than once. I said to her: Today I'll come with you, Leah. It's too much for Noa, she's so young, she has her life to live and we shouldn't burden her. But she stubbornly refused. And Noa bore a grudge against me because she couldn't understand her mother's refusal of my help except as a rejection. Leah hid from me. After the operation she began sleeping in the guest room. She stopped getting undressed in front of me. She was ashamed of her illness. Once she said: I want you to remember me the way I was before—a whole woman. I didn't know how to console her. She didn't want to invite people here or to go out to visit; she secluded herself with her illness as if with a lover. Once she said: "A disease of this kind can be understood only as punishment. It has no other meaning. Tell me, what am I being punished for? What harm have I done?" I tried to treat it as a joke. I said: "I would never have believed that you could be so superstitious." But of course my words made no impression on her.

I take the letter from the envelope without looking. My eyes take in the neat, restrained writing, automatically. Straight margins. A word here, a word there. I turn the pages over, looking for the signature. And there it is: Yours, Elisheva Green.

So I wasn't mistaken. A different handwriting, perhaps a different woman, but the same name. She hasn't forgotten me, I think with some satisfaction. I imagine that when I passed her that time in the street, when I was in Tel Aviv to give a lecture, and I didn't greet her, or even signal with a nod of my head that I remembered, that I recognized her, I imagine she was hurt. And at this moment, because of the wound I inflicted on her, because of this letter whose contents are still unknown to me—at this moment, the possibility that everyone dreams of opens before me: the possibility of love. And I am suddenly overcome by terrible longings for the faraway girl I once knew, the one I lightheartedly called Flora because there was something about her coloring, her essence, that reminded me of Botticelli. I go to the bookcase and take down a volume, leafing through until I find the picture I'm looking for. Here she is, draped in pink; with a touch of the hand a girl turns into spring and scatters flowers on the grass, while Cupid shoots an apple among the three graces. I know: years have passed and the die was cast long ago. Nevertheless, dazzled by hope, I begin to read.

Dear Professor Licht [Good Lord, what formality. Doesn't she remember my name!], Unless I am mistaken you once met my Greek friend Yanis. [Rubbish, I never met him.] He

was very ill for a number of years. About a year before he died
he invited me to come and live with him in his home in
Athens. For reasons which I will not explain here, I accepted
his invitation and I was with him in his last moments. I hope
that I was able to be of some help to him. Perhaps you
remember that we were a kind of foursome, and of course you
must remember my good friend Henrietta, who was your
student too, like me. [What's she hinting at, for God's sake?
Surely it's not possible that anything could have come to her
ears. . . . Snow white skin and coal black hair, with a surprising resemblance to Gauguin's Tahitian women. I always
wondered if she dyed her hair. But her eyes were very black
too, really black, a very unusual kind of black. Henrietta was
a beautiful girl, in her way, but in those days, when Elisheva
was going around with her, I didn't like her. There was
something alien about her, arrogant and withdrawn, and I
couldn't bear her Hungarian accent, although it was very
faint. She had a wonderful voice, and sensuous. . . . But she
was a refugee, and we never felt quite at our ease with
them. . . .]

In a certain sense we four were connected to each other
by a common destiny. And, in the end, even by family ties.
Henrietta was like a sister to me, and she was the person
closest to me after my parents were killed. I don't know if I
ever told you about that. They were passengers on a plane
that was blown up. We were really like sisters. Henrietta married Alexander Segal, Yanis' friend, who had loved her for
many years, a barren love, incurable and hopeless.
Defining our relationship in terms of a common destiny
must sound pretentious, but I don't know any other way of
describing the peculiar circumstances of our situation. And
there was something else we three had in common. We three,
but not Henrietta, were frustrated writers, although for a
long time none of us admitted it. It was only at the end of his
life that Yanis recognized that writing was his true vocation,
and he attempted then to write his autobiography, an abor-
tive attempt because he was a man without a language. Greek
was his mother tongue, but he had been cut off from it at an
early age and he never acquired another language to replace

it. And so he wrote in English, a language he had learned at school and which he had grown accustomed to thinking in. Yanis knew many languages, he was a polyglot. But since he decided that his vocation lay in science, he never refined his linguistic tools; and this was the reason, it seems to me today, that he could not become a writer.

As for Alexander Segal, he is a compulsive letter writer. This is one of the aspects of his disease, which the doctors have diagnosed as paranoia, but which no one really properly understands. I don't think that Alexander is conscious of his literary inclinations. Literature was something that he always affected to despise. Once Yanis said to me: Alexander has read everything, everything that is important, but he always reads with contempt, like a scientist looking at an insect through a microscope.

And I kept a diary. Today I know that I did this because I wanted to describe the reality I was living in, in order to preserve it in words, so that it wouldn't be lost. And perhaps that is too elegant an interpretation. Perhaps I wrote out of narcissism, in order to preserve myself, in order not to lose myself. In any case, the truth is that I wanted to be a writer, but I was afraid of failure. I have never had any faith in myself. When I felt the desire to write a story, I would sit down at my desk and look at the blank pages before me, and a terrible darkness would come over me. The story, which was already arranged in my head in all its details, would suddenly slip away, and I would be gripped with paralysis. On the other hand, I had no difficulty with my diary. At the beginning it really was a diary, but as time went on I filled it with writing exercises. When you read it, you'll see what I mean. And so none of us realized his true and secret desire.

And now that Yanis and Henrietta are dead, and Alexander is a dead man as far as I am concerned, I would like to commemorate them. And despite the time that has passed, it seems to me that you may be wishing for the same thing, even if you are not conscious of it. Since I am not capable of carrying out this project, whereas you are a man of many gifts and there can be no doubt as to your talent, I am making a bundle of these papers to send to you: Alexander's letters, the ones Yanis never managed to destroy, the rough draft of Yanis' autobiography, a rather slim notebook, no more than a kind of outline for an extensive book, and passages from my diary.

I can imagine your astonishment, perhaps your anger, as you read this. Since our last encounter, when you pretended not to know me, almost a year has passed. Surely you couldn't have guessed then that one day I would write to you. After I saw you that day, I read the diary that I started writing when I was living in Haifa. I added a few notes later, and while I was staying with Yanis I tried to improve the style of a few passages. I am thus entrusting you with my literary remains.

Our accidental meeting in the street seemed symbolic to me. It was no accident, of course, that you ignored me, nor was this the first time that you treated me rudely. For you I was never more than a passing episode, a flirtation that was fine while it lasted, as you said. And even during that episode you managed essentially to ignore me. You were ready to accept my desire for you. You wanted my youth and my gaiety, but that was all. When I used to ask if you loved me, you would turn hard and say: My dear young lady, what do you know about love? This has got nothing at all to do with love. And I, not wanting to lose you, played the game according to your rules. But when other aspects of my nature showed themselves, you made haste to escape.

But the game, as it seemed to you, wasn't the real game. It was far more complex than you can imagine, and it had certain consequences. I think the time has come for you to know about this. Whatever you do with the material I'm putting at your disposal, I am sure that you will learn from it. I am aware of the impertinence and lack of consideration in this invasion of your life, and perhaps there may even be some hidden desire for revenge on my part, some wish to inflict pain indirectly, through the past. And perhaps also there is the wish to inform you of my continuing existence, a selfish desire to announce, I'm still here, and if today you are prepared to play the game by my rules we can begin again from the beginning. But, I know you do not want this, and I know also that it's impossible to begin anything from the beginning, ever. And this makes me feel bitter, and the bitterness breeds a vengefulness, of course.

I know that your situation now is difficult, and that you

have hard problems to contend with. There are moments when I am full of compassion, the compassion of love, the protective feeling a baby's tears evoke in a mother; but, at the same time, I discover in myself a kind of hardness. In the face of your despair, at which I can only guess, I discover in myself the ability to do things which I could not have done in the past, like the ability to impose myself, like the ability to strike a blow. I am not setting myself up as a judge, although I have, in fact, passed judgment. We all pass judgment all the time, sometimes even against our will; it's human nature. I know that there is something arrogant about imagining I know what is good for you in your present situation, and so I will not claim that I am doing what I'm doing in the wish to be of help. I have never pretended to know too much about others. To me the other is an enigma we never succeed in deciphering and today I understand why my longing for you was strongest and most terrible precisely at those moments when I felt closest to you. For it was then that the gap between us seemed deepest, when in the middle of an embrace part of you remained remote and apart, detached from the embrace that we seemed to share.

In any case, it seems to me that I'm doing you a good turn, providing you with a distracting occupation, but I cannot be certain. All that is certain is the impertinence, and the desire, which has not yet completely died, to be as close to you as possible. This desire is no longer as strong as it once was. Today our relations look to me like a war, and I have no wish for war. I'm too tired, I want to rest, to forget. I prefer to be free, free of desires, free of the torture of the will.

Tomorrow I'm leaving Yanis' house and going far away. I do not think that we shall meet again.

Yours,
Elisheva Green

The letter had no return address.

I placed the pages on my desk. Such a confused letter. I don't know what to think. Now I feel hungry and I go back to the kitchen. There's a big mess on the table. I gather up the empty envelopes and the superfluous invitations and, holding my nose, push the lot into the garbage bin and hastily shut the cupboard door. But the smell has pervaded the kitchen and there is nothing to eat. I leave the room and the smell pursues me. I must go downstairs and empty the garbage bin. I'll wash it out with Lysol. I like the smell of Lysol. Afterwards I'll go and buy something to eat. And then I'll go to the post office and collect the parcel.

ELISHEVA

As usual, the flower seller on the corner greets me. His hair is gray and falling out, and even in the summer he wraps a woolen scarf around his neck when evening falls. He stands there, leaning against an iron fence, with a transistor to his ear and his bleary eyes half shut. He couldn't possibly guess that he may never see me again, for tomorrow, the day after tomorrow, I'm going away from here. Thoughts of Yanis fill me with warmth and sorrow. The thought that somewhere in the world there is a man who needs me fills me with joy. Confirms, in a way, my existence. For what does a person want if not to make sense of his existence, give meaning and deeper purpose to a life whose only end is the reproduction of the species, like the animals and the plants and the amoebae. Anyone who knows anything about nature knows that this is its one and only purpose and that we human beings, although we are obliged to obey the laws of nature, try to evade them, to give life a meaning beyond its blind laws. But if not for the blind force of nature, what would prevent millions of miserable, depressed people from taking their own lives? We don't think about it and we call it hope. We deceive ourselves all the time and all we can do is defy the doom we refuse to acknowledge, mock our fate and endow life with a meaning beyond the blind laws of nature, beyond the absurd, by creating something which is outside nature. Perhaps this is what Alexander was trying to do with his Chinese gardens. Henrietta told me about it. She came specially to tell me about it. She asked my advice, but I couldn't help her.

And perhaps this is why I keep a diary, to satisfy the desire to leave something behind, some sign, some trace. A desire that never goes much further than a desire. I lack the vitality of the executive, like Avigdor Licht, who spends his life rushing from place to place, from book to book, from subject to subject, and from woman to woman. An inexhaustible appetite, the appetite of an animal toward what is not animal-like, but in a form which is completely so. It seems as if I'm jealous of him. He used to mock me, saying, You're jealous, Elisheva, you're jealous, a jealous little woman, that's what you are. And I'm still jealous of his enormous vitality, of his stubbornness, of his forcefulness, and even of his crude, uninhibited ambition. But he lacks sensitivity, responsiveness to others, to the universe. A man who wants to devour the whole world has no time for trivialities. To know everything, to taste everything, to do everything to perfection down to the last detail. The skilled lover, the connoisseur of food and wine, the universal scholar—how inferior I felt in comparison. My spiritual laxity makes my writing undisciplined, lacking even the merit of self-exposure. . . .

Before I set out for my evening walk I gave myself a pedicure. When I rubbed the skin off my heels I thought how my feet had grown dead, cracked skin and lost all their delicacy. How my belly had coarsened since I gave birth to Michael, how my neck had stiffened, the skin wrinkled, and how my head creaks now when I turn it from side to side, the faint crunching sound made by the contraction. No wonder that Avigdor did not recognize me. Yes. Henrietta was right when she asked me who it was that once called me Flora.

Stop it, Elisheva! Self-pity is despicable. Look at Yanis, he's going to die and I'm sure he knows how to accept his situation. I know he's going to die. Otherwise he wouldn't have sent for me. He wrote that he's sick. He didn't write the name of the illness. His fingers must seem even longer now than usual. I remember them, so brown and lean and dry. Transparent, hovering over my body, feeling their way carefully. Avigdor didn't make any use of his fingers, as if they weren't separated at all from the palm of his hand—heavy, impatient, demanding. Perhaps that's why I called him Pierre. Because he reminded, always reminds me, of Bezuhov. Like a bear he was, a big heavy yellow bear. A kind of Syrian bear. And still the memory of him stirs a love in me. Even today. After so many years.

Today I went to visit Leon's mother. I'd never met her. When I was waiting at the bus stop for the bus that goes to the southern neighborhoods it began to rain, a lazy rain. The drops fell slowly, singly, and when each drop hit a small puddle, it trembled there like a living heart. Then I walked down the noisy, crowded streets, passing wholesale shops with sacks of fragrant lentils and dried peas and beans, sawdust heaped at the corners of the road, or drifting out of the carpentry shops, grocery shops crammed with sausages suspended on hooks, pickled fish in wooden barrels—here you learn to know people's tastes, their desires, their pleasures—and a wine shop, with the musk of wine pouring out into the street. There was a wonderful picturesqueness in all that commotion, a marvelous vitality, as if the street were saying: As long as people are alive, they have demands, wishes, wants. They want food, they want nice apartments and nice furniture, they want luxury, beauty, things. And people are still living here in the upper floors, above the shops, above the workshops, in crumbling houses. And your heart contracts at the sight of their efforts to beautify a balcony whose plaster is falling and exposing the bent, rusty pipes underneath, but, inside, the ceiling is covered with wood, there are potted plants in the corners, and in the living room the light is on on this winter day, a grand chandelier with glass droplets glitters. . . . The rain went on falling and people hurried purposively through the mud and the puddles, the wet sticky sawdust, and pushed through the shops to buy. Repressed appetites bursting out after the war. Liberated people, who had been poor all their lives, descended like barbarians on the loot. The new wealth reveling without shame.

Mrs. Dantes' shop was shut, as I had expected, and I went to the little café to look for her address in the telephone directory, perhaps she had a telephone, and there were little red mullets there, fried in bread crumbs, and slices of grey mullet in a sharp sauce, and slices of fried aubergine, sprinkled with garlic and chopped parsley, and chick peas boiled in salted water and strewn with crushed black pepper. Men with moustaches in blue overalls went in and out and drank beer in huge mugs and tore the tiny fish in their hands and chewed their bones with gusto. They spoke a different Hebrew and sometimes they spoke Ladino. If the place hadn't been so close and stuffy, and if the men hadn't stared at me so strangely, and if the marble tops of the small square tables hadn't been so full of filthy black cracks, I would have probably been overcome with a desire to sit down and eat my fill of these Balkan delicacies.

I found Mrs. Dantes' address and bought cigarettes and some chickpeas in a piece of newspaper which the man behind the counter twisted into a cone around his finger, then made my way again through the narrow, crowded streets, filling my lungs with the aroma of baking bread, of sacks of grain, so sweet and overpowering, of sawdust, of braided garlic and frying onions. At a cake stall the big black trays and the round aluminum trays piled high with sweetmeats seemed to smile at me, and I couldn't control myself, I bought a cake made of straw-thin noodles filled with nuts that made my fingers and lips sticky with the sweet honey. The sweet smell of vanilla pursued me all the way down the street until it was overpowered by an odor of melting wax that came pouring out of one of the houses. Someone, somewhere, had given thought to her hairy legs, her smelly armpits, and had decided to do something about her life, to improve herself. But that was a ridiculous way to interpret things. Perhaps it was a purely mechanical act, part of the weekly routine of a woman who paid attention to the way she looked.

Saffron, cardamom, coriander, cumin, cinnamon, and roasting peanuts and coffee. Brightly colored hairclips for little girls—butterflies and flowers—hung two by two on strips of white paper, toys and dolls' prams hanging from toyshop ceilings. Red motorcars, a tricycle, plastic tractors, little nylon raincoats with false fur, shining polyester fibers, cosmetics, piles of jeans. . . .

At last I came to the house and made my way up a dark marble stairway, worn and broken, to an old wooden door, painted a nauseous blue in oil paint. I knocked and heard shuffling footsteps, the heels tapping as if her shoes were too big for her feet. The door opened on a small bowed woman. She beckoned me inside, and sat down on a little, low stool. A broken old woman, very thin, her face fallen, withered, and dark with grief; and looking out of that face, the marvelous black eyes of her son. In the gloomy room, the heavy, dusty curtains were drawn, and the tiled floor was sunken and dented; the tiles clattered when you walked across it. In places the old Arab tiles had been pulled up and replaced with new, yellowish ones, and the pattern was no longer complete. But the old ones still shone and the new ones had empty faces.

I said to the woman: "I knew Leon. We were friends. How did he die?" And she told me all that I had guessed. "It was the asthma," she said, "that killed him. He died of suffocation. Alone, far away." And I told her that I would be going to Greece soon, and if she would give me the address I would go to the landlords and ask them about his last days. She took out a little notebook from the bureau and said to me, 39 Ormou Street, apartment number 10. I remembered Ormou Street, near Syndagna Square, a long, busy street.

Mrs. Dantes was wearing a black dress and long black stockings too wide or long for her legs, falling around her thin ankles in ugly folds. On her head a black georgette scarf, which she adjusted from time to time when it slipped backwards, revealing straight metallic grey hair severely pulled back into a bun. And she said, "I told him not to go, I told him, don't go. Hijiko mio, it's not good for you. You've got a shop here, a nice little shop, stay and look after the shop. Hijiko mio, I said to him, I'm too old for it now, the work is not hard. I said to him, It's not right to go away and leave your old mother all alone, what is this craziness with the guitar?, I said to him. All of a sudden at your age? You're too old for the guitar. But if you must, aren't there any teachers here? Leave all that nonsense, Hijiko mio, I said to him, don't be like your father.

"Spain I said, your father was never in Spain, he was only there in his imagination. There's no inheritance waiting for you there. I lied to him. I didn't want him to leave me. But he didn't listen. He found himself a loose woman there, a goya, an Inglesa, a fine lady. That was the first time he went away. And he married her, without a rabbi, without a bridal canopy, like the goyim marry. And that was the only wife he ever had, because she refused to give him a divorce. She wanted him to stay with her and wash her father's car and clean their palace, like some servant. My Leon, a servant. And you know why she didn't want to give him a divorce? Because over there the state pays money to girls whose husbands don't support them, and she didn't want to lose the money. Like social security over here. You know there are old people here today who don't get married because they don't want to lose their social security. The state makes people live in sin, that's what it does.

In the end he came back to me. He was sick, so sick. One attack after another he had. He didn't want to work in the shop, I don't know why. He went to teach English in Berlitz, he would lose his temper with the students, he wouldn't even come to live with me. And then he suddenly started with the guitar and said he was going to Greece. He went away from his mother, that boy, he disobeyed her. I said to him, Don't go, here you have mother who'll look after you as long as she lives, God willing, and call the doctor in time. Come and stay with me, with your old mother. This house is big, the rooms are empty, You don't hear the sound of a voice all day long. But he wouldn't listen, caro. He wouldn't listen. He didn't keep the commandment 'honor thy mother.' "

She said all this through tight lips, with a kind of malevolence, and she fixed her black eyes on me with a terrible aggression, the aggression of the just, the accuser. But I understood her. Suddenly she cried: He deserved to die alone, in exile! He deserved it! And then she covered her face with her vein-knotted hands, white and rigid, her fingers digging into her temples, hurting herself, scratching her face. I went to her, put my hand on her head, on the steel-gray hair gathered into a bun, thin and oily, and I said something to her that I have never said to anyone else, perhaps not even to myself. "I had a child once, too," I said to her, "and the child died." But she shook off my hand with irritation, adjusting her scarf, and said: "That's life, . . . that's life. All the time you think tomorrow will be better, but every day is worse. You're still young, niña, but when you're my age, you'll understand. . . ."

Going down the black broken stairs toward the light and noise of the streets, I was pursued by the stale smell of empty rooms; and I asked myself why she should go on living now that her son is dead. To crack sunflower seeds on Friday night, to sit in front of the television on Saturday nights and crack sunflower seeds again, to sit on the wobbly chair out in the doorway in the evening, in summer, after the shops are shut, with the other old women who live here alone. Only old people still live here. Neon lights hung low on chains in the street, shedding their light on looms, on knitting machines or sewing machines in the large spacious rooms of still handsome houses with ornamental cornices, arched windows, all sweatshops now. And in the smaller houses, the old people live.

Nobody will bother to repair those houses, I think, they'll let them slowly disintegrate, and one day they'll bring bulldozers and nothing will remain of what was once the neighborhood of Ahu-at-Bayit. But in the meantime old women still sit on their chairs in the evening, on the pavement, when the workshops are silent and the shops shut, and nothing moves but the mice and the prowling cats. What do they talk about to each other, about grandchildren, nephews and nieces, about old men who died yesterday or last week, sons who fell in the war, suitors who courted them fifty years ago or more. She sits in her room, waiting for death, fries little pink fish, buys a sweet plaited loaf for Friday night, covers it with an embroidered cloth, blanches almonds for marzipan, whips egg whites for meringues, grows herbs on the balcony where nobody sits anymore. She sits alone at the window, looking at the street, contemplating the lives of others. She drinks mint tea, perhaps she reads romances in Ladino. Dead. Her only son is dead. She brought him up, she pampered him, she did not spare the rod either, and he is dead. And I, even this was not granted me. I had no child to bring up, to spoil, to scold. I had a baby and he died in agony.

LICHT

So—a package deal. It amuses me to such an extent that I laugh aloud. My laughter sounds sick. Why does it amuse me actually? Was it that I was expecting something else, or perhaps because Elisheva has revealed certain characteristics I would never have thought her capable of. The proposal definitely attracts me, it comes as a challenge. Haven't I always had ambitions in that direction? When I was a student at Oxford I wrote a story. In English, naturally. I only write in English. It's a shocking waste to write for such a small audience. So, I wrote a story, a number of stories, as a matter of fact, but I sent only one of them to a literary magazine that doesn't exist anymore.

The editor then was the writer Kingsley Amis, and he published the story. He wanted to meet me and he asked me to send him more. When I told him my profession and the field I was working in, he said: "Listen, your story's okay, and if you go on writing you'll be a third- or even a second-rate writer, but you'll never make the top grade. Don't you think you'd be better off concentrating on your own field? You're a talented man with a promising career in front of you, but if you disperse your energies you won't succeed in anything." I was young and I didn't resent what he said, I felt no more than a slight disappointment. In a way I was even grateful.

I believed him and I took his advice. I stopped writing fiction. Research, essays, from time to time newspaper articles, but no more fiction. Today, when I think about what he said, I ask myself how he dared deliver a judgement of that kind—pronounce sentence, in fact. On the basis of a single story? It was impudence, worse than that, conceit. On the other hand, he's a clever man; I've read his books and I know. Perhaps he took into account that if I was a real writer I wouldn't take any notice of what he said, and his words would only spur me on. Maybe he wanted to put me to a test. And, who knows, perhaps he saw right through me, perhaps with his writer's sensibility he sensed the essential rottenness of the young man standing before him, whose only ambition was to become famous as quickly as possible.

So there we have it. On the one hand, Kingsley Amis, and on the other—Elisheva Green, with her proposition for a package deal. Elisheva, I accept your offer. I think the challenge suits my character and my situation. I imagine you took this into account. You're more complicated than I thought, I seem to have misjudged you, as I misjudged others, as I misjudged my daughter Noa. The work appeals to me. There are plenty of problems of course, difficult problems of structure, of editing. . . . Yanis will have to be translated into Hebrew, yes, this time I'll do it in Hebrew.

Elisheva hasn't forgotten me. She certainly chose a strange way of showing it, but she hasn't forgotten me. What is she getting at when she speaks of consequences? I don't know. But she promises that things will become clear as I read. Why hasn't she forgotten? I treated her badly enough. Revenge? Maybe . . . but that's a way of relating too, it shows she cares, cares deeply. . . .What is the secret of my charm? I really don't understand how I've always succeeded in arousing the admiration of others. Perhaps because I always strove so persistently to get ahead, perhaps because I never took my relationships with others seriously. I always made other people feel a certain sense of inferiority; in other words, I took care not to let anyone relate to me as an equal. The other was never important to me. What was more important to me than anything was to prove to the world that I was worthy of the honors it bestowed on me, and therefore I did everything I did in absolute seriousness. Even if it was only cooking a meal, I did it like a professional cook. The need to distinguish myself. . . . I needed other people to acknowledge my superiority. And today it all seems like a bad joke.

Soon I'll go and empty the trash, and wash out the pail with Lysol. Then I'll go to the store and buy bread, butter, milk, a few olives. I expect the grocer will be embarrassed when he sees me. He'll evade my eyes and perhaps he'll have a hard time for a minute. Maybe he'll try to say something, but I won't let him. I'll say straight away, a loaf of rye bread, please, and a bottle of milk. . . then I'll go to the post office, to get Elisheva's parcel. . . . In the meantime, I'll go through the mail again. I have to pay the bills, go to the bank, and get things organized. And I'll have to answer a few letters. If she's given her address, I'd write a reply. But she didn't want that. She didn't want a reply, I don't know why.

I feel guilty, of course. And all the time, ever since I found Noa dead on her bed, I want and don't want to die. But the strength of the two wishes isn't equal, the not wanting is much stronger.

Since I'm guilty I feel ashamed and I think that I deserve to be punished. Therefore, shouldn't the wish to die be stronger? Next to the man who wants and doesn't want to die there's another one who observes him, or observes them both, the one who wants to die and the one who doesn't, and the observer says, Never mind what you want and what you don't want, the important thing is you're guilty, and if you're guilty then you must pay. You must bear your punishment, you must atone, and your death will be atonement for Noa. And there is yet another who asks, Tell me, how much does Noa's absence hurt you? This one wants to measure my pain, because perhaps my guilt lies in the fact that it doesn't hurt enough. And he asks, What hurts you more, her absence, the fact that you will never never see her again, that you'll be lonely and sick with longing (and just how sick will you be with longing?); or perhaps what hurts you isn't that she's dead, but the way she died, pointing an accusing finger, as if she wanted to protest.

And is there any other explanation of what she did? She wanted to punish you. She wanted to hurt. And if that's what she wanted, then she must have had a reason, and what was the reason if not my standing by, indifferent to her suffering, not participating in what she was going through? And then I say to myself, But she turned her back on me, she didn't want my help; if she wanted it, she would have asked, appealed to me, she would have tried.

She hated me. She didn't want me to play any part in her life. And what do I know about that life? Nothing. Dry facts from which you can draw quite contradictory conclusions. She was my daughter and I didn't know her, I didn't know what she was doing; although we lived under the same roof I didn't know what was going on inside her. I didn't guess, and in fact I didn't have the time to spare. All my life I've been interested only in myself. All my life I was occupied travelling, studying, working, writing. All my life I've been busy proving myself worthy. To whom, and worthy of what? I don't know. Of what am I guilty? I paid my debts to this country. I fought and I was even taken prisoner. I did reserve duty. I was always a law-abiding citizen. I paid my taxes, I never cheated. I was thorough in my work. I tried to be perfect in everything I put my hand to.

True, I was unfaithful to my wife. And once I'd begun I never stopped. But she didn't know about it. She couldn't have known and if Noa found out what did it have to do with her? What could she know about my needs, about my despair, about my terrible longing for youth, about the old age creeping up on me, about the desire to seize more and more of life. . . . But the guilt can't be formulated in a causal sentence, a factual statement. It's a kind of metaphysical guilt.

Your heart, says the observer, is tied up in knots which you have never tried to undo. You always kept on the right side of everyone. You offered help where it was needed, you listened when it was required, you perfected the game of love, so that no woman who went to bed with you would feel deprived. You outdid yourself as a host, you were fair with your students. But you never never really opened your heart to anyone. No one was permitted to touch you, you thought that that tangle was your business, yours and nobody else's. When anyone tried to come close to you, you shrank, you hit out. When they came too near, you became violent, cruel, rough; your Israeli abrasiveness, of which you never managed to rid yourself, asserted itself. When it came to your daughter, you did your duty, with presents, sometimes extravagant presents, you did your duty with a kiss on the forehead. Not that you didn't sometimes want to devour her with kisses. You did want to, sometimes, but you never did. You devoured life without a thought for the people you devoured. You never allowed yourself to show tenderness. You treated your daughter exactly as your father treated you, your father, who imprisoned your fears and your failings, the tenderness in you, behind locks and bars.

More than anything else, you were afraid of tenderness. You were afraid of being soft, of being unmanly. That's what your father did to you. He locked up all the tenderness inside you and you never took the trouble to break the locks. That was what you feared most. And others paid the price. When you kissed the women you loved, you kissed them with passion, you kissed them with lust, but not with love. And you didn't let them love you. Everything else was permitted, but not that.

Did you ever ask yourself about the suffering you caused them because of what you deprived them of? Of course not. You were convinced that what you were giving them was enough. And when they demanded what you were incapable of giving, what you couldn't allow yourself to give, you were cruel. And now, a little too late, you realize that it wasn't enough, that your own private tangle of knots isn't only your own business when a fellow human being wants to be part of it, that unfinished words are like nothing at all.

You protest. You say: I couldn't behave differently, that's how I'm built. I had to defend myself. That's understandable, of course. But it doesn't exempt you from guilt. It doesn't exempt you from the fact that you treated other people as if they were a joke. That you said to them, This far and no further. You make everything conditional, like a contract: This is what I'm prepared to give and this is what I expect to receive, no more and no less.

What am I guilty of, you ask. I couldn't, you say. Well then, if it's more convenient for you that way, go ahead and see it as a kind of metaphysical guilt. That way you can retreat to the comfortable position you've taken all your life. You say, But everyone's the same, didn't Noa behave like that? Did she undo the knots in her heart? But I say to you: Here, and precisely here, lies your guilt, in that you imposed the same locks on your daughter that were imposed on you. You treated her the way you were treated. And yet you hated it! You were furious with your father for treating you like that! And nevertheless you were unable to liberate yourself from the prison he imposed on you. How pathetic!

Certainly, untying knots involves a lot of pain. And why suffer? After all, it's only an abstract kind of guilt and all it takes to dispel it and to revive your spirits is for the postman to ring the doorbell. And you want to die of shame because you don't know how to behave, and you reassure yourself with banalities about life having to go on, or that suicide would be pointless, or cowardice. Of course, dying, in this case, would be the easiest way out. So why think about it? You wipe out all these oppressive feelings, as if you can sweep them under the carpet forever. No more guilt, no more loneliness, no more longings. No more terrible loss. No more murky tangle of feelings, confusion and embarrassment and sorrow that you don't know how to cope with. You obliterate them all, including the fact that you want to die, including the fact that you want to live and you're ashamed of it, including that observer who keeps on mocking you and saying to you, Look at yourself, egoist, look at yourself and see how you aren't sorry enough, how you are already capable of thinking about food, about green olives, and going to the grocer's, and going to the post office to get the parcel that a certain woman far away has sent you, of buying things, of Lysol. You'd do better to drink the Lysol.

What an ugly creature you are, incapable of sorrow. Why don't you scream? What an ugly creature you are. Who can go on living and making plans after everything that's happened? And even to hope for love. Love? In the first place, you don't even know where she is. Secondly, she's no longer the girl she was. She's a mature woman, soon she'll be old and charmless. A woman you haven't talked to, for fifteen or who knows how many years, sends you an idiotic letter, a crazy letter, about things that have nothing to do with you. You didn't even love her, you only used her to feed your self-love, yet you grab at the possibility now without a moment's hesitation.

And she knew it, too, she knew how you would react, it was exactly what she intended, the cunning creature. There's no doubt that's what she intended, inventing something for you to do in your hour of need. Occupational therapy, that's all it is. And she chose just the right time, too, tempting you to take a bit of interest in other people's lives, something you've never done before. I finger the blue envelope in my hand. No return address.

And did you take any interest in your daughter's life? You thought she was grown up and could look after herself. Sometimes you regretted that she hadn't found a husband yet, but you did not think it was too serious. There was always a boy here, a boy there. There was always someone, and maybe she didn't like boys at all. She always had girl friends, single girls like herself. No, it didn't break your heart. You had your own fish to fry, why should you bother about anyone else's troubles? Noa. My daughter, I want to cry and I don't know how. How shall I atone for not knowing? How? She left a letter, but she didn't favor me with an explanation. She argued that she had the right to do what she liked with her life, she said she was sorry. She said that I was a strong person and would surely get over it. And she wished me success, the little bitch! How I hate her for that letter. How cruel it was! Did she really hate me so much? She said she hoped I would write a lot of books and she didn't express any regret or sorrow.

I always knew, of course, that I wasn't close to her. That I never took enough of an interest in her life. Did she ever let me? I grind my teeth, did she ever let me? The two of them were united against me. They turned their backs on me, she and her mother. How devotedly she looked after Leah, right up to the last minute. No daughter could have been more devoted. When I said I would go with her for the radiation treatment, to spare Noa the suffering, she wouldn't let me. You have your own affairs to attend to, she said, why bother? It's not for you, they said. She mocked me, and Leah supported her, she always supported her.

Naturally, I wanted her to study. To make something of herself.

Naturally I was disappointed that she hadn't inherited my merits, what I consider my merits, my intellectual curiosity, my studiousness, my ambition. True, I made a lot of mistakes. Show me one father or one mother who never makes a mistake. And what's so bad about the fact that I was so wrapped up in the work I labored over day and night? My own family were like strangers to me. Actually, they provided a background against which I might shine. Perhaps I was the one who made them the way they were. Perhaps I did it on purpose, so that I could shine at their expense. Oh God, how sick I am of these questions. What ends do they serve, now that everything is lost? The truth is that I never had the patience to listen to them. I only pretended to listen. That's all. Out of politeness.

I attached no importance to the things they were capable of talking about. Little things. The trivialities of women. Sometimes I was jealous. A kind of crazy jealousy. Noa's mine too, I would think, not only Leah's. Why doesn't she come to me? Why is she so remote? But I repressed these thoughts. I would say to myself, It's natural. Women are close to women. I was under no obligation to think about these things. Leah did not trouble me with her problems, and Noa took her cue from her mother. Once when I was making love to Leah she suddenly burst into tears. And when I asked her about it she gave me an evasive answer. I didn't press her. I didn't want to know. Maybe I was afraid of her secret. . . .

I wonder why I should think of this now—in all those years it never occurred to me to ask her if she was satisfied. I took it for granted. I think that it was in our sexual relations that my indifference expressed itself most strongly. Indifference isn't the right word, and neither is selfishness. It's a lot of things together: fear, indifference, unwillingness to get involved. And this is characteristic of me in every sphere, even the scientific one, which is why I'll never go far. My achievements always will be mediocre.

I cultivated an arrogant, detached way of life. To call a spade a spade—I became a snob, the dreariest kind of snob—a jumped-up peasant giving himself the airs of a man of the world. And in this, too, I am not unique, I know dozens of Israelis like me. Artists in Paris selling cheap the cultural wares they brought with them from here: the Zohar, Judaism, the Kabbalah. Canny merchants who know how to capitalize on the spirit of the times. Scientists in American universities, many of them sons of the bankrupt old aristocracy. Once the founding fathers, the old colonists, the citrus farmers were our aristocracy. Crude, ignorant people for the most part, but at least they had some kind of dream. And what have we got today? Building contractors. People who are even cruder and more ignorant than their predecessors, and who do everything in their power to prove their sophistication.

To see the difference between them just look at the houses they built for themselves, the old and the new. Go and have a look at the old houses still standing in places like Nes Ziona and Petah Tikva, Rishon L'Zion and Rehovot. The style could be called colonial, perhaps, and it would be out of place to call it simple. I remember one house in particular, pink, with Greek pillars and arches, but with all its vulgarity, it isn't ostentatious. It has a certain rural modesty, a certain true grandeur, the grandeur of actual conquest.

But above all I remember the Eretz Israel of little square houses, sometimes with flat roofs, sometimes tiled, and here and there with a shed built onto the side. Go, for instance, to Rosh Pinna, to Yesod Hama'alah, and see the simplicity of the lines, the tranquility of the houses and the gardens. You can learn a lot about the character of the people who lived in them, their demands from life, their attitude to the world. And most significant of all is that they didn't cultivate lawns, there were fruit trees in their gardens, olives and loquats, bananas, oranges and lemons, and later on apples and pears, too. Because land was respected in those days. It wasn't exploited for decoration, ostentation, or social status. It was cultivated. When land has value in people's lives, then people have value, too, whatever their style of life.

Compare the old houses with the houses of the contractors, the new rich—how did my friend, Professor A. describe them? He said that they were built by people who got their ideas of culture and beauty from the Hollywood of the thirties and forties, and created a monstrous hybrid from their false ideas of wealth and aristocracy. They built demonstrations of status, they took the stage sets of movies like *A Thousand and One Nights* and *Thief of Bagdad* and built them in concrete: they imported a phony American idea of the Orient and made it into a local status symbol. A brilliant man, my friend. How well he understood our new aristocracy, and how their architecture exposes the baseness of their values. Cheap Hollywood movies they saw when they were children . . . .

I'm trying to escape again. Where can I escape to?

ELISHEVA

On the way to the travel bureau I suddenly felt desperately tired and went home again. I asked myself, Am I ready for this trip, do I have the strength to care for a dying person again? And if not, can I get out of it, can I refuse? How could I say no to Yanis? I thought of how I had managed to pull myself together again, how I would not allow myself to break down . . . to think of the dead more than once in a while. And now a long, thin, brown finger was beckoning me back . . . .

Yesterday, in the evening, after lying on my bed all day, I felt somewhat restored and I went out. My feet took me to Carmela's door, but not by the shortcut through the grevillea avenue. I was afraid. It's so dark there. I made a big detour, as if I didn't want to get there at all.

Carmela's apartment is full of rubbish. I always scold her for her mania for collecting things. "That's why you never got married," I say to her, "because you love things more than people. Things don't threaten you with demands." She isn't offended. "It's my own choice," she says, "I want to be free." Carmela talks a lot, but she isn't really open. I don't know what ties us to each other, apart from the fact that we're both single women, no longer young. She is so different from me. She had such energy and vitality, there's something almost vulgar about her, with her loud clothes, the tattered furs she wraps herself in in winter, her heavy makeup. There's something crude about her boisterous, superficial gaiety. She takes so much trouble with her disguises that they proclaim the chasms beneath, aching to be exposed. But they remain hidden. I don't know what attracts me to her. Perhaps that enormous vitality itself, the tireless motor consuming people and things and never turned inward on itself. People with great energy have always fascinated me. I look at them in amazement, in utter incomprehension . . .

but they turn away from me, like Avigdor. . . .

For the most part I don't understand what Carmela is getting at, especially when she talks about authenticity in personal relations, or the way she goes on and on about women's liberation. How remote I am from all that. The truth is that Carmela is such an unliberated woman that her longing for liberation is perfectly understandable. And, in spite of everything, I have to admit that it's cozy at her place. Especially in winter.

When she opened the door she said: "What on earth are you doing here? It's my birthday tomorrow, and you're invited for tomorrow."

I said: "That's alright. I can go if it's not convenient." But she invited me in. She was in a despondent mood. "My customers are driving me crazy," she said. "You have no idea what they demand today. It's perverse, I tell you. You have no idea. . . nobody wants anything simple or elegant today. They themselves know nothing, of course. But they pick things up from the air, or from the newspapers. And they dictate to me. One insists on Louis Quinze and another wants Chippendale, or Persian. Someone else heard about Victoriana and that's what he has to have, without knowing the first thing about it. I'm telling you, it makes me want to vomit. I've been running around all day for an imbecilic woman who must have oriental decor for her villa. I felt like offering her an Arab lavatory, a hole in the ground instead of a commode. And if you think I wouldn't have been able to sell it to her you're mistaken. I've had it. . . ."

"Then change your job," I said.

"And what will I do? Work for the municipality, like you? Where they won't let me do anything at all. And for a lousy salary, too. Tell me, do you think they are really comfortable in their villas? They don't live in them at all. They just put on a performance."

But afterwards Carmela began to talk about her longings for a real, honest life, and I realized that her bad mood had nothing to do with her professional troubles. She spoke of personal relations, of the possibility of deeper relations with others. I told her it was a pretty fairy tale. I tried to explain, but it was no good. She doesn't understand that each of us is a monad, a closed cell drifting alone in the void, each with our own perception of the world that no one can share. Even the adjacent monad doesn't have the same view, the difference may be minute but it's decisive. True, they sometimes meet, but it's an illusory meeting. The walls of the cells brush against each other and the friction creates a kind of warmth, but that's all. There is no real coupling apart from the physical, and even that is hardly ever successful, in my experience. But anyone who refuses to be satisfied with this is doomed to a lifetime of unhappiness. And physical coupling, too, doesn't join people, it lasts no more than a moment. The warmth it generates may be greater than that of simple friction, but nevertheless it doesn't join two people together. The only way we can come close to another is through our children, but children leave us, they too are separate beings. Nevertheless they provide a kind of consolation. That is why I wasn't willing to relinquish Michael, even though I felt like a criminal every time he asked me, Where's my daddy; or, Why haven't I got a father like all the other children?

I wanted to explain to Carmela that the very fact that we are what we are, closed autonomous cells, gives rise to the longing to be united with another, and so we invent fairy tales about that possibility. And anyone who invests in these fairy tales is bound to end, just like her, with a slap in the face. But Carmela is not ripe for such insights, and I pity her. Perhaps all the things she buys are some compensation. . . .

"When are you leaving?" Carmela asked, and I didn't know what to say.

She said: "Tell me, do you really have a boyfriend in Greece?"

I said to her: "Look, Greece is just an allegory. When you think about Greece—what do you think about? What do you know about the Greeks of today, the country of today? And when you go there, what moves you? It's only an allegory. I don't know what it feels like to live an allegory. But our lives here are a kind of allegory, too, without our being conscious of it, of course: the chosen people, the Holy Land, we drink it in with our mother's milk. But in our daily lives we live like people who live in any country, just another country. But we are still an allegory and we live that allegory in spite of ourselves. Perhaps the Greece of today and its people are not in the least interesting. But it still moves us to think about Greece, you and me and many others. And my friend in Greece, too, is only an allegory and there is very little that is Greek about him. He has a Greek name, and a tenuous attachment to his people. But what he really is, before anything else, is a sick man who's going to die. And I think I would like to go and be with him in his last days. I'm used to looking after dying people, it doesn't frighten me."

Carmela looked at me in astonishment, and I was tempted to tell her about Michael. To say, as I said to Leon's mother, I had a son once, and he died. But I didn't say anything, and she didn't ask, except with her eyes.

"How did you meet him, your Greek friend?" she asked.

"It's a long story," I said, "but I'll tell you the bare facts. I met him here. He grew up here. He studied here, he worked here. And one day he left, and went back to the land of his birth."

Carmela replied: "The chap who's coming tomorrow, he's got a friend in Greece, too. So you'll have something in common to talk about while I'm cooking."

PART THREE

The Visit to Carmela's

The poet Hart Crane (1899-1932) committed suicide by jumping from the deck of the S.S. Orizaba *during a voyage en route from Mexico to New York.*

ELISHEVA

Carmela's celebrating her birthday today. I am in no hurry to get there. I don't really want to go. What do I care about Carmela? What do I care about the man she's invited? Carmela inspires very little affection in me. It's only that we're lonely, only because both of us are so alone. And why is it so important to her that I come this evening? I don't know. It is a clear evening and I enjoy walking. Sometimes Tel Aviv seems to me like an inferno. At dusk after a sweltering *hamsin* day, when the dust hangs over the town and the heat shimmers in the headlamps of the cars, grains of dust scattered in the light, and everything blurred in the haze, the city is a monster of noise and filth. But in winter it's different. The air is clear, clean and at certain hours there's something almost European about it.

Now my feet hurt because of the new shoes. Italian. I bought them this morning to give myself a treat. When I get home I'll bathe my feet in warm salt water and paint my toenails pink. Avigdor—I don't call him Pierre anymore—Avigdor liked my feet, small, soft, always clean. Now that I call him Avigdor they're not the same anymore. They're hard and calloused, neglected for years. Nowadays it's hard for me to think about anything else: a man I once loved walked past me in the street and he didn't recognize me. Or pretended not to. And all the pain that was silent for so many years has suddenly begun to scream. I know very well that my hopes mock me, that I will never again feel his fond hand in my hair, and words that once were said never will be said again. Then I hear the poet's cry:

> *Of old there was a promise, and thy sails*
> *Have kept no faith but wind, the cold stream*
> *The hot fickle wind. . . .*

I know I'm treading the brink of an abyss. I can jump or step aside. The choice is mine. But the dream is so seductive. It alone is not limited by hope and dread, by fear and pity, by flattery and love. And from fear of the poet, for fear of the lure of his call, like the sirens' song seducing ships to smash against the rocks of death, I turn back to groundless fantasies, sweet and forbidden as the fruit of the Tree of Knowledge to Adam and Eve. Melting snow on distant mountains and a river flooding its banks.

Today I can understand why Yanis and Henrietta never believed my stories. I would tell them about a man I called Pierre Bezuhov in exactly the same way that I talked about Hart Crane—a poet who died when I was a child, a man I never met. But how could I not have invented stories? How could I have revealed that my love was always accompanied by an image of death and that it caused me untold suffering, suffering transmuted by love into the exclusive object of my desire? Henrietta was always matter-of-fact, and Yanis was not close to me at that time. . . .

Boys and girls in blue shirts with red laces at their necks go noisily past full of rudeness and self-confidence. They remind me of the children in the Home. They always spoke in a kind of whisper, hesitantly, and with downcast eyes. Even those that shouted shouted their fears and their insecurity, and their shout was like a whisper. Their secret whispers filled the little rooms, pressing against the walls as if they wanted to tear down the barriers that separated them from the confident, cheerful world outside.

In those days Henrietta denied God and I believed in him. When we grew up, it was I who was the heretic and Henrietta who rebuked me. But although she disapproved of my way of life and her strictures were a burden to me, we never stopped loving one another. If I could tell her my story now, she would know that I am no longer a woman of little faith. Nevertheless, I ask myself whether she never pretended, never hid things, whether she was really frank with me. We were very close, we loved each other, and yet she remained an enigma. And, above all, there is her death . . . .

The memories are disturbing my peace of mind.

"Your hair's hard," the man I used to call Pierre, the man who was my lover long ago, said to me the other day, "you're still using the same shampoo, and you're still as flirtatious as ever."

And as he spoke to me on that chance encounter in the street, detached and alien as he was, I remembered the hard, rough hand in my hair, massaging my scalp, sliding down to the nape of my neck, lingering on my shoulders, crushing my breasts, a big hand, broad and strong. Its grip was firm and it tore off my clothes impatiently, pushing my body to the ground almost roughly. Take your clothes off, Pierre. It's hot in the room and dark. And now slap me in the face, make me desist from grief and insane desire, make me be modest and grateful for anything this empty life may offer. The strong fingers dig through my flesh into bone, trying to mold my body into a different shape.

But that's not really how it happened. He simply walked past me without a greeting. In his eyes I saw nothing, not a spark.

"You've got delicate bones," he said to me once.

"You're hurting me," I replied, "my bones are soft and it feels good when you hurt me."

Tomorrow I'll make the final arrangements and I'll leave. And perhaps, halfway between Haifa and Piraeus, in the early afternoon, when the rays of the sun are slanting onto the sea, making the water gleam like a vast, flat expanse of brass, I'll go up to the deck, rest my arms on the damp railing, and look at the water flowing and splashing murky foam onto the black prow. Perhaps I'll take off my coat, my watch and my jewelry, and lay them down, perhaps I'll think of Hart Crane, and do as he did thirty-seven years ago, sailing on the steamship *Orizaba* from Mexico to New York. Or perhaps, if I choose to, I'll sail with the ship to Piraeus, and late in the afternoon I'll take the subway from the harbor to Kefissia, to Yanis' house. The housekeeper will open the door and Yanis will welcome me gladly and kiss me on the mouth like a relative, not like a lover.

To be with Yanis, as in Rome, liberated from this crushing compulsion. At dawn the swallows and the finches singing in the blooming gardens of Kefissia will wake me, and I shall find myself in his arms. He will be sprawled on his back, as usual, his head facing the ceiling, his mouth slightly open and his pointed black beard tousled. In my heart I shall compare him to Michelangelo, as I did in Rome, in Florence and in Venice, some years ago, and I will not think about the fact that he is a failed poet, and a weak man. I shall lie in Yanis' bed and look at him, and my longings will brim over like water, into another continent, another sky; like flotsam and jetsam my longings will float, the memory of a shipwreck whose planks are rent apart, borne back to their point of departure on murky waves.

Yanis planted a magnolia tree in the garden of his house. In summer its great white flowers will bloom and I shall pick them and decorate the rooms. In the middle of the drawing room, on a low wooden table made of oak, in the daytime when the big room is flooded with dry, pure light, I shall sit opposite the Corinthian vase and quietly contemplate the curving, sensuous roundnesses and watch them wither. I shall be able to reflect calmly and quietly on Henrietta and Pierre, my beloved. I shall no longer have any vague expectations of catastrophe and sorrow, of a beloved man who does not come.

A beloved man who does not come.

I shall be lonely and my body quiet. And, like everybody else, anguished and lost, sometimes, but only sometimes, demented with grief. Like everyone else, like my beloved, whom I called by that funny name, Pierre Bezuhov, a big-bodied man with a heavy tread, red-gold hair, and a loud, exulting laugh, which sometimes makes him whoop and choke, and when he bends over me my eyes are blinded. Like Yanis and Henrietta, and even like Alexander, Yanis' friend, a man I have never met. All the people I know and all the people I don't know; all people everywhere, at all times. I shall be like North Labrador:

> *Cold-hushed, there is only the shifting of moments.*
> *That journey toward no Spring—*
> *No birth, no death, no time nor sun*
> *In answer.*

◆

Again and again Avigdor-Pierre comes back into my thoughts. And whenever my thoughts encounter him something dangerous wakes in me, something threatening, and I am filled with fear. For I still yearn for him, yearn to know again the joy in life that was mine long ago, when, hiding in a hotel for whores and sailors, furtive, frightened and thrilled, I knew unimaginable happiness. I was no longer alone, and nevertheless I wanted to die. I prayed for it never to end although I knew the transience of this happiness, how it lasted, like lightning, no more than seconds. I tried to hang onto it, and I wanted to end when it ended, to be lost when it perished, to die with its loss.

But when I told him about it, about my desire for death, he looked at me blankly and rejected this alien being I had so carelessly and unthinkingly revealed.

In Kefissia, in Yanis' warm and elegant house, I will be granted peace, and in the quiet which will prevail there, I will be able, perhaps, to subdue my sorrow, and it will become a dull, blunted knife.

No, I don't want to meet him again. I'm afraid. I'll take off my clothes and he'll see how I've changed, looking at me with his critical eye. My feet have grown clumsy, my ankles are swollen, my backbone is a little curved and there are wrinkles in the smoothness of my neck. There's something humiliating and depressing in not being sure, and I have never been sure of anything in my life. And thus, in Yanis' drawing room, opposite the wooden table, I shall sit and be quiet. I shall sit there day and night and watch the big white flower dying slowly, submissively. For that is what is needed, sub-mission and humility. I will attend to this perfect, rounded and airy structure, whose tumescence is white as a northern face with golden hair, as a full, fortunate moon. Day and night. One day or two. Swollen and rounded as a pregnant woman. You may not touch its skin, which is soft and tender and fragile as a butterfly's wing. And my love, too, will slowly die. I have never been in Athens in the winter. It's years since I last saw Yanis, but I can still see him now with great clarity. I can hear him talking to me in his strong, clear voice about his friend Slavos. I can see him standing near Henrietta, whose black hair falls to her shoulders and breasts.

Yanis looks at her with loving eyes, he contemplates her with yearning and his sorrow is unspeakable. I say: This is my friend Henrietta, whom I first met in the shade of a tall tree with a lucky flower in her hand—the most beautiful flower I have ever seen.

This is what I say, and Yanis smiles at me compassionately and says nothing. His face has aged and I am seized with dread at the sight of its thinness. I saw him last four years ago in Rome. From there we went to Athens, trying in vain to resurrect the joy of our first trip together. In Rome we walked in the gardens of the Villa Borghese and in the magnolia avenues, and I told him about my first meeting with Henrietta in the Home, and about the terrible slow death of the lucky flower. I described its scent, wonderfully delicate, immediately dissolved, yet which remained.

The grevillea with its silver leaves, the butterflies whose wings are dusted with magnificent spots of color, the glint of the light on the waves—others have spoken of them and given them names. The smell of a green lemon. Little bunches of violets.

> *No more violets*
> *And the year*
> *Broken into smoky panels.*
> *What woods remember now*
> *Her calls, her enthusiasms?*

Thus wrote Hart Crane, and shortly afterwards he leaped overboard into the sea. It was on the way from Mexico to New York. The sky was the color of a half-ripe mango. At the end of April 1932, a few minutes before twelve o'clock, on the deck of the *Orizaba*, three hundred miles north of Havana. The sea was green and calm.

> *Summer scarcely begun*
> *And violets,*
> *A few picked, the rest dead?*

This is how he saw the world on one of the days in the short span allotted him. Yanis once told me that he would prefer such a death to the death foretold him by the woman who read the coffee grounds. A nonaccidental death, noble, and chosen. But for him it would have been the Mediterranean, among the Dodecanese islands, next to Delos. As close as possible to the birthplace of Apollo.

In that same conversation he said: "I want to be ready for it when it comes. I wouldn't like it to be sudden, like an ambush, a knife in the back. That would be humiliating. I would like to go forward to meet it calmly, heroically, in the knowledge of what awaits me. Like my father. . . . What did he think about the end? What does a man feel when he is about to be executed? I know that the fascists tortured him first. They hoped that he would break and tell them the names of his comrades and their hiding places. He stood firm, and I envy him. I'm not at all sure that I would have been able to endure it . . . this doubt often tortures me. I am afraid that I would have disappointed him, I'm afraid that I'm not worthy to bear the name of his grandfather, who also was executed after torture, in another time and place. In Crete, during the revolt against the Turks. . . . Perhaps these are the only moments in a man's life when he has the opportunity of proving that he is worthy of respect. I hope very much that when my time comes I won't let him down, that I'll know, like him, how to face death without bitterness or resentment, like a whole man, who lived the right life."

Poor Yanis. He was not given that chance. He is too ill now to fight. His enemies and the enemies of his father are in power and he is helpless. His friends are in prison, their fingerjoints beaten with rulers, electric shocks, Turkish whiplashes. And he sits at home tied to a wheelchair, waiting for death.

Will I really travel all the way to Piraeus, to Kefissia, to the house of a stranger?

I remember a sad evening in Rome. Yanis stood at the hotel window, looking down at the square below. I was lying naked on the wide hotel bed with its lumpy mattress, as his desolation stalked the room, anxiously waiting for love. I said with feigned lightness, Come over here, I want to give you a kiss. Yanis stayed at the window, his back to me. And because he blamed me for his disappointment and the failure of his dreams, he chose this moment to ask me about what had impelled me, a few years previously, to try to do what Hart Crane had done in April 1932, on the *Orizaba*. I told him some story or other, and in my heart I thought about the stupid way in which we were losing the chance of happiness which might have been ours. I spoke for a long time about all kinds of irrelevant things, and finally he replied: I don't understand a thing. And I couldn't make out the letter I found on your desk then, either.

"There are no stars tonight, but those of memory," the poet said.

I am late of course, and Carmela is angry. As I walk into the hall I catch sight of a man sitting in the rocking chair in the living room. He raises his head and looks at me, and for a moment I feel like running for my life. The phonograph is playing and I can catch the words of the song:

> *When I am dead and buried*
> *don't you weep for me. . . .*
> *On the good ship Zion*
> *don't you weep for me. . . .*

The man does not get up when I come into the room. He looks at me, nods, and puffs on his pipe, which has gone out.

> *King Peter is the Captain*
> *don't you weep for me.*
> *I don't want you*
> *to weep for me.*

He doesn't get up. He doesn't hold out his hand. He just says his name curtly: Alex. I almost laugh with the surprise. I think that if this man turns out to be Henrietta's Alexander, Yanis' Alexander, it would be an astonishing coincidence.

"Alex or Alexander?" I ask him, and he raises his eyes for the first time from his pipe.

"Once I was called Alexander, by my mother and my friends and my late wife. Now I prefer Alex. Yes, Alex, please."

His late wife. . . .Once after Yanis had complained to me in a letter that Alexander wasn't answering his letters, I offered to visit him and find out how he was. Yanis sent me an urgent telegram. You must never meet Alexander. Never.

I obeyed. I phoned Alexander once, at his request. It was a strange conversation, I couldn't succeed in making contact.

And now here is Alex, sitting at his ease in the depths of the rocking chair. A tall, thin man, black straight hair falling onto his brow and sometimes covering one of his eyes. He brushes it back with his fingers, using them like a comb. His fist is closed round the bowl of the pipe while he stuffs tobacco into it with his thumb. He rocks comfortably and looks at me with apparent indifference and insolence. I know nothing about him, except for the way he clenches his fist around the bowl of his pipe, except for the way his narrow eyes peer at me, except for the way he fills the room with the sweet, nauseating smoke of his tobacco, the funny, jerky way he turns his head, the cold, amused look in his eyes.

We won't be able to be friends, I think. He is a scornful man who despises his fellow beings.

Carmela says to him: "It's a profession that has to be studied."

She is talking about antique furniture, her favorite subject. She takes from the bookcase a lavish volume and sets it, opened, on Alexander's knees.

"Here, you see? It's a complicated subject. There are different styles, different periods. . . ."

Alex pages through the book, looking at the sketches and photographs with a mocking indifference. Carmela leans over him intently. From time to time she points to one of the photographs and makes some remark.

Alex says: "I have never attached any importance to furniture. Like everything else that serves us, all that is required of them is that they be functional."

Carmela shrugs her shoulders and says nothing.

Suddenly Alex turns to me and asks: "Are you really a landscape architect?"

"When I have work," I reply, with studied indifference and a certain rudeness. He goes on asking me questions. His questions are routine, insultingly banal. And I answer casually, as if I am accustomed to the curiosity of others.

Then he says: "Do you know anything about Chinese gardens?"

Suddenly I feel a sense of alarm, a dim memory flickers at the threshold of my consciousness. I answer hastily: "No. But I know something about Japanese gardens."

Carmela places on the table almonds, a selection of salty pastries, lemonade.

I had never met Alexander. His presence here is startling, like a blast of wind full of dust and dirt. He reaches for the almonds and takes some in his fist. I don't look at him directly, but at the same time I can't take my eyes off him. I sip my sherry, and a pleasant warmth seeps through me.

One can't go on repeating the same stories forever. They grow old and tired with the passage of time. I can't go on drawing out this love which doesn't change. I must lead it carefully and gently through everything it does not understand, building bridges over any pitfalls on the way. I must leave this place. Go far away, to a place where I have no friend or savior, to a remote corner of the world where an ancient tranquility prevails, a primordial peace, the deathly stillness of a distant time. And so tomorrow, or perhaps next week, I shall travel the long road from the sea to the olive groves and the vines trailing over the wooden beams in the inner courtyards, to the land of bald mountains and meager water and whose narrow valleys sunder it in pieces. And there, at twilight, when the darkness threatens the sea and flames consume the sky, Yanis will be waiting for me in the milling crowds of Syndagma Square, opposite the El-Al offices. He will bring his friend Slavos with him—a man I have never met, who perhaps does not even exist—and on our way perhaps we will also meet Henrietta.

I can no longer hope for love affairs on Kerkyra, the island of the sun, where I once dreamed of unexpected meetings with the man I called Pierre Bezuhov and the uninhibited consummation of desire. My hair is going white and my complexion is turning sallow. Nevertheless, precisely now the possibilities are unlimited and everything is to be expected.

In that land there are still peasants who walk home from the fields when evening falls, carrying wooden ploughs on their shoulders; the vines still wind their tendrils round the wooden trellises at the doors of little restaurants; the olive trees are still an ashy green; the white jasmine flowers still smell sweet in the evening, and the light pours steadily onto the land of dreams and stripes with shining silver the bluest water in the world.

There I can be content. For the sly and fickle spring of the Aegean sea will no longer awaken hopeless longings in my heart. At last I shall be able to call my love by pet names, calmly, without excessive excitement; I shall be able to name him by the tender names a woman speaks to a beloved man in a whisper, in pleasure, when her heart is full to overflowing.

And as I reflect upon my approaching journey, it seems to me that if I knew how to write love poems I would not have to jump like Hart Crane from the ship into the sea on the way from Mexico to New York, as he died in the year 1932, in the month of April, in the noon of the day. Oh, then I would have sung words like music to the honey and the green figs and the flowering, fragrant laurel, and grown lucky flowers in my vase.

There is no need to go away. All I have to do is shut my eyes and I can see Yanis. He's waiting for me outside the big office building. I see him from the distance, thinner, with his face eaten by the sun. He hasn't seen me yet and his black eyes, which always twinkled with amusement, are sunken. I ask myself if he is ill. With a feeling of dread I remember that a number of years ago a malignant tumor was removed from his body. He's going to die, I think in terror, he's going down to Hades to seek for Henrietta, the beloved of his soul.

"I've brought a friend," Yanis will say to me, "he's waiting for us in the car. Be nice to him."

"Who is he?" I ask.

"A Greek,"—he says, with a forced laugh, "a Greek who only knows Greek."

"Then I won't be able to talk to him," I say, obscurely happy.

"He's waiting for us. Come along."

We walk up the square and turn right. Opposite lie the gardens of the defeated, exiled king, hiding behind a tall hedge and a crowd of bus stops. On the corner, a little motorcar is parked at the side of the road.

Yanis has a pointed fox face and sly eyes which no longer laugh, yet are still laughing. I think about how he has succeeded in preserving his joy in life, despite his fatal illness. In the past he was plump, with a little paunch. He is shrivelled now, his paunch a soft little swelling in the middle of his body. And his cheeks, dry and brown as a tobacco leaf left in the sun, furrowed by deep lines, seem to have receded, like ebbing waves, to the shelter of his heavy brows. His little black eyes peep out of their sockets with a merry gleam—tiny dark pools overhung by mountains.

A man in his early youth emerges from the little white car parked and comes towards us with heavy, deliberate steps. His body is big and clumsy, his gait that of a peasant; warm and friendly.

The fascination of the rudimentary is hard to withstand. It inspires a missionary zeal to give it meaning; a wish to knead and mold, to tame it.

Yanis introduces his friend and I can't catch his name. I am a little excited, evidently.

The man gives me a friendly smile and presses my hand so hard that it hurts. His hand is huge, and it encompasses my hand with a grip as tight as an iron hoop on a cartwheel. The pathetic wail of a puppy comes from the building in whose shade we are standing. "A little dog," says Yanis, "he must have been left alone. Maybe he's hungry. Maybe he's lonely."

I am a woman in the evening of her days, I say to myself again and again. I am a woman who can no longer hope for love affairs, not even on Kerkyra, the island of the sun, an island made for love. . . .

"Put on that Black gospel singer again, I prefer him to Deller. Deller's voice disgusts me," says Alexander.

Carmela changes the record, and once more the tender, husky voice of the Black singer fills the room:

> *When I am dead and buried*
> *don't you weep for me. . . .*

I prefer it that way, too. I don't want anyone to weep for me. I don't want my death to sadden anybody. Because I choose it. But perhaps Pierre will be haunted by guilt and remorse for the rest of his life. And perhaps he will take no notice at all.

Carmela pours me another drink without my asking for it, and I sip it slowly. I wouldn't mind getting drunk. A few days ago I saw Pierre in the street. What he was doing here, in Tel Aviv, I don't know. He didn't notice me. I walked past him without saying anything. He's aged, the years haven't been good to him. But at that moment, in spite of the bitter insult, my love for him was as fresh as the day I fell in love with him. As if it too was subject to the seasonal renewal of the plants.

We had a few experiences in common, Pierre and I, I think bitterly, a few happy days together. In my imagination I see piles of clouds tumbling down the mountainside, like huge pink-feathered birds, and there is something as tender as Henrietta's cheeks in the stillness spilling all around, in the infinite quiet of the landscape sloping down to the sea. We stood on the top of the mountain, looking at the sweet sight together, and I said his name in a whisper, lovingly. He laid his heavy hands on my head and pressed it to his shoulder, and for a moment I no longer heard the buzz of the crickets and singing of the songbirds and I no longer saw anything. And in the heart of the stillness, in the heart of the detached, alien beauty of rough mountain flanks, spiky burnet bushes, sticky pink rockroses, the current of love streamed in an agitated, unquiet flow. Pierre's hands groped the lower reaches of my belly and my eyes glazed. One day we'll go to Kerkyra together, won't we, I said. Pierre laughed. The remnants of the warmth of the day enveloped us like a mantle of vast dimensions, the clarity and transparency of the evening air, and the premonition of the cold, stinging night wind.

I remember the first time we met, in the lecture hall where I remained behind after the other students had left. The windows of the hall were open because of the *hamsin* which was just about to break. It was the beginning of the autumn semester, and the weather was still unsettled. We had a funny lecturer in art history who wrote his lecture notes on little bits of paper. After his lectures he would stay behind to put his notes in order. These notes were the object of many jokes among his students, who found him an odd and intriguing figure. He would extract them from a little cardboard box, one note after the other, and it would sometimes take him a considerable amount of time to find the one he was looking for.

A sudden gust of wind from the big open windows scattered the lecturer's notes, which landed all across the room. The burly, red-headed man stood there in confusion, looking at the flying papers, and he suddenly burst out laughing. He was laughing at himself. Immediately, I went to help him collect his scattered notes. There were strange signs on them, neither Hebrew nor Latin, more like cuneiform characters, or hieroglyphics. And a lot of numbers. I could not control my curiosity, and although I knew it was not polite I asked: "What is it? What kind of writing is it?"

He looked at me as if he had been caught red-handed and said: "So, you've discovered my secret. It's a kind of code, my own private invention. Signs that help me to remember."

Afterwards he asked my name, thanked me and shook my hand. The handshake of the man who had invented a code to help him remember, the man I was later to call Pierre Bezuhov, sent a stream of warmth through my hand, and I felt as if he was a great bird spreading vast wings to shelter me. Love budded in my heart. I did not know exactly what it meant at the time, but later on I came to understand the signs.

I can't go on thinking about him. He's an old man. I must get away from here. I have to go somewhere far away, where love is taken for granted and life is simple.

There will be no need to tell Yanis why I have come to Greece for an extended stay. Yanis knows my restless nature, the nature of my longings. He has a good idea, too, of my hopeless love for Pierre. He still has the letter I left on my desk on that unhappy day, and it can shed light on the way things are today, too.

Alexander asks me if I had studied at the Technion.

I nod my head and think about how Pierre taught me about art history, and many other things, too, more important things perhaps. He taught me the pain unto death, the sorrow of despair, and the joy of existing. I did not know the meaning of joy before I met him and I did not know it again after he left. The presence of

Pierre was life itself, and his absence the chaos of emptiness. I remember the day when I met him by chance in the street and he invited me to sit in the garden of a café overlooking the sea. It was evening and we sat in an arbor and looked at the mountain darkening beneath us and at the flaming horizon of the sea. There was the smell of fresh rose from the water-saturated earth and the plants growing around us.

I was embarrassed, nervous. I couldn't understand why a professor should be interested in a second-year student. I was so young. I couldn't understand why he had invited me to sit with him. But he was in a good mood and, seeing my embarrassment, he tried to put me at ease and suggested that we celebrate with a bottle of wine. I responded enthusiastically, and when we parted I was a little drunk.

"What are you celebrating today?" I asked curiously.

"Every day is a celebration. I'm celebrating life. I'm celebrating the joy of existence. You must learn to do that, too. I suspect that you have a tendency to depression."

"I had a friend who studied at the Technion. But she never completed her degree," Alexander says hesitantly, "maybe you knew her. She studied architecture too."

Yanis warned me against him. Yanis forbade me to meet him. Quickly, I lie: "I only studied for a year in Haifa."

"My friend had a number of extremely interesting ideas about architecture," he says.

"How do you know?" I inquire, deliberately provocative. I want to change the subject to something less dangerous.

"She showed me her projects," he says.

"Are you in the profession too?"

"No. I'm a physicist," he says, "but I have certain hobbies."

How slowly and deliberately he pronounces the words "certain hobbies." Perhaps he wants me to ask about his hobbies. But it was precisely his "hobbies," according to Yanis, which were dangerous. Henrietta wasn't afraid of him. When she followed him to that remote settlement in the desert, Yanis and I had already left the country. I had gone to Vienna as soon as I came out of the hospital, on Yanis' advice. He was the only one who knew my secret. When I came back to complete my studies I wasn't risking anything, for Avigdor was out of the country on sabbatical, and one year was all I needed.

"Where did you study?" Alexander asks.

"In Vienna, in the Vienna Polytechnic." A lie. And perhaps it was a lie, too, that he was a dangerous person? Henrietta didn't believe Yanis. "He's biased," she would say, "he's jealous, I can't believe him. And supposing he's right, supposing Alexander is a little mad, so what? What difference does that make to me? I love him . . . ."

Henrietta's love for Alexander, Yanis' love for Henrietta, Elisheva's love for her Pierre Bezuhov. For a moment it seems to me, sitting opposite Alexander, that I now can understand, that there is something inside us which we love more than we love each other, more than we love the object of our love. But even if I do understand, I can't be kind to him, to the man sitting opposite me, I can't bring myself to forgive. Yanis' words stand between us. There is no doubt that he possesses a certain strength, this man, a self-flagellating strength. For some reason, he makes me think of Torquemada. He should have been incarcerated in the monastic dungeons of Spain. Someone should have built him a sophisticated laboratory there and left him to his own devices.

Hobbies. What hobbies? Driving like a lunatic in the rain on dangerous roads? Gambling with human lives? I feel like screaming.

"My wife had a friend whose name was the same as yours. Elisheva. They were childhood friends, they went to primary school together, to the Technion. I never met her. My wife told me that when they lived together in Haifa, Elisheva tried to commit suicide. . . . how strange. I've never been able to understand what drives a person to do such a thing. . . ."

"Yes," I reply, "I don't understand it either. What nonsense! To kill yourself for love."

The horror of that day, the day when I saw Pierre off at the airport. I took the first train to Tel Aviv in the morning, to get one of the buses to Lydda leaving from the square outside the railway station. I said nothing to Pierre. I wanted to see him off without telling him. It was very silly of me.

When I entered the compartment and Pierre looked up I saw the expression of annoyance on his face, but it was too late to withdraw. I said nothing and neither did he. I sat opposite his wife, watching him paging absent-mindedly through the newspaper.

A little girl stood silently at the window, looking at the passing landscape. From time to time they spoke to each other. His wife said something. He replied. The little girl asked a question. The woman replied.

Pierre had no idea, he couldn't have had any idea, that I was going to see him off at the airport. He must have been furious when he saw me come into the compartment and sit down opposite him. Perhaps he thought that I would try to talk to him, make a scene, betray his secret. But I didn't say a word. I didn't even ask him for the time, I didn't even ask if I could look at the newspaper, which he soon stopped reading and put down in the seat. I was surprised that his wife didn't recognize me, didn't remember the girl who used to come to their house, her husband's student. Only once did I catch him looking at me, his eyes flashing with a cold fire.

He sat opposite me, a strange, silent man who had detached himself from my life, a man to whom I could no longer turn, a man who wanted to escape from my love which was a burden to him. Here, in the compartment of the train, bending over the morning newspaper, dressed in an ill-fitting elegant suit—how clumsy he looked in these well-cut clothes—he was no longer the man I had known on joyful nights, the man to whom I had been as close as it is possible for one person to be to another.

Cold and denying and withdrawn into himself, he sat there afraid of catching my eye. And I—I have never again felt so alone except in one terrible hour, three years later, an hour which I would prefer to erase from consciousness. A wall rose between us—the newspaper, the silent child, the elegant woman. And I cursed myself for my foolishness.

It is this miserable hour that I remember most distinctly, that makes me rail at fate for not putting more perfect happiness in my way.

I returned to Haifa immediately, on the same train. Yanis and Henrietta, I thought enviously, why not disturb them? Why not?

I found them in the flat. Yanis was lecturing her about some new theory in physics and she was asking questions. I teased and provoked them mercilessly, very gay and chattering incessantly. I told them silly stories. About Hart Crane, I think. Yanis said: "What's the matter with you? You're behaving as if you're drunk." I said: "My love, my love went away today. He left me a long time ago, but today he went away and I'll never see him again." Henrietta stared at me in bewilderment. "Who are you talking about?" she said. "Who went away today?" "Pierre," I said, "haven't I told you about Pierre?"

They tried to ignore me. And every time Yanis tried to resume his conversation with Henrietta, I made some nonsensical remark. In the end they couldn't stand it any longer and got up and went out. They left angrily and demonstratively. "You're unbearable today," said Henrietta. "A manic fit," said Yanis. But I was delighted that I had finally managed to get rid of them. When they were gone I sat down to write a letter. Yanis has this letter. I don't think he has thrown it away. Now I ask myself if I'm grateful to them for saving my life. It would require greater honesty and courage than I possess to answer that question. Besides, things have changed. In the years that have passed I have learned to adjust myself to an empty life, I have learned to adjust myself to his absence, to the death of Michael, my little son. I have allowed myself to love strangers, being under no obligation to keep faith with the man who fled from me. And this time it is I who will flee. Like Jonah I shall flee. I shall go far away. I shall hide in the belly of the whale—a dark place, closed and protected.

The car crosses the suburban alleys, driving in the direction of Phaleron. You can see the sea in the distance, a dull, dark expanse with a pale sky crouching over it. You can see the lights of the ships flickering and swaying in the humid air hanging over the sea. Behind us the Acropolis looms against the sky, lit up like a lighthouse. A pleasant breeze is blowing and I feel calm and relaxed. Gradually the town is behind us, and the houses fewer and apart. A wide road stretches out before us, sloping down to the sea. We soon pass the wealthy suburbs on the seashore, the cafés and nightclubs with their loud Greek music blaring. And then we emerge into the open spaces, climbing the cliffs which once, in very ancient times, erupted in violent protest from the sea.

A deep little bay, in whose pellucid waters the overhanging rocks are reflected, revealed, illuminated, and left behind. Some of the bays are dotted with tiny, uninhabited islands, where seabirds nest, and I can see flocks of white seagulls swooping on the aqueduct. I open the window for a moment, and beyond the wind roaring in my ears I can hear their demented, terrifying shrieks.

Suddenly Yanis shouts something in Greek and Slavos stops the car.

A figure stands at the side of the road, a tall solitary woman with straight black hair falling over her shoulders and her face. She holds something in her hands, close to her breasts—something white, which shines in the dusk. She approaches us and, as she walks, slowly sheds her clothes, a naked woman, bigger than any woman I had ever seen, holding a huge white flower in her hands. The flower is perfect, round and fragrant. The hand of decay had not yet touched it.

Henrietta! I cry.

She smiles at me, and in the dim light of our headlamps I see the serenity shining from her white face, like the twilight in the evening sky. Her face is wonderfully kind and gentle, and the voices of the angels, singing to God at daybreak, reach my ears.

Henrietta, I say to myself, beautiful Henrietta, who died so many years ago in the rain.

"Come into the car," says Yanis, "come inside."

Alexander leans back and says lazily, "I don't really know how to appreciate food. I eat when I'm hungry. But my friend Yanis, he would really have enjoyed this. . . ."

And there are no more doubts.

"It's a shame that your Greeks are so far away. I've made too much to eat," Carmela says.

"Your Greeks?" Alexander asks.

"Yes, I forgot to tell you, Elisheva has a friend in Greece, too."

"What's his name?"

I break in quickly with my lie: "It's Alek—Aleko."

We go on eating slowly without talking. At last Carmela collects the plates and carries them to the kitchen. There is a sound of running water and clattering dishes.

"Do you need any help?" I call loudly, hoping for a reprieve.

But Carmela calls back, "No thanks. You sit and talk to Alexander."

For a while we sit in silence.

Suddenly Alexander says, "Once I had a Chinese garden." A light danced in his hazel eyes, like speckled flames.

Hart Crane, I think, was wiser than any of us. He knew exactly what had to be done. Running away doesn't solve anything. It only puts off the end. We have to face ourselves, rouse ourselves from our slumbers, go down into the gutters of our selfishness, our self-love, our lust for honor, money, fame. Cleanse the gutters. Learn to open our hearts to the suffering of others. And so I cannot stay here. I have to exile myself from myself. Not run away, but go into exile, in order to clear things up.

I am back there, on that night in Greece. Yanis and Henrietta are sitting in the back of the car and I can't see them. I can see only Slavos' profile, tense and solemn, reflected in the window at my right. His nearness gives me the same feeling of restfulness I knew when my father took me into his arms. He was a big man too, and his walk was clumsy and awkward. Slavos says something in Greek, soft and guttural, a language which is foreign music, spellbinding.

I cannot understand what he says, but his meaning is unmistakable. His soft, warm voice pours into my body like wine, making me feel warm and peaceful. I say to him in Hebrew: You're like a big father. You should sing me a nice lullaby.

Slavos turns his head. He smiles at me and puts out his hand to stroke my hair.

From behind me I hear Henrietta: "A woman who told fortunes from coffee grounds told Yanis that the woman he truly loved would cut his throat with a kitchen knife. And ever since he's lived in fear, poor man, he has no way of telling who his true love is. And ever since he's been afraid of love and he never goes into a kitchen. He's always believed that I am his true love, and now he's confused. He wonders if she was telling the truth, if his heart tells him the truth. Ever since he heard the words of the fortune teller he's been suspicious, mistrustful, tortured by doubts. . . ."

Slavos lays his hand on my greying hair and his fingers caress me, fingers broad and strong, like the fingers of my beloved. A sensation of pure pleasure seeps slowly through my body and I begin to forget. My memories dissolve between the little drops of water falling on the windscreen. Very gently his fingertips caress my head, stroke my hair. When he has to make a sharp turn, he lifts his hand away to hold the wheel, and as soon as the road straightens his fingers return.

Slavos speaks to me with soft foreign sounds, and with the rhythmic movement of his fingers, which lulls me into a profound peace.

From behind me, I hear Henrietta saying: "Alexander discovered the formula of life. He wanted to rule the world. But Yanis disclosed the secret of the Chinese gardens to him and he changed his mind. And that's how Yanis succeeded in saving the human race from a madman. We should all be grateful to him, we owe him a great debt. Imagine what would have happened to the world if it fell into the hands of a madman like Alexander. I would have refused to live in such a world, even though I was his lover. I would have escaped to another world, even if it was dry and desolate as the moon . . . ."

Then suddenly she claps her hands, and cries in her childish ways: We should be happy and gay! We should live life as if it were a celebration!

And she begins to sing a children's song, which the fat singing teacher taught us when we were in the sixth grade:

Sun, sun in the sky
Give us lots of shining light,
Light on the rivers and light on the seas,
Light on the forests and light on the trees. . . .

Her sweet, childish voice fills the little car with sounds of distant childhood. And I can see her clearly as she was then: a refugee child from Hungary, sad-eyed and white-faced. A beautiful little girl, the most beautiful little girl I have ever seen.

The fat singing teacher loved Henrietta, and during the singing lessons, as he passed among the rows of desks, conducting with his plump hands, he would linger at her side and stroke her hair. Once, when I was sitting next to her, I heard his whisper, above the choir of girlish voices: Golden flower, golden-hearted flower. . . . But Henrietta paid no attention.

And I see her again, at the end of a mossy avenue of casuarina trees, waiting for me with a big white flower in her hands.

Henrietta was full of secrets, the mysteries of her childhood in a remote and tragic land, a childhood hounded by calamity. A quiet little girl, who kept locked in her heart a great terror and cruel memories of which she never spoke. A child-woman, whose prematurely adult world I could not then share.

When I approached, she offered me her flower.

Smell, she said, and I did as she asked.

The children at the Home say that it's a lucky flower. A flower that makes you lucky in love, she said—breathe the smell in deeply. It's a good smell.

In those days I didn't yet know that you need luck in love. But Henrietta and the other refugee children already understood, it seems. They knew many secrets, terrible, dangerous secrets: the terror of death, the fear of betrayal, the pangs of hunger, false prayers to alien gods in monastic shelters, the sweetness of kisses and the anxieties of love.

And again I remember her laughing and embarrassed with Yanis, whose love she could not requite.

Henrietta's lovely face, the faces of the dead and the unwanted memories.

How pointless, this ceaseless retreat into lost, impossible happiness. The touch of Michael's cheek, so soft and fair, and the crown of golden curls like his father's. His father's hands digging into my flesh, down to the slender bones. The restlessness in his hard, almost cruel caresses, the penetration which made me swoon with joy. . . .

The memory of the moment of joy seeps through my body, flows to my groin, to my legs which are suddenly weak. I close my eyes in order to abandon myself to this thrilling carnal memory.

I have to get away. I really must go away from here. I must go, to a blue, transparent place, a grassy place, where the scent of flowering laurel freshens the spring air, sweet beyond measure, making the world radiant. A faraway place, where the grass is green in your eyes.

We have left the town far behind us, and now we are driving along the top of the cliff. Slavos' fingers are still woven in my hair, like the branches of the tree entangled in Absalom's locks. We drive along the cliffs and rocks on the road to Cape Sounion, at the edge of Attica. The bays brim with water, darkening as evening falls. Here and there white foam gleams, and I imagine the glistening fishes darting through the water in shoals. Flocks of pink clouds sail through the sky, angels' wings and white water lilies, and the radiance glows like broken columns of marble. A roar of waves breaks on the shore, and the wind cries.

The stars have not yet spread across the night, and there is little room for human memories of love. The universe is full of itself and its beauty, complete and calm.

I sit close to Slavos, whose hand is firm on the wheel, absorbing the fullness of the world, the murmurous silence of the sky.

"Yes, tall, inseparably our days / Pass sunward. . ." Hart Crane wrote in one of his poems, perhaps one of his last. What has he to do with me. I came here, I made my way all the way from the sea, and the gardens of the sea made a shining rainbow in the eyes that I found. I did not jump off the ship into the sea, halfway from Haifa to Piraeus. . . .

We cross skies breaking into flames as evening falls and hold out our hands imploringly. But our plea goes unanswered.

Hart Crane was born in Ohio and loved the Caribbean Sea, where I will go one day to know the unbearable abundance of beauty. I will obey Henrietta and celebrate life. In Mexico he discovered the ancient cult of death of the Aztec gods—cruel as the sacrifice-demanding sea. Perhaps it was there and then that the yearning awoke in him more insistently, as it sometimes awakens in me, when I allow the memories to rise. Perhaps he was unable to withstand the chaos in his heart. Hades demanded a blood-sacrifice.

The car gathers speed, screeching round the bends of the winding mountain road. Sparse vegetation grows between the big boulders strewn over the mountainside, raked by day and by night by the eternal wind which blows here. Grey bushes with no sap in them; bushes whose salt-saturated leaves are small and wretched. Unceasingly they are swept hither and thither in the wind. When their day comes they will be uprooted from the soil, the sun will dry out the last drop of their moisture and they will roll down to the sea, dragging with them twigs and thorns and small stones.

Our car climbs the steep cliff and suddenly an ancient temple appears on the horizon. The marble columns are tall and slender as the body of a boy, their plain pediments already obscured by the darkness stand out against the still pale horizon, evoking ancient glories and a sacred covenant.

At the edge of Attica, on the peak of a rock erupting in opposition to the sky, a rock exposed on every side, falling steeply to the sea, in solitary desolation stands the temple of Aesculapius the healer.

The temple of Poseidon, says Yanis, so I am mistaken. This, then, is the place of Poseidon, the god who brings down disaster on rebellious sons, the god who terrified the horses of Hippolytus until they dragged him to his death. Poseidon—the god who maddened the soul of Hart Crane until he was enchanted by the lure of the depths and the singing of the sea nymphs.

But it isn't the temple of Poseidon. I know the secret of the ruined temple. In a dream long ago its secret was revealed to me— the secret of the marble columns erect against the sky and the precipice, the secret of the marble floor, worn by the wind and washed by the rain for generations until its stones look like the white bones of the dead.

We leave the car at the side of the road and the night wind roars in our faces, lifts my skirt and exposes my white thighs.

Henrietta is slowly climbing up to the temple. The wind blowing from every side gives us no rest: it cries and howls and buffets us without stopping. Now Henrietta is standing in the temple: a large-limbed ancient goddess. Her hands are crossed on her chest, and between her breasts a full white flower shines.

Henrietta, chaste as the moon, a pure light glowing in the night, a shower of pearls, and trains of gold gather in the crevices of the rough, barren mountainside. The radiance shines from her nakedness into the stillness, strewing it with small, delicate voices:

words of benediction. Henrietta is singing in the world. The radiance of her countenance dazzles the eyes of God.

I walk towards the temple and Slavos follows with soft, secret footsteps, a cat hunting its prey. I climb the temple stairs to pray to the god of healing. Perhaps I will find mandrakes, make a potion from them, and, like Reuben who gave them to the woman he loved, I shall fill my love with golden intoxication.

Night has fallen and the sea is dull and threatening beneath the sky bending over it with moon and stars. All around the sea clutches at the rock, rending and tearing, besetting it with dangerous battalions.

When Alexander speaks again, as if out of a trance, I cannot believe my ears, although I know. ''I found her at the bottom of the valley. Her marvelous face, on which the rain fell, was mangled beyond recognition. It was not granted to us to be like the butterflies who die when they mate.''

I will go away from here soon.

When spring comes the magnolia planted in Yanis' garden will bloom, and I shall pick myself a flower, a lucky flower. I shall contemplate it quietly. I shall sit by the window and watch the dying of the days passing sunward. I shall contemplate the white flower like a northern face with golden hair, and see how it fades and dies without a struggle, without bitterness. Then I will be able to think of Henrietta and Pierre and Yanis and Michael in perfect peace.

One after the other the threads of corruption will appear in the budding whiteness. It will wilt and turn brown like stagnant water. And there will be nothing pitiful about it: a glorious bud with many expectations which did not mature and whose secret was never known.

New beauty will be born, and flower like a legend.

PART FOUR

Pentothal

*Thiopental sodium: A central nervous depressant;
intravenous anesthetic.*

ALEXANDER

Dear Yanis,

This time I am writing to you from my room in the institution. I was so agitated yesterday that I returned here immediately; I felt that I couldn't cope without help. Now I'm calm and I can write reasonably. The coincidence was astonishing. And I still haven't made up my mind if it really was an astonishing coincidence, or a bad dream.

The day before yesterday I was sitting in a café in Dizengoff street in Tel Aviv and writing you about a certain voice I heard over the phone years ago. Not so many years ago, actually. I don't know, I've lost my sense of time. But have a good memory for voices and when I heard that voice again, and this time face to face, I recognized it instantly. Just imagine, it happened the very next day. One day I was writing about it, describing the voice to you, trying to be accurate, and the next day I hear it, and I recognize the voice I had heard only once, long ago.

Is it really the same voice, or is it my imagination? But I have no doubts whatsoever, although the lady denies it. There are too many facts supporting my version. She's part of the conspiracy, of course, but she's not prepared to admit it. And if I had any doubts yesterday, now I'm quite sure: what other explanation can there be for her denial? But I still haven't finished telling you about the telephone call.

Well, this woman phones to give me regards from you. And her voice fills me with yearnings I do not want at all. Because of her, I am invaded by the sounds of laughter and song from another time, sounds which—to my relief—grow fainter every time she forces me to answer her questions. I answer her indifferently, you understand, and she gets angry. I try to lie, to keep cool, and when she becomes insistent, pleading, I simply retreat and begin to talk about my own affairs, my Chinese garden. I am busy with my excavations, so I tell her about it. While I'm talking a strong wind blows up, and a column of dust rises from my little mound and is borne towards the whirlwind devastating the dunes. Here it's always like this—every mound is an illusion, for when the wind drops everything is changed. One day the footsteps of people and animals will vanish, and only the thorns rolling over the sand will leave their delicate trail. I hear the desert bushes exploding like earthquakes, flung here and there. The sands will stop them and gather around them, forming new mounds. The wind brings forth voices in the stillness, disrupts it, ruffles it as it does to a woman's skirt, exposing her nakedness, destroying the silence, as the voice coming through the telephone can destroy me.

"Alexander! Alexander!" the woman cries, "can you hear me?"

"Yes, I can hear you."

Everything you say is true. Henrietta sat next to me in the car. You were abroad then and you are not familiar with the details. What a fool I was to believe that I loved her, that we could be happy together. I explained to her many times that a Chinese garden is unlike any other garden in the world. For the plants in it are not ordinary plants, but the gardener makes them himself, with his own hands, and consequently he is godlike. I explained to her that a Chinese gardener does not need narcissi, lilies or Dutch tulips. The flowers that he creates are far more beautiful. He makes them out of colored paper, bright scraps of material, delicate twigs. The result is not spectacular, but modest, like its elements, like the structure of a living cell.

"Alexander!" the woman cries, "why don't you answer my questions?"

"Yes, yes," I reply, "I receive his letters. They come once a month. I'll answer them, one day I'll answer them. Don't worry."

And, as you see, I'm keeping my promise. I'm answering.

I think about the countless times I explained the principles of the garden to Henrietta, strict principles, which may not be ignored. But she refused to listen. She objected to my garden. She said that she loved me and wanted to live with me, but without the garden. I can't stand conditions. What's that supposed to mean: she loves me, but without the garden? I informed her that I was not prepared to make any concessions, and that nobody could accuse me of not fulfilling all my obligations. After all, I only devoted my leisure time to the garden. A Chinese garden needs care, and I'm sure that if only I had been left in peace to look after it, to cultivate it, it would have flourished. But the kibbutz members had it in for my garden, just like they had it in for me at the institute.

"Alexander," says the woman, "Yanis wants to know. Why don't you write to him?"

"I'll write, don't worry," I say. I imagine that Yanis told her that I wrote to them about my formula. I wrote to the directors of the institute, to my professors, to well-known scientists. I explained in my letter that everything was ready, that I needed a special laboratory to carry out my project. The formula was perfect. I am sure that there was no error in it. If my expectations had been realized then, I would have brought about the greatest revolution in the history of science, and everything would have been different.

This woman is relentless. She goes on showering me with questions and I begin to get nervous. Until now I have succeeded in maintaining a tone of indifference and detachment, but I can't keep it up much longer.

"Right," I say to her, "right, you're right. It was in the evening, shortly after I came home from the hospital, after the land mine, on the way to the theater. Henrietta was sitting next to me and I was driving. It was raining, and I was thinking all kinds of thoughts. . . . Why are you cross-examining me? You must know all this; you must have asked at the kibbutz and they must have told you. You can't bluff me. . . ."

That's what she phoned for, you understand. She didn't give a damn about how I was, or why I didn't answer your letters. All that was just an excuse. All she wanted was to drive me crazy. She wanted to make me tell her about that journey, in the night, in the rain. She wanted to hurt me.

Henrietta was sitting next to me and I was driving for the first time since I was nearly killed. I don't know whether you know that a few months before this I had been driving along the same road when I hit a mine. So obviously I was apprehensive. I was afraid, really afraid, my hands were shaking. Before we set out people tried to persuade me to let somebody else take the wheel, although I was the one who always drove, but I refused. I told them that if I gave in this time, I would never get over it. That I had to test myself. But when I started driving along that dark road in the rain I was seized by a great fear, and so instead of thinking about mines and terrorists, I thought about you and Henrietta and your treachery, which I will never be able to forgive.

We crossed the dark desert; it was a moonless night, and I tell you that I was sure that this time, too, there would be a disaster. I knew that the wadis would flood. My head was still bandaged and the wound hurt a little. Henrietta was laughing at how ridiculous I looked. Her laughter annoyed me and she knew it. I said to her: Stop it, if you don't stop it I'll have an accident. But I think she was just as tense and nervous as I. Perhaps she, too, had a premonition of disaster, and she couldn't stop her nervous laughter. I'm telling you, I felt like stopping the car and giving her a good slap in the face, and it's a pity I didn't. I didn't do it because I was in a hurry to get there, to get the journey over with.

On the way, she told me that when I was in the hospital the kibbutz had come to a decision about my Chinese garden. They wanted to take advantage of my absence to destroy my garden once and for all. It disturbed them. My garden disturbed them. Henrietta opposed them, she said. She called them cowards. She said to them: Let's see what you do when Alexander's here. Now that he's lying wounded in the hospital, you're big heroes. Miserable cowards that you are. And they were ashamed.

But I must stress again: Henrietta did not object on principle. At the general meeting, I mean. As you know, she too objected to my garden. And now that I was back from the hospital, there was no evading the issue any longer. It was clear that at the next general meeting the question would finally be decided, and it was clear that all of them, including Henrietta, would vote against me. What did it have to do with them? It cost them nothing. I never worked there during working hours. I really can't understand it at all, unless you want to say that it's in the nature of a collective to act that way. . . .

To return to the telephone conversation. Listen, it was a long conversation. The woman told me that she had recently been abroad, that she had visited Greece and met you. I felt that she expected some sort of sympathy from me, some response. She knows that I loved you once; what she doesn't know is that you betrayed me, and that even though you are the man who revealed the secret of the Chinese gardens, the Paran desert, and Henrietta to me, I will never be able to forgive you. You deceived me, Yanis, admit it. One day, one day you'll have to admit it. Time will pass, Elisheva's memories will fade, and then I will be prepared to listen to her, and then I'll tell her about your treachery. Why not? But now, when she's giving me regards from a man whose treachery sears my heart. I cannot. I simply cannot.

It's hard to explain. You have to know the circumstances to understand. One thing added to another: nervousness, rain, a sudden panic, troubling thoughts. Listen, actually it's quite simple. I panicked and lost control of the wheel. Suddenly I saw shadows moving at the side of the road, and before I could tell the others to get ready to fire, the car crashed into the valley.

When I pulled Henrietta from the crushed cabin her face was mangled, and I thought that if only they had allowed me to develop my formula as I requested, we would not have reached this pass. But they placed obstacles in my way, as in the matter of the Chinese gardens.

At first they pretended and let me use the lab after working hours. They were happy to exploit my talents for their own ends. They weren't interested in my formula, of course. They claimed that biology was out of their province, and that my invention had no value, certainly no commercial value. . . .

"Alexander," says the woman, "please, Yanis is waiting for a letter. He wants you to come and stay with him. He misses you. . . ."

"Well," I say to her, "maybe I'll write to him tomorrow. We'll see how things work out. In any case, thanks for phoning."

What a lie. That's not how the conversation ended. You know very well how it ended. It ended with an ice-bath and injections.

Alexander

Dear Yanis,

I'm still here in the institution. Ever since I met Elisheva—and I'm sure it was the same Elisheva, in spite of the fact that she pretended not to know who I was, and denied that she was yours and Henrietta's Elisheva—I don't dare to leave the grounds. You understand, I'm confused. There are moments when I doubt my sanity. And what if I'm wrong? But nevertheless, Yanis, I'm quite sure. You know me, after all, and you know that I'm never wrong. The old doctor, the one I told you about, never stops trying to convince me that I'm off my rocker, and usually I don't believe him, but now, now I'm beginning to have my doubts. Maybe he's right. After all, how else can you explain it? What reason could Elisheva have had to lie to me like that? I can't think of any logical reason, any reason that makes sense.

Yesterday the old doctor paid me a visit, and I was so debilitated that I agreed to answer his questions. He asked me why I came back, and why I don't take advantage of the permission I've been given to come and go. I told him that I'm afraid, that it seems to me that I really am beginning to lose my mind. And he laughed, and said—now of all times, when you're so much better. . . . I couldn't explain the business about Elisheva to him. I suspected that his reaction might be extreme.

Afterwards we talked a bit about my formula. I told him that I could not agree with the assumption that the whole business of the formula stemmed from certain circumstances in my life history. What bullshit, I said to him, and that's exactly what I think, too. I hardly knew my father, for example, and it's very unlikely that he could have had any influence on me. He spent most of his life on the West Coast, obsessed by the gold rush in the Nevada desert.

I sometimes use pompous phrases, I know, I'm quite aware of it. And don't think I don't know why I need them. To cover up the truth. I've never told you about my father, have I? I hardly dare to tell myself about him. In any event, his face, as I remember it from his infrequent visits to our house in the Bronx, was innocent and clean-cut, and only his eyes, which were glassy blue, sometimes had a somewhat frightening expression. He was a tall thin man, a fancy dresser, he always wore elegant suits and white shoes with holes punched in them. He was a kind of clown, and he laughed a lot. Towards my mother, a sour-faced woman who had no idea of how to enjoy life and who behaved coldly and formally with him, he showed great gentleness. Whenever he came he would shower us with kisses and presents. She would frown and evade his demonstrations of affection, and I would be overwhelmed by helpless rage. I couldn't understand why she hated him, why she rejected him. They would shut themselves up in her bedroom and speak in whispers. Sometimes I tried to eavesdrop, but I never succeeded in overhearing more than a few words.

What can I say, Yanis, it was impossible to guess that that man was a crook, and it was only from the photograph that appeared one day with the stories in all the newspapers that I was able to guess his true nature. In that photograph he was sprawled on the floor next to a bed in the corner of a luxurious room, his face and chest bleeding and full of bullet holes. His face was twisted and one of his eyes was spilling out of its socket.

I was on my way home from school one day, and I stopped as usual at the newsstand to buy my mother a copy of the *New York Times*. I always managed to read all the headlines before I got home. It was a huge picture and the caption read: Underworld Accounts Settled. For a moment I didn't recognize him, and perhaps I wouldn't have suspected it was my father, but for the name. But still I didn't believe it, I thought it was a coincidence. After all, there are a lot of Segals in the world, and even the fact that the first name was the same didn't necessarily mean anything. But when I got home and saw my mother packing, I knew. She said to me, Hurry up Alexander, pack your things. We're moving. And when I showed her the paper she said: It's got nothing to do with you. Things like that aren't inherited.

My father died in his sleep and he could not have known the terror of death or imagined its nature. Unlike your father, the illustrious Iorgis Stephanides, who faced a firing squad. My father was alone, in a strange place, far from the people who may have been fond of him. I, in any case, was fond of him.

We went to live somewhere else, and we never mentioned his name. My mother wouldn't talk about him. Whenever I tried, she silenced me. Today I know everything about my father. When I visited the United States for my grandmother's funeral, I went on a sort of pilgrimage, searched the press archives, and learned everything they had to tell. I can assure you, he had no influence on my life. For me he was a charming, laughing father who sometimes unexpectedly appeared and brought lots of presents.

The old doctor argues that my mother taught me to hate violence, but that the hatred of violence itself contains a lot of hidden violence: that she taught me to hate my father, and that this is the root of the trouble. I disagree. His reasoning is too simple. True, my mother taught me to hate violence and crime. On that day when I brought home the newspaper, she snatched it from me with a fury which I never would have imagined her capable. She waved it in the air and yelled: Look, look, this is what happens to all gangsters in the end. And that certainly made an impression on me. The picture is one that I find hard to forget.

My mother certainly had a great influence on my life, that I admit, but I can't see the connection between this influence and my so-called madness. Morning, noon, and night she dinned it into me: My son, say your prayers with true intent, and never forget to say "Hear Oh Israel" when you go to bed. She was a pious woman, and she was always preaching at me: "There's a God in Heaven, my son, and He pays people back for their deeds on earth. You must learn to be modest in your demands, my son. God loves only the poor and the humble and the innocent. Pray to God, my son, for your soul, to keep you from evil, from being like your father. . . ." Over and over she drew my attention to the retribution that overtakes gangsters and evildoers. Tirelessly she lectured me on the vanity of earthly possessions and the virtue of charity, and told me that money and luxury were corrupt, inventions of the devil. And she threw away all the expensive toys my father had brought me. But, I ask you, what did she live on? Where did she get the money to keep us, to pay our rent, and my tuition? I never asked. I didn't want to embarrass her.

In my last talk with the old doctor, I explained to him that I had inherited the puritanism so foreign to my people from my mother. He agreed that this outlook was connected to my history. I told him that my father arouses profound compassion in me, because, in my opinion, he was a man driven by demons; and that I'm not at all sure that people of his type deserve to be hated and despised. I also told him that your stories about your father, for whom you showed such admiration, made me laugh, because the two stories bear such a twisted, outrageous resemblance to each other: on the one hand, a hitman and a gambler; and on the other, a fanatical freedom fighter. Both of them driven and persecuted relentlessly, until their violent and stupid deaths. In my opinion, I told him, every unnatural death is senseless, even if it is in a sacred cause, and for this reason I can't see any essential difference between the two men, and your stories still make me laugh.

You remember that when you used to talk about your father, and I smiled, you would apologize and say: "You have to understand, Alexander, I have no option but to be a Communist. Anything else would be tantamount to a betrayal of my father and my country. You know that the fascist bastards caught him in the mountains and tortured him to make him betray his comrades. Their depravity and cruelty were so great they were capable of torturing, and even executing, members of the rebels' families, as a means of intimidation. It was because of this that my mother and I were forced to flee the country, and because of everything she'd been through my mother died with her unborn baby in her belly. There's nothing I can do but hate them, Alexander, hate and seek revenge."

And I would think to myself that my mother and I had fled for reasons which were quite similar, and that my father's associates were quite capable of killing my mother to make her tell them where my father had hidden his money. But I didn't tell you that. I only said: "Yanis, I hate violence." And you would reply: "That's a form of hatred, too, and hatred is a form of violence."

I don't know why I'm writing to you about all this now. After all, you're not my friend. You betrayed me, you lied to me, and you never saw a squashed head in a wrecked car, whereas I still can see it, see it every day, although a lot of time has passed. If Henrietta was alive she would probably blame the Chinese gardens for everything. The fact that I got the idea from you never made any impression on her. She used to say, What do I care if you learned about it from Yanis? What I want to know is why you do it, what you get out of it.

It made her angry to see me sitting in the evenings bending over my desk and making little plants from colored paper and twigs, sorting out the smooth pebbles I found the in dry wadi beds and painstakingly planning irrigation systems.

She would sit opposite me and leaf through the Chinese journals you used to send me. The Chinese like illustrated magazines, you once explained to me; they like miniature pictures painted with the thinnest of brushes, and their delicate colors; they like exquisitely carved ornaments. In China, life is conducted according to unchanging rites and ceremonies. People's lives are organized in obedience to clear and precise rules, and they are calm and contented with their lot. But Henrietta didn't understand. She thought I was incapable of love. Is that true? My love for you proves otherwise. But you betrayed me. Confess, confess that you betrayed me. Listen, if you had told me that you were lovers, I would have accepted it. I don't know what I would have done. Perhaps I wouldn't have married Henrietta, perhaps I would have, I don't know. But what's certain is that everything would have been different. You deceived me, and I have no doubt, Yanis, that you'll pay for it.

LICHT

Elisheva never forgot, and this puzzles me. Naturally, just like anyone else, I too remember all kinds of encounters. But what puzzles me is the passion, the emotional investment. None of this has ever seemed necessary to me. Not that I've never been in love. I have, in my way. But it never involved the kind of torments that she writes about, nor the passion. I wanted a woman, courted her, enjoyed her, and that was it. This kind of affair doesn't last long, and if you make too much of it, it brings nothing but destruction to yourself and others. . . . That, in any case, is my view of the matter, and I'm sorry that she sees it differently.

I don't understand what she saw in me, why I so fascinated her. Nor do I understand why I've always succeeded at everything I've turned my hand to, without ever being really satisfied. Everything's always fallen into my lap—girls, fame. . . . On the other hand, I ask myself if a man like me, a man whose daughter committed suicide, can be considered a success. Can I simply dismiss it by saying that it was a blow of fate? I know that I'm supposed to feel guilty towards everyone, towards Noa, towards Elisheva, and even towards Henrietta. I'm supposed to feel guilty, and I reject the guilt and ask: Am I really guilty? In all these cases, the problems weren't my problems, and they had nothing to do with me.

Or perhaps my guilt lies in the fact that I demand admiration from others, thus denying the equality between us and making them seem inferior to me. And perhaps I'm guilty of not being prepared to offer anything of equal value in exchange?

Isn't it true that I regard most people as inferior? Leah, in any event, submitted to my demands and never made any of her own in return. She never even criticized me, except on rare occasions. And Noa followed suit, but only outwardly, it seems. Noa rebelled against me, but instead of doing it constructively she gradually destroyed herself. She had so many gifts, but in order to spite me she never made the least attempt to realize them. When I was at home, I was the pivot about which everything turned. But now I know that they had a life of their own, a life I never touched, a life I knew nothing about. It's quite possible, for example, that Leah had a lover, and she may even have had a number of love affairs. I never once suspected anything of the kind—I took her faithfulness to me completely for granted. But now I'm not so sure any more. . . . I'm beginning to feel like the hero of a Strindberg play, something which is utterly foreign to my nature. . . .

If only Noa had left something behind her, notes, a diary. . . . But they, my daughter and wife, were mute, speechless souls. Whereas these people I hardly knew, who were strangers to me, really—they filled reams of paper with their yearnings, their sorrows, their life stories. What have they to do with me? And yet someone must do them some sort of justice. This task will keep me occupied for a time, and once again shall I build myself up on the ruins of the lives of others? But no, I deny this charge. I was asked to do it, and this time I will honor them with my attention. . . .

What arrogance, what crap. . . .

I know very well what my real task is. I know that I should be embarking now on a voyage into myself, diving into the depths and coming up with a verdict. But I can't do it. I don't want to be made to feel guilt. Somewhere in my distant childhood I see my father standing opposite me and pointing an accusing finger. Taking off his belt and getting ready to whip me. And what had I done, for God's sake? Stolen a few watermelons from a neighbor's field and sold them in the market to buy a book I longed to possess. Ever since that day, I've refused to be made to feel guilty; ever since then I haven't taken a single relationship seriously. And now I'm glad that Elisheva has provided me with a way of killing a little time. As for what will happen afterwards, after I've done the job, we'll have to wait and see. It's not important now. Maybe I'll learn to write. I've always known that my work, the studies I write, are parasites on the body of the really important thing, which is the work of art itself. Like a parasite I fed on the material which others created. I've never tried to produce anything of my own. Proust or nothing, I thought. I listened to Kingsley Amis. And now that I'm facing the void, with a pain that cannot be defined or written about, the kind of pain I've had no practice in feeling—the axiomatic need to write something "great" suddenly seems ridiculous. The act of creation itself is the important thing, not the degree of perfection, the doing and not the result. I'll compromise. I'll teach myself to compromise. I'll forego greatness. Mediocrity too can provide satisfaction.

Maybe one great love is all you need, maybe after death comes and reveals your love, your need, your loneliness to you, the heavy guilt that you feel, for all your defiance—maybe this is enough. In any case, I no longer aspire to greatness. I'm taking a risk with an experiment of whose success I am not at all sure, and instead of sinking into despair, I'm absorbing myself in the preparation of this book, playing around with the time sequence, fitting the pieces of the puzzle together. My role is merely that of editor, and I'm not even sure that I'm any good at it. All I myself am contributing to the book is a few chapters, to facilitate understanding and put things in context. My role in the book, as I say, is marginal, although it seems that I certainly played a role in the lives of its heroes, however uninvolved and unwitting.

I am like a man who peeps into an abyss and is overcome by terror—and the terror purifies his soul. When I read Elisheva's notes, I arrived at a certain understanding of suffering, or so it seems to me. And now I understand—I hope I'm not mistaken in this—that suffering has no logic; in other words, it has no specific reason. It resembles, rather, a state of accumulation. When this applies to a liquid or a gas it's one thing—but in the case of solids, the material can break. This is what happened to Noa, to Elisheva. Perhaps it's what happened to Alexander. And again I ask: Am I to blame? A rock can be broken with a pick, but it can also break from within, when it reaches boiling point, for example, or when the earth quakes.

Perhaps this is the place to say that I knew Henrietta. I don't think that I would have taken any notice of her if she and Elisheva hadn't always gone around together, because she wasn't a student of mine and, consequently, we never came into contact with each other. Henrietta knew nothing about the relations between us until the day that I myself told her about them. I was alarmed when I realized what I had done. Who could have guessed that a thing like that could have been kept a secret between two such close friends, as close as sisters? To this day I don't understand why she didn't tell her, why she made such a mystery of the affair. Henrietta told me about it later on, after Elisheva was no longer living in Haifa. She said: "She was always talking about some mysterious lover. She talked about it half in a joke. My ginger bear, she would say, and she called him Pierre, because he reminded her of Bezuhov in *War and Peace*. And she would say: Actually, the one I love isn't Pierre, but Andrei; but since the two of them are friends, I love Pierre a little bit too. Now I realize that she was talking about you, but I could never have guessed. She was always full of nonsense, of fantasies, and she related to people in books as if they were real. It was very hard with her, to distinguish between reality and imagination. There was that American poet, for example, Hart Crane, that she was so crazy about. The way she talked about him, as if she had known him intimately, as if she was speaking of some friend from Haifa . . . ."

And Henrietta laughed: If there's anyone in the world you

don't resemble it's Bezuhov. Where on earth did she get such a nonsensical idea? And then she said: Do you know that she tried to kill herself after you went to America?

When I returned, about six months later, I tried to contact her, and Henrietta answered the phone. I told her that I had been going through my papers and found an old seminar paper of Elisheva's, and I asked her how I could return it. She said that if I gave it to her she would send it to Elisheva. And when we met I said to Henrietta that it was a pity Elisheva had dropped out without finishing her degree, because she was quite a gifted girl. And Henrietta said: She suddenly took it into her head that she wanted to study in Vienna. But she may still come back. She underwent some kind of crisis and she needs time to recover.

Henrietta didn't have the faintest idea about us: and when I told her about it later on, when we were already lovers, she was shocked.

Henrietta only told me that she and her Greek friend had found Elisheva unconscious, with a letter on the blanket, and that they had taken her to the hospital. She didn't tell me about the child. In any event, from the minute that I told her about my relations with Elisheva, our own relations began to fall apart. At first, she said, "I chose to keep our affair secret for your sake, but now I feel like a criminal. . . . I'm afraid that she might somehow get to hear about it. It would hurt her, I know that it would hurt her. And there's something wrong about it, as if I stole you from her. It even smacks of incest."

I laughed at her. I said: "Don't be silly—if it wasn't you it would be someone else. And, in general, in matters of this kind there's no point in considering others. We make each other happy, and that's all there is to it. Whatever there was between Elisheva and me is over, so what difference can it possibly make? And as for saying that it smacks of incest—that's simply ridiculous. It's idiotic!" But Henrietta wasn't convinced. And the more I talked, the worse I made things. "How lightly you take things," she would protest. "If not me—then somebody else. What kind of a way is that to talk?" And I would reply: "What would you prefer—for me to make a tragedy out of everything? Things like this should be taken lightly, otherwise they lose their point. Either we enjoy each other, in which case we go on seeing each other; or we don't, in which case it's good-bye. There's nothing deeper to it. You don't love me and I don't love you. We like each other and have a good time in bed together. That's all."

"How do you know that I don't love you?" she asked.

"One can sense these things," I replied. "Elisheva loved me and it was intolerable. She made a nuisance of herself. And then I left the country. You don't love me, Henrietta. I don't know if you love anyone else. Maybe you do, but not me. Maybe you love that Greek of yours, who looks like some desiccated monk."

Henrietta said nothing.

In the end, in utter desperation, she married Alexander Segal. I must be under some kind of curse, she would sometimes laugh, the men I love are always the ones that are forbidden to me. Who else, I would ask, but she would not say. But now I know, and I find it in myself to envy the dead man, even though my feeling for Henrietta was no deeper than for the other women in my life. But there was something about her—a kind of glow of innocence and honesty and inner integrity—that makes it impossible not to envy the man she loved. He must have been worthy of it.

ALEXANDER

Dear Yanis,

Don't you think it's funny that I always open with "Dear Yanis," as if you were still in some way dear to me? I won't deny that I feel a deep bond, otherwise I wouldn't have been so hurt. And in spite of all my hatred and anger, it's impossible to say that my salutation is perfunctory or meaningless. You really are dear to my heart, and despite this, or perhaps because of it, I want to kill you.

Today I went out, for the first time in ages. It was so hot and stuffy in my room that I thought it would do me good to take a little walk. Outside I was greeted by a light breeze, and the walking really did make me feel better and more tranquil. Suddenly I felt like a man with time on his hands and nothing in particular on his mind. I took a bus to town, where, somehow or other, my feet carried me to the municipal park where we sometimes sat when we lived in Tel Aviv. I walked down that narrow street, you remember, the one with the attached houses, as in old towns of Europe. You always were dragging me to such places that reminded you of Athens. I imagine you must be wandering through the streets of your city a lot nowadays, trying to retrieve all that you missed out on. Do you remember how, a few years ago when I came to visit you, we would go for walks through the old quarters together and peep into the courtyards? You wanted to give me a taste of the way of life in Greece. Look, you said, it's a good, simple life: I saw sopping wet washing hanging from wall to wall and piles of wooden and copper tubs; herbs growing in clay pots and people doing their work; and I asked myself if those people really were happy and content. I asked myself if those women, laboring over their washtubs, didn't really long for washing machines. But I didn't express my doubts aloud. I didn't want to spoil things for you. You were so crazy about Athens! I've never felt like that about any place.

In any case, this street reminded me of you and of the alleys we roamed together in Athens. How odd that the doctor insists I've never been to Athens. He shows me my passport and says: Look, you see, you've never in your life been to Greece. What rubbish! I remember perfectly peeping into those courtyards, and there, too, as here, there were vines trailing over little trellises made of rough planks of wood.

There was nobody in the street. I could hear the breathing of the people taking their afternoon naps. Suddenly I felt that I was alive, that I belonged to something. One of the gates—an iron gate painted a rusty red—was wide open. I went into a courtyard paved with crooked stones. An old man was lying asleep in the courtyard on an easy chair, with his face to the sun. He had a long, white beard and a pink face. There was a wooden table with a glass of water next to him, and I vividly remembered the glasses of cold water which we sipped slowly, sitting in out-of-the-way little squares in Athens, the retsina we drank in the evening in inns where they played sweet melodies. I thought of Elisheva and asked myself if you spoke words of love when you sat with her in dusty little squares planted with faded plane trees. I asked myself if you whispered the words of the sad song, sung by the man passing between the tables with his stringed instrument, into her ear, if you whispered them passionately.

I want to know, I want to understand, how you loved them, why you loved them. I want to reach some kind of clarity. I love your Greek songs. They're songs full of sadness, like your dark, ascetic face, like the bare mountains that dominate your country. Suddenly I see your image and feel suffocated with love. Why did you leave us, Yanis, why did you go away? I must stop this, I must control my feelings; I can't allow myself to sink into bitter longings that poison the soul. I must always remember that you're nothing but a traitor.

And so, I sat down next to the old man and waited for him to wake up. I wanted to ask him about the dovecote stuck up on a pole in the corner of the walled courtyard, I wanted to ask him where the doves had gone. Had they died? Or perhaps he had chased them away. And if he had—why had he done so? I wanted to tell him that I would take the doves and look after them, if it was too much for him. It would be wonderful to have a living creature to look after.

Did you know that after I left my work in the scientific institute, because of the intrigues against me, I joined the Society for the Prevention of Cruelty to Animals? My mother taught me to love animals and take care of them. She used to say: Anyone who loves animals and cares for them will never harm a human being. Love animals, Alexander, and perhaps in that way you will learn how to love people, too.

She was a naive woman, and perhaps she didn't know that the cruelest of the Nazi murderers had pet dogs they doted on. In any case, she believed what she said, and she filled our house with animals and birds. Cages of budgies and canaries hung from the walls, and we fed them with seeds and lettuce leaves. Every available space was taken up by stray dogs and alley cats. Sometimes I think that my mother gave me a harmful education. She was an innocent, and her intentions were pure, but these things don't necessarily help. This became quite clear when I was working at the scientific institute. You must remember. I was young and innocent, and the institute staff hatched their plots against me with cold calculation. And you proved yourself a false friend even then. You supported them, Yanis. I won't say you that you were implicated in the plot, but you supported them. You were the chief opponent of my formula, of my plans. Then I thought that I understood your motives, for in spite of your scientific inclinations, in spite of your vaunted freedom from superstition and your so-called atheism, you're a Greek after all, and as such you can't really be free from all kinds of traditional beliefs.

True, you didn't like the idea of my project right from the beginning, when I first described it to you in our first year as students together. But I loved you anyway. Your foreignness and loneliness tugged at my heart. In a certain sense, you were like me. I loved your stories about your country. I loved your *joie de vivre*—you were always singing in the lab and it drove the other students mad. You taught me a lot of things I didn't know: how to drink wine, slowly and sensuously; to eat fine food with relish; to love women. You even taught me to dance, so that I wouldn't be bored at all those parties you dragged me to. You were fun to be with. (What are you like now, I wonder? Have you changed?) Nevertheless, the business of the formula weighed on our relations; you didn't hide your anxiety and revulsion. You didn't like to hear me talk about it and you would say to me: "You must understand, Alexander, that even though I don't believe in God, there are limits. Life is sacred; and you're about to do something extremely dangerous. You should think about it very carefully. Life was created in the flash of an eye, and it's wrong for us to try to reconstruct that act. It's a sin, a grave sin. Conception and birth should take place naturally, according to the laws of nature. If we destroy nature, it will destroy us." Those were your words, I remember them exactly. And I replied: "You're an Orthodox Greek. The priests are talking out of your mouth."

How we argued! You would shout: "Me? I'm a Marxist! You're not listening to what I say. I'm talking about nature, about the physical world, not about God. I'm talking about creation, about genesis. It's forbidden for man to become the creator of life. It could have disastrous consequences. . . ."

Actually, I enjoyed those arguments. They made me feel closer to you. And you would often talk about the Chinese, one of your favorite subjects. You would say in a solemn, serious tone: "I can understand what drives you. We all would like to play God. Nietzsche realized this. But you're taking the wrong direction. We should be constructive. We should do things on a human scale, like the Chinese when they plant their gardens. . . ."

It took me a long time to understand you, Yanis, but, even now, I only agree with you because I have no choice, because, of course, I've forgotten everything. You were influenced by the monks, admit it. An unconscious heritage, like my own thirst for knowledge, which is so characteristic of my people. And in the end you ran away. Admit that you ran away from me. You told Henrietta that my tragedy broke your heart and you couldn't bear it. But I know the truth. You simply ran away, ran like a criminal, and abandoned me in my darkest hour. When I think about it I am filled with rage. I can't go on writing. We'll meet again, Yanis. We'll settle our account. I hope that you live in fear of that day.

Alexander

Yanis, greetings,

What slaves we are to convention and habit! So today I decided not to write, as usual, "Dear Yanis."

Today I tidied up the few possessions I brought with me to the institution. Yes, I'm back here, still here. I left most of my things on the kibbutz. I brought with me only the most essential things, including, it appears, a letter of yours which I found today in the pocket of a pair of trousers I haven't worn for a long time. There was no design on my part in this—in other words, I had no intention of keeping the letter, or of bringing it with me. I destroyed all your letters, and this one is the sole survivor. I received it on the kibbutz in the Paran desert, in my place of exile. You never visited me there. Actually, you couldn't have, because I went into exile there after you left the country. You left, of course, before the wedding, which is something I can understand, even though I think that a true friend should have been able to overcome his feelings for my sake. What do you think? Do you think that I don't know why you ran away? Why you were unable to be present at our wedding? Okay, I can forgive you that.

But you know the kibbutz, you must remember. We stayed

there for a night when we were on one of our hikes to the south. It was a fine letter you wrote me, delivered to me there, and it moved me—my suspicions had not yet crystallized at that time. To remind you, I'll copy it out for you now. An idiotic thing to do, but I feel a need to do it. Not that need explains anything, of course—it's the ends of our actions that illuminate them, and what the end of this action is—I leave it to you to judge.

Here's the letter:

You'll be excited when you get this letter, just as excited as I am writing it. I don't want you to go on reading it now. I want you to get up now, take a bus, ride for six or seven hours, or however long it takes to get to Jaffa. I want you to get as far away as possible, even if only for one day, from your Chinese gardens, and go to the Greek restaurant where we sometimes used to eat. I want you to sit down alone at a little table and order a real Greek salad. You know: tomatoes and black olives, olive oil and feta. I want you to order a glass of ouzo, and, while you sip it slowly as I taught you, read my letter. Imagine that I'm sitting opposite you, as in the good old days. We'll talk at our ease and we'll even be happy. We'll talk of the light-filled lands on the shores of the Mediterranean, our consanguine lands, the lands we love. We'll talk of the olive groves, of the shepherds, of the simple life and simple people. The things that have been lost in our era, things that you are capable of finding and perhaps have found, and perhaps that's why you went there, in your kibbutz in the desert. I'm a little sorry that you chose to go to the desert. I would have been happier if you had gone to the Galilee and become a shepherd, for example. I'm not sure that the desert is good for you. But let's leave that alone—we decided to be happy, no? Nevertheless we won't be able to ignore the question of the degeneration of life in our time, and the fact that we too are in some way accomplices in the crime. In spite of everything, during the course of our conversation you'll forget that whole sorry business of the formula, and the injustice that was done you. By Christ, life is worth a lot more than science. Raise your glass, Alexander! I'm raising mine. We'll drink a toast to blue skies, the blue sea, the green and black olives.

I'm not working as a scientist anymore, I've retired like you. People are far more important, and curiosity is a loathsome and dangerous thing. Because of it we forget the present, for it is always directed to the future. But only the present is real, is true. It is the only eternity that we are capable of knowing, this eternal flux of all things, Heraclitus' *panta rei*.

Now listen. After you've eaten, go to the travel agency whose address I enclose. There you'll find a return ticket in your name, for Greece, of course.

I'm expecting you.

Yours, with love,
Yanis

Well, that's the letter. I did as you said, of course, I went to Greece. Or I didn't, as they tell me here at the institution. Perhaps I really didn't, but I remember it all vividly. I remember the streets, the taverns, the markets. Together we climbed the Acropolis and you explained everything to me in precise detail, as usual. I remember how we sat in the shade of a huge plane tree in a little square. I remember the trip to Delphi, the little villages on the way. I remember everything. And what counts is the memory, not the facts. And I want to ask you now, do you think that memory, too, is in constant flux? Your words about Heraclitus and the eternal present give rise to this question. Does memory possess a dynamism of its own? And do you know how, exactly, things are stored in this warehouse?

Don't you think that these are fascinating questions?

When I allow myself to reflect on matters of this kind, I feel a tremendous desire to go back to my scientific work. This is something that I would like to investigate—the structure of the brain, the operations of memory, dreams, hallucinations. How Pentothal works and what screws it loosens.

Today, when I found your letter and I sat down to write to you, for some reason my hatred cooled, and for a few moments I forgot my grievances against you. Somehow your letter restored a long-lost happiness. But now it's all coming back again. And I can't avoid asking myself a question which I have managed to evade until now, an important question: why am I writing to you? You betrayed me, you knifed me in the back, you deceived me, you hid things from me, you went to bed with my beloved, and I go on writing to you. Sometimes I even begin, out of habit, "Dear Yanis." Can you explain it, this urge that I cannot withstand? Why should I want to write to you of all people, to you, who sinned against me?

I took a short break, to try to find an answer. I thought about people, how they cling with such passion to feeble ties and how far they're prepared to go in order to keep up their connections with each other. Why? What is this need for these doubtful connections? Is it a way of declaring: I'm alive, I exist? Or perhaps it's a way of attracting attention; or both. I don't know. I'll put these pages in my pocket and go out now. I'll take a pen with me. I want to go back to that courtyard where the old man sleeps in his easy chair, the courtyard with the empty dovecote. I want to look into his face and ask myself these questions again. The face of an old man may give me some kind of answer.

Yanis, I'm here now, in the courtyard. There's a table and chair here, and I broke into the courtyard and I'm sitting down to write. I'm afraid they'll send for the police. But I don't really care, I'm not doing anything wrong. The worst they can do is take me back where I came from, and that doesn't frighten me so much. The old man is still asleep. I look at him and my memories well up. According to my doctor, doubtful memories, but I don't give a damn what he says. In the last resort they're my memories, that no one can take away, I hope. I'm never going to let anyone inject me with Pentothal, or anything like it, again.

I've been waiting a long time for the old man to wake up. The sun has disappeared behind the low wall that surrounds the house and a shadow has fallen across the old man's face. I'm amazed that he can sleep so soundly. This courtyard is paved with big, irregular flagstones, and I think that if it were mine I would certainly plant a Chinese garden here. Are you annoyed that I return to this subject? If you are, I don't care. The neighbors wouldn't mind, because they can't see over the wall.

A fly which has been buzzing around the table just fell drunkenly into the glass of water, and I'm afraid the old man will wake up and drink the polluted water before I can stop him. I shall certainly be blamed. I must get away.

I'm in the municipal park. When I fled from the courtyard into the narrow street, people were awakening from their afternoon naps, I sensed them stirring in the houses, and some children were playing with a ball. I was frightened but I walked slowly, so as not to arouse suspicions. But I wanted to run, and for some reason all I could think about was the theft of my formula. It was the fly falling into the glass that reminded me; because I was the same then, a fly falling into a deathtrap, mesmerized, unable to escape. I can't understand what made him suddenly fall like that, he was so full of life. But suddenly he grew dizzy and fell. Went on swimming desperately for a moment, and drowned.

I arrived at the lab one morning, opened my private drawer—it had no lock—and it was empty. All of my notes were gone, not a scrap of paper remained. I was astounded and not astounded at the same time, because I had been expecting this for a long time, I knew that people were plotting against me. And in fact, it didn't worry me too much, because the formula was safely filed away in my mind, where nobody could steal it. That, in any case, was what I believed then, in my innocence, as I stood in front of the empty drawer. And that is what I told you, when we talked about what had happened—that my formula was still safe in spite of this theft.

But you, Yanis, did not seem too pleased to hear this; and it was then that a suspicion crept into my heart, a tiny suspicion, only the hint of a suspicion, but that was when it began. And what did you say to me? You put on a sad expression and said: Listen, Alex, this is only the first move in the war game. Or perhaps you didn't say that, perhaps you only said: You'd better forget the whole thing, Alex. Remember, I warned you.

Yes, you were part of the plot. . . .

I feel a terrible weariness now. These emotional upheavals are bad for me. I'll sit here a little longer and then I'll forget the whole thing again. I'm sick of it, I don't want to write to you anymore. You never answer me.

Alex

ELISHEVA

Meeting Alex at Carmela's upset me so much that the next day I handed in my resignation to the municipality. But I haven't gone to the travel agent's yet. I hardly leave the house. I want to phone Carmela and warn her, but I can't. I haven't the right. After all, Alexander's not a murderer, and if he's not locked up I suppose he must be cured. How he pressed me! But I withstood him, even though it cost me a lot. And when Carmela told me that Licht's wife had died I nearly gave way. It's lucky he didn't notice. Or perhaps he did, perhaps he was pretending, too. Perhaps it was hard for him, too. In any case, I managed to get her alone for a moment in the kitchen, and warned her not to mention that I had studied at the Technion.

My first impulse was to run, to get on a bus and go straight to Haifa. Which was foolish, of course. His wife's death doesn't change anything. I'm sure he must have some mistress or other now, he's probably consoling himself in her arms at this very moment. He never greeted me. He pretended not to see me, not to recognize me, the bastard! How I could have entertained such a vain and stupid hope, even for one moment. . . .

Since that evening, Alexander's image is constantly before me, it haunts me. . . . Why did I refuse to admit who I was? What did I fear? Was it only because Yanis warned me against him, just as I now want to warn Carmela? Is that fair?

Suddenly I felt like eating chocolate, a lot of chocolate, and I went down to the delicatessen. I'll buy chocolate and marzipan, I thought, and what else. . . maybe a jar of Roumanian walnut preserves. When I got there the owner of the shop was mopping the floor, and he asked me to wait outside, if I would be so kind, if I had the time to spare. . . . And I waited, I had all the time in the world. Although he was a grim, surly, unsmiling character I suddenly felt a surge of affection for him. After he had washed the floor—his wife was never there anymore, perhaps she was ill, or dead—he began to sweep the pavement in front of the shop. He swept conscientiously, collecting the dead, fallen leaves in his iron dustpan. Always, summer and winter, he wore khaki, left over, perhaps, from British army days. Now he was turned out in knee-length khaki trousers, his shabby shoes brilliantly polished, and only the grey socks falling around his skinny ankles seemed to betray his age. His broad-brimmed hat seemed to have gone grey with his hair, a kind of faded peasant's hat which must have been fifty years old, a summer hat. . . .

For some reason, he reminds me of Yanis, lean, sinewy, sun-burnt like him. He's always at it, sweeping, telling people off for lit-tering the pavement, washing the floor, weighing everything scrupulously. On his counter the sweets and chocolates are carefully arranged by kind, and each kind has a separate serving spoon; I've never seen him touch a piece of candy with his fingers. He never smiles at his customers, but treats them with a kind of civility. And when he reckons up the bill, he writes the figures slowly, round and neat and clear. Perhaps it is this which reminds me of Yanis, the order, the attention to detail, the punctilious-ness. . . . When the floor was dry I went in and asked for marzipan, Swiss nut chocolate, Roumanian walnut preserves, rose-petal jam—I like its sourish taste. . . then I left, passing the stationer's on my way. It's been closed for about six months now, and dust has gathered on the pens and inkwells, the pencil boxes and the children's toys. The owners were old and they died one after the other. I liked to linger there, smelling the paper, in that dark, cramped shop. Behind the counter hung the picture of a young man in a black frame. One day the lame proprietress of the shop told me that her son had been killed in the War of Independence, their only son. They kept different kinds of ink, and even oil paints, and they kept old writing paper in their storeroom, smooth and thick and shining. You could find old fountain pens, too. I would drop in and we would chat about the weather, the political situa-tion. They kept the evening paper for each day, and I would buy airmail envelopes, glue, drawing paper, India ink. . .

Today I went to the travel agent's at last. Everything's arranged, if I wanted to I could leave tomorrow. But I'll go in May, in early spring. On the way I saw the head of a sunflower, dry and seedless, lying on the pavement; a flowerhead like an empty, abandoned honeycomb lying forlorn in the sun. As superfluous as I, walking through these city streets, cast off, gradually withering. Soon I'll leave this place, there's somebody waiting for me, there's a man looking for a little love in the evening of his life. Yanis is dying. His death will carry me even further from the girl I once was. I imagine I see her, a young woman in a Monet garden, in a white dress. She holds a pink parasol, there are flowers in her lap, and she sits on the grass beneath a tree near a pale pathway, half in the shade, white roses behind her and a flutter of fresh leaves. The wind blows through the branches of the tree and the low bushes, and the pure air caresses her young skin. . . narcissism! Wisdom comes slowly, but the body learns nothing, it only loses. Wisdom is a kind of compensation. The slow dulling of the senses. Soon wisdom, too, is lost. . . .

What is left of Michael? I still hear his screams steady and monotonous, the screams of his dying. But I cannot remember his face, I need a photograph album for that. But his screams I will always remember.

He looked like you, Pierre, did you know? But you don't know, of course, how could you? What nonsense to call him by this ridiculous name, Pierre! Licht, that's what I should call him, as he refers to himself with such pomposity. I sometimes ask myself what made me love him, and why I let my love for him ruin my life. Even when I see him today, my knees turn to water and I have to stop myself from running towards him, from touching him. Is that what the whole thing amounts to, this terrible urge of one body for another. . . .

I remember and I begin to shiver. In the quiet street simple sounds fall like blows. Lights have appeared in the windows, and in the twilight air the humidity is heavy and suffocating. Beneath the grass the earth drinks in the dew. A small corner of a big city on a mountain in the evening. It seems like countryside, because of the lawns, the flowers, the pungent scent of the pines. . . .

Take me to a grassy place, to a quiet distant place. There I shall still the sounds of memory.

Standing on the threshold, my books under my arm, shivering.

My dress is flimsy and it's not yet summer. I hear the muffled sound of the bell and then footsteps. The door opens and I shyly step inside. I follow the teacher silently into his study. There are books everywhere, and in the corner a philodendron in a big pot. I sit down near the desk, take out a pen, polish my glasses. His daughter calls him and he goes to her, I hear the little girl's voice and his gentle but impatient answers.

Then he returns, smiling an empty smile. He begins to question me, periods, dates. I try to answer, but I've forgotten everything. I make an effort to remember. First a hut in a laurel grove, then a temple with columns. Describe the structure, he repeats, and I try. Three steps leading to a paved area. What's it called? What's it called? He helps me: a stylobate. I go on: there are six columns, composed of a shaft, a capital, and a square tablet above it. What's the tablet called? I can't remember. An abacus, he says. Yes, an abacus, I remember now.

Through the window I can see the night taking hold of the crests of the trees. The branches move. I can hear them moving. Abacus, he says. I hear the trees, I hear voices: aba, aba, abacus, architrave, frieze—beautiful, polished words. I open the book on Doric columns, friezes decorated with triglyphs. He says impatiently: You're not concentrating, what are you thinking about?

I am thinking of a painting by de Chirico, *Piazze d'Italia*, a building with dark, arched doorways. I want to go into one of the doorways, to escape from the exposed, empty square with the yellow light, the frozen world, without flux. I say, "The temples were open, but they were afraid of things that were open, of flux, of movement." I speak haltingly, as if my mouth were full of stones. My teacher bends over me with his big, black-framed spectacles. His golden beard nearly touches my arm. "Is anything the matter," he asks, "is something troubling you?" He speaks in a quiet, deliberate voice, trying to be kind, paternal. My hands are trembling, and I cover my face with my hands. The darkness of evening lies heavily upon the pines, lies heavily upon my heart. I am unable to speak. "Never mind," he says, "come next week. Prepare yourself properly, and we'll go over the material again." I get up. I gather my books, my purse, and unable to look up, leave the study. He accompanies me to the door. On the threshold, I lift my face to look at him; I lift my hand to touch him, I stroke his bare arm. Then my hand falls. For a moment we look at each other, and then I turn and go quickly down the stairs. I don't look back.

Tonight I couldn't sleep, a baby was crying in a neighbor's apartment. I had imagined that if I resigned my job I would be free and there would be nothing to prevent me leaving the country. But apparently it's not so simple. Why I can't tear myself away. Why is it so difficult. Is it the death of Avigdor's wife that's holding me back? Do I cherish a secret hope that the story will now have a "happy ending"? But I know that it's impossible. I say to myself, you don't love him anymore, it's your memories that you love. You love your image of him and of yourself as you once were. You love something that belongs to you alone, that has nothing to do with the man he really is. The true classics of romance end with defeat, the only real possibility. Now a situation has arisen in which it seems possible to realize an old dream, a dream whose realization has never seemed possible before. An obstacle has been removed. His wife is dead. Surely the old wrong will now be righted. But I know that that's not really true. Even if Michael were alive still, it couldn't happen because it's based on a lie. That's why I must get away.

In the morning, after a sleepless night, I opened the windows on a fine winter day, almost like a summer day in Europe. There was a transparency in the air and the sky was brilliant. But the roof-tops, with their forests of antennas, oppressed me. In the end, I took a bus to Mikve-Yisrael. I like the botanical gardens there, the old buildings of the agricultural school. I wanted to see the Bengal ficus tree again, to sit on the limestone wall in the shade, and drink in the tranquility. But I did not find the little square with the Bengal ficus. I walked instead to the eucalyptus grove, and there, at the edge of the grove, at the end of an avenue of old, black cypress trees, were three graves.

Would I have allowed myself to lead the kind of life I have led if my parents were alive? It would have caused them terrible sorrow. This place was one I had never visited before, although I once had lived nearby. I never explored it then, but now my feet had led me here, to the modest tombstone of one Ya'akov Netter, and another neglected stone whose letters were nearly obliterated; and one tombstone commemorating two children, Jaques and Jean Hirsh, three and six years old, who had died within nine days of each other, the children of a certain Shmuel Hirsh. Who was this man, and how had he overcome the death of his children back in 1887? I took the bus back to town and went to the library to search for answers. This is what I found: Shmuel Hirsh, the fourth principal of the "Mikve-Yisrael" high school, had been a harsh, resolute man, who ran the school on military lines. He remained in his post for twelve years, until "for family reasons he resigned in 1891 and returned to Paris." There are no answers. We must invent them for ourselves.

ALEXANDER

Yanis, Yanis,

All my resolutions break against the rock of this intense desire to go on writing to you, to go on bothering you, to let you know again and again that I'm still here, still full of suspicions, still hoping for revenge. Last time I began a story I didn't finish because the devils overcame me. But now I'll return to that stopping place. . . .

As I walked down the street I was overcome with excitement, and my heart beat wildly. I had a feeling that someone was following me, but when I turned to look no one was there. The walls of the houses cast shadows on the paving stones, and the only light came from above, a pale light as pure and transparent as the petals of the Chinese flowers in my garden. You know how scenes like this affect me. I love light, pale, azure shades. Strong, bright colors irritate me. The colors of my Chinese flowers, too, were very delicate, and they blended with the yellow sand of the desert, so that it was impossible to see them from a distance. You know, Henrietta never understood how soothing this occupation was for me. She didn't understand how much I need this kind of tranquility.

I stopped at the bottom of the alley and thought of you and the formula. Lately the business of the formula has begun to disturb me again, and that's a bad sign. However hard I try not to think

about it, I can't help myself. . . . I remembered how frivolously
you always behaved with women. Women were always falling in
love with you, and I've never understood why. After all, you
weren't a handsome man, so thin and swarthy, with your sharp,
foxy face: a Mediterranean type, but certainly no Valentino. I think
I'm better looking than you are, but I've never had any success
with women. The fact is that you know how to court them, with
such ease, with a kind of elegance, and exuberance. Whereas I have
always been inhibited by my shyness, and to this day I'm stiff and
awkward.

But you are cunning. I think you never really loved any of those
women you courted. I think that, like me, you were afraid of love.
Once you confessed to me that a fortune-teller had told you you
would die at the hands of a woman you loved very much. Maybe
it's nonsense, but I'm sure you don't want to die before your time.
You're one of those people who are madly in love with life, aren't
you, despite your black moods. You're one of those people who
want to exhaust every possibility. You didn't spare me, and you
didn't spare Henrietta, and, if I'm not mistaken, you didn't spare
Elisheva either. You had to devour us all.

It grieves me to think that if I were still in possession of the formula, you wouldn't have to be afraid of love. On the other hand, I
haven't the least desire to save you. I wonder how I would act if I
had to make a vital decision and I was still in possession of the formula. I'm sure that my father, for example, never asked himself
about the harm that he might cause his victims. He wasn't
squeamish about the means he used, nor the results. The people at
the scientific institute weren't squeamish either, as you know, the
bastards. They used against me the most effective methods
available, cruel methods used to make secret agents talk. It seems to
me, Yanis, that people are always hostile to those who want to bring
them salvation. If you were familiar with our history, you would
see this clearly. Shabbtai Zvi, the false Messiah, for example, have
you ever heard of him? How they persecuted him! They even made
trouble for Herzl, our great leader. I don't know Greek history, but
you consider it and see if I'm not right. Socrates, for example—just
look what they did to him. It's always the same; to destroy the
messiahs, the saviors, people resort to violence. I'm beginning to

suspect that they don't want to be saved, maybe they're afraid of the limitless good of the Garden of Eden. Maybe that's why you too, Yanis, were so opposed to my formula.

The fortune-teller told you that a woman you loved would cut your throat with a kitchen knife, and that's why you never enter a kitchen when there's a woman there. And you're always cautious and alert when you meet a strange woman. But you weren't afraid of Henrietta. You weren't afraid to sleep in her kitchen. Not that I really believe that you slept in the kitchen.

After thinking these thoughts, and succeeding somehow in suppressing that tormenting matter which I don't want to mention now, I returned to the unpleasant municipal park. You probably remember it. The trees are old and very tall, and they cast shadows which are precise, but changing. One day I'll go there and measure the changes in the shadows, in other words, their expansion and contraction in the course of the day. When I was a child I liked to stand on the street corner and write down the models and colors of passing cars; and at home I would make tables and calculate how many Chevrolets had passed in the course of an hour, how many Fords, and so on. Even now I enjoy this kind of game. . . . The shadows annoy me because they falsify the true color of the earth. And they create images, and I hate images. The truth should always be evident to the naked eye, capable of being immediately and clearly perceived. But here a difficult question arises. What is color? Is there such a thing as a true color, a pure color? Well, I won't weary you with these questions. It's enough that I myself am harried by them. They torture me, because I can find no exact answers. And you know me, you know how I hate things that are obscure, questions that have no unequivocal answers.

In certain places the park is planted with grassy lawns—ugly and artificial. That's appropriate to England, but not to Israel. The land here is too precious, and, besides, green grass doesn't suit its nature. Altogether, everything here is too neat and symmetrical, the lawns mowed, the trees pruned, the bushes trimmed into artificial shapes like balls, there's nothing that's wild or subtle. I've just remembered Elisheva. Because of the park. That's her profession, landscape architecture. She should learn the principles of the Chinese garden. I'll write to her about it, if you send me her address. This park hasn't a drop of Chinese imagination, with its stupid, arbitrary symmetry, its rows and parallel lines. The division is so simple as to be idiotic. And a few flower beds smacked down here and there with insolent colors that sting your eyes.

Yanis, Yanis, the sight of our park is so dreary. I feel a great weariness. I look for a bench and sit down. What am I doing here? Perhaps I'll fall asleep, have a little nap. In a little while I'll close my eyes and forget the ugliness around me. I'm desperate for rest, Yanis, I'm very tired. I try to escape, but my persecutors follow me. I can see my little garden: tender seedlings, transparent paper wrapped around bits of wood, tiny scraps of felt threaded onto invisible wires. . . . I made it all with my own hands that still remember their labor: the feel of the cool pebbles, of the paper on which I inscribed my delicate drawings. And, remembering, something exquisite, something godlike flows through my writing hand, the power of birth and life, of sacred creation. . . . Oh, my lost gardens!. . . Tomorrow I shall go out again and wait. Perhaps I shall be granted a sign, an omen. . . .

Yanis, Yanis, you have no idea of people's cruelty and envy. You're naive. You can't imagine what they did to me at the scientific institute. Even though you were there, you were blind and saw nothing. You don't believe me, I know. But I'm going to tell you again how they used that stuff against me, that drug they use to brainwash dangerous spies, thiopental sodium. Pentothal. They inject it intravenously and it affects the central nervous system, it paralyses the control centers of the conscious mind. You remember how I was sick and consulted the institute doctor? They'd been waiting a long time, Yanis, for such an opportunity. I had no suspicion that the doctor would inject me with that stuff. He told me it was penicillin. And, idiot that I was, I believed him. When I woke up I didn't remember anything. Years of work down the drain. And you said to me: You forgot, so what? Maybe it's for the best. You never understood, and I loved you. . . . I'll think of something else, I'll write about something else. I don't want to remember. I don't want to remember your stupidity, your treachery. I don't want to lose you.

Here in the park there's a hollow tree. The animal that decided to make his home there did a good job. He destroyed the tree, hollowed it out, planning it in advance, savagely, against all the rules. That's the way to act, Yanis, against the rules! Elisheva should come here one day and learn the principles. She should come and observe. I love wildness and disorder, but I don't understand them. How is it possible to understand anarchy? It's so different from the rules that govern the design of Chinese gardens. There everything hinges on refinement, on order. Yanis, I have to understand this tree trunk. Perhaps a new horizon will open up before me. Perhaps I will be able to exchange the Chinese gardens for the principle of the hollow tree. Yanis! All the trees in all the avenues must be hollowed out! You hear? Something wild and astounding has to be done!

Night is falling, Yanis, and I'm still here writing. The rounded bushes stand in rows like giant globes in a travel agent's office. I'm waiting patiently for the occupant of the hollow tree. I'm sure he'll come. I'm sure there's no way of resisting Pentothal, not even for people with strong nerves. Not even for people who've been trained for a long time.

Yanis, listen!. . .something's going on here. Something's happening. Little people are coming towards me from all directions, a long line of them walking behind a small white coffin. They're crying. Why are they crying? I know they're crying, Yanis, by the expression on their faces. Now they're surrounding me and sobbing soundlessly. Now four of them step forward, the coffin bearers, and walk towards me. They're coming towards me, Yanis! I must escape. . . .

I don't understand what they want of me. I'm afraid. I want to go away and I can't; like then, like when they injected me with the Pentothal. My legs are growing as heavy as lead, and the world is getting smaller and farther away. . . .

They lay the white coffin at my feet. They speak to me, and I can't understand them. My friends. . .all my friends. I can see everyone who was with me in the car that night, when we went to the theatre. Henrietta, too, Yanis, with her mangled face, in the rain, in the creek on the other side of the road. Now she's all yours. With her mangled face, she's all yours, Yanis, she's all yours!

They surround me, their airy bodies hovering and gliding in a kind of dance. In their pale, transparent clothes, Yanis, they are dancing slowly and lightly, suspended above the ground.

I'm tired. I must sleep.

Dear Yanis,

I can't begin with how are you and all the rest of that polite cant. I don't give a damn for all that shit. The truth is, I couldn't care less how you are. As far as I'm concerned, you can go to hell. If I write to you it's not out of friendship or affection. It's because I've got an account to settle with you.

As you can imagine, I wasn't particularly communicative at the institution. I told them that if they had decided among themselves that I was crazy, good luck to them, it was their business and it had nothing to do with me. I told them that as far as I was concerned they could do what they liked with me, as long as they didn't expect my cooperation. Go ahead and use force, I said, I had no objections—on the contrary, it suited me very well. Afterwards it occurred to me that if it suited me, it meant I was cooperating with them. But they, of course, didn't notice anything so subtle and I certainly didn't draw their attention to it.

As I say, I was uncommunicative, but there was one old doctor there, a pensioner who refused to be reconciled to his age and turned up to work once a week. I don't know what his function was, exactly. Maybe he was only a volunteer, and maybe he loved madmen so much that he couldn't live without them. I sometimes talked to this old man. I would provoke him and ask him what I was doing there with all those lunatics (by the way, I loathed them). They didn't look insane, with the exception of one or two, and for the entire duration of my stay there I don't think I said a single word to any of them. When I asked him this question, he would agree with me and say that the best way for me to think of it was simply that it was preferable to going to jail. I think that he really did accept my version; in any case, he never treated me like a sick man. And once he said to me, "Listen, you've always been an active person, working, doing research, you read a lot and did a lot of experiments, you took an interest in a great many fields of study, and here you do nothing. You idle your days away, occasionally you read a newspaper, and you spend most of your time pointlessly digging up the sand." (Pointlessly, you hear! Pointlessly digging up the sand, that was his opinion, damn him.) And he said that he knew Dr. X had suggested to me that instead of digging aimlessly in the sand I should make a garden, and that they were prepared to give me a bit of land for that purpose, where I could grow vegetables or flowers. I understand, said the old man, that you weren't interested. But this idleness is bad for you. You're a gifted man, and you're simply wasting yourself like this. (As if I were still capable of doing anything after that business with the Pentothal.)

And he said: "Why don't you write? You have interesting ideas, and you used to write for scientific journals. I'm not familiar with your subjects, but, if I'm not mistaken, you still have some interesting ideas, so why not write about them?" Then he began to talk about the creativity of the scientist. All kinds of bullshit. How I hate all those clichés. In any case, thanks to him I had a brilliant idea, Yanis. I stood up and kissed him on the cheek and said, Listen, doctor, you've saved my life; and he looked at me in astonishment. I explained to him that if he would get me access to a computer, in other words, permission to leave the hospital, say, once a week, I had an idea that I would like to develop.

You know how I've always wanted to return to the sources. What were the primal urges, if not to create life? And what is modern physics, if not the development, in more sophisticated form, of course, of the theories expounded by Democritus, or in the time of the alchemists: the idea of creating one substance from another, transmuting one element into another. Today this idea no longer seems absurd, and it wouldn't surprise me if someday soon gold, indeed, will be produced from other substances. Theoretically, everything's possible. If I were working in an atomic reactor I would conduct experiments along these lines. And it occurred to me, quite a long time ago, that it would be a good idea to return to the sources of music too and begin again where Pythagoras left off: with the relationship between mathematics and music.

I know that this is not an original idea, I've never had any pretensions to being original. There's no such thing as originality in science, as you know. There may be such a thing as chance, but not originality. The next step is always connected to the step before, and originality is simply that next step, the small step forward;

whereas the great leap is usually the result of chance. I also know that small step forward has, in fact, already been taken, and by a compatriot of yours, too. Ever since I came across the name of Yanis Xanakis in the newspaper, I haven't been able to stop thinking about it.

The report I read didn't give any details about the direction or methods of his research. But it was enough, it sparked off something in me. And now I had the opportunity to do something about it. I'm not talking about a mathematical description of music, but the opposite, a musical description of mathematical principles. It's a complicated matter and I won't go into details here. I had a number of ideas about the utilization of computers in the field of creativity. For example, writing poetry with the aid of a computer. The possibilities are fascinating. Or sculpture, for example, investigating the relation between light and shade, or light and movement.

The doctor didn't understand exactly what I was talking about, but he promised to help me. Two weeks later he informed me that the hospital would not consent at this stage to any outside activities on my part, since they had not observed any significant improvement in my condition. As long as I went on digging in the yard from morning till night it was out of the question. They said they would reconsider the matter only if I took up a more reasonable occupation. This was a serious blow, but I made up my mind to deceive them. Okay, I would take up another occupation. Since the old man had recommended writing, I would write. And so I began to write to you. I wrote whatever came into my head and afterwards I destroyed most of it because it wasn't any good. But I didn't destroy everything I had written. In the meantime I left the hospital, although not forever, since, as you see, I'm back here again, on account of meeting Elisheva.

In any case, I've decided to settle my accounts with you, and I'm sending you all my abusive letters. I think you'll find them interesting, and maybe this will liberate me from my nightmares. Perhaps you remember my telling you once how I pass my bad moods on to others. And if you don't remember, I'll remind you. When I get into a bad mood that prevents me from thinking and working, I need to get rid of it as quickly as possible. So I go out and select a victim, usually a chance victim, someone I don't know. I follow him, while exerting telepathy to transfer my bad mood to him by force. Sometimes it takes a long time, but it always works. It works even better when I use someone I know. In this case, I attach myself to him and, during the course of conversation, I transfer my depression to him. When I feel relief I know that I'm free, and then I conclude the conversation and go away. It's essential to make a quick getaway, otherwise there's the danger of the victim returning to you what you transferred to him.

You have to understand that it's hard to get rid of a depression when you live alone. Secretly and without being conscious of what they're doing, everybody uses the method I've just described. People always transfer their misery to others, it's part of the human game. But because I'm alone, without a wife or children to take it out on, I have to use others, whoever is handy. Now I'm trying to learn to operate my system from a distance. I shall call this experimental method "teledepression." Neat, don't you think? And why, in fact, shouldn't it be possible? Why shouldn't the mind communicate as well as the radio? I've concentrated all my depressions in my letters, and in this letter, too, I am transferring my depression to you. What you do with it is your business, of course. I hope that after reading this letter of mine you'll sink into a depression that is agonizing and prolonged. If this happens, it will make me happier than I've been in a long time.

Yours in teledepression,
Alexander

Editor's Note: *PROFESSOR LICHT*

Here Alexander's letters end. There are four remaining entries from Elisheva's diary, three dated from her first year of studies at the Technion, and one five years later. These are her earliest diary entries. It's difficult to say why she chose to preserve only these of all the entries she must have written between these years, and after them too. In any case, since I was unable to fit these early entries into the body of the book which I have constructed from the materials made available to me by Elisheva, I have decided to present them here, as the conclusion to this section of the book.

ELISHEVA'S JOURNALS: The Past

Yesterday Henrietta had a little party for her birthday. A few students came, and a paratrooper I didn't know. I asked him about Shmulik, whom I regretted not meeting again. Foolish to imagine there might be more of a chance for a relationship with Shmulik than with others. But I really liked him. The paratrooper looked at me in astonishment. He said only, "I knew him." I said: "Maybe you know where he is now, what he's up to, where I could find him." Shmulik was a paratrooper, too. I thought I might write to him. The paratrooper replied coldly, "Sure I know where you can find him. You can find him in the cemetery. Tell me, don't you read the newspapers? He was killed in Kalkiliyeh."

The blood drained from my face. Blond, curly-haired, handsome Shmulik. He treated me with gentleness, even a certain chivalry. I didn't know. . . .

Yesterday Yanis showed up again, and Henrietta made up a bed, as usual, on the kitchen floor. I don't like it but I don't say anything. On the one hand she rejects him, and, on the other, she encourages his advances. It's not right. The friendship between them doesn't seem natural to me, there's something false about it. I think she's simply playing with his feelings. But Henrietta is a woman of principle: a Gentile is a Gentile, and that's that. Even if she loves him, she won't admit it. I like Yanis. Every time I meet him I like him more. Sometimes, when I let myself, I even feel attracted to him. But I don't let myself. Yesterday he told me that when he was a boy he wanted to be a writer. "But I knew that I would never be a real writer, not as I understand it," he said. "I'll never be a Dostoevsky, I'm not deep enough. And I can't compromise. So I gave up the idea. Better to be a good scientist than a third-rate writer."

The trouble with Yanis is that he doesn't have a language, he was divorced too young from his mother tongue. But there have been writers in the same situation. Conrad, for example. Why doesn't he go home? This isn't his home, even though he grew up here. He's a bitter man, but I like his bitterness, I feel close to him.

◆

Today I went to Professor Licht's. It went off smoothly, more
or less. For some reason, he frightens me, this man. But he was very
nice to me, he even made a few jokes. His wife brought us coffee,
and gradually I relaxed. Sometimes it's so hard for me with people,
exchanging small talk with people I don't know well. The need to
smile, to be friendly. This Licht is like a big, yellow bear, a teddy
bear. But frightening.

In the evening the paratrooper came again and invited me to
the movies. But I didn't feel like it. I made coffee and we listened to
records, and I thought how it might have been with Shmulik. I felt
at ease in his company.

It's a cloudless night, hot and humid. I'm sitting on the verandah, my dress sticking to my skin. When a breeze blows a chill runs
down my spine and my skin comes out in goose pimples. Michael is
quiet now. I came outside to smoke a cigarette and write a few lines
in this diary. I didn't bring a toothbrush or a change of clothes, but
I remembered to bring my diary.

I know that there's no hope. It's a matter of days. I pray for his
death, for his sake, for mine. It isn't an illness that can be cured, and
I don't want my son to suffer hopelessly all his life. I should think
of him as a gift, carelessly received and then lost one day—and be
thankful that he is being taken away from me. I needed him for
myself, for selfish reasons, so that I could go on living. And what
did I have to give him, a fatherless child who constantly asks me
about his absent father without my being able to tell him the truth.
I have no right to wish for his life to be prolonged, only that his suffering may come to an end.

Now he does not even sense my presence. When he screams, I
refuse to allow myself to scream with him. But I know that my
scream will break out one day, when his screams are stilled. What
can I say about the loss, the sorrow, the pain. I tell myself that I
should have given him up at the start, that this is my punishment.
But this is nonsense, I know. It's bad luck, not a punishment.

This young woman, for instance, sitting on the bench opposite
me, why is she being punished? A good wife, a good mother, a good
housewife. Last year one of her children died of the same disease,
now the second is dying. It's pure chance that a germ found its way

into the membrane of this child's brain rather than another. There's no meaning to it, no purpose. I should find consolation in the thought that my life will no longer be full of anxieties, worries, duties, that I shall be free. I want to scream. Free. Free to die?

What a good thing I didn't call him Uri. At first I thought, Uri, what a pretty name. Then I thought, a boy shouldn't be saddled with too sweet a name. If I'd been married I might have felt differently. . . .

A gift I received thoughtlessly, and now I'm losing it. I need my strength now. Later I'll be able to cry as much as I like. Now he still needs me, even if he no longer knows that I'm at his side, trying to ease the pain.

That moonlit statue by Reder on the patio seems to mock me, it looms out of the darkness like a Gorgon, and I want to scream. I'll remember it forever, the mockery and my silent scream.

This wound that I feel in the center of my body, between my abdomen and my heart, hollow yet immeasurably heavy. Let it be, if only for a single moment, this pain.

She sits opposite me stunned, her hands in her lap, staring into space. Soundless tears stream down her face. Ever since her arrival here she has scarcely eaten a thing. She hardly ever goes inside. Her husband watches over the child's bed. Hour after hour, by day and by night she sits here erect, with her high cheekbones, her thick, arched eyebrows meeting at the top of her nose. Her Eskimo hair is drawn tightly back and gathered in a bun. Sometimes tall, broad-boned, thick-browed, scowling men stand over her, huge men with Mongoloid cheekbones and straight black hair surround her and coax her to have something to eat, to go home and sleep. One of them peels an orange and offers it, they bring her cookies, thick sandwiches, a bottle with a straw. She consents to a sip of Coca-Cola, and they stand round her with sullen faces, huge and concerned and very hairy, with curls of black hair peeping out of their shirt collars. They stay a while and then go quietly away. At first, they laid the food by her side, kissed her, one by one, on the forehead, and then went away without a word. Sometimes she would fall asleep on the bench, her head dropping onto her chest, and start awake, looking around her with bewildered eyes. Who knows what dreams visited her, what sweet memories redeemed her for a second as she dreamed.

I sleep inside, next to Michael, on two chairs. There is no one to bring me a folding bed, no one to bring food and cigarettes. I have to pay strangers for this help. When the screaming stops, I go out and pace the verandah, look at the statue, and smoke one cigarette after the other. I gaze with an empty heart at the woman sitting on the bench, day after day, night after night, her second child dying; see the night nurse bustling in and out, the duty doctor arriving in a rush, besieged by mothers, fathers. . . . I ask a man passing to buy some cigarettes, a sandwich, afraid that if I leave he will die in my absence. To be there in case he wakens, as if my presence binds him to life. And all the time wishing for his death, afraid that he might live. And all the time my ears are alert for his screams, the terrible, monotonous screams of his poor sick brain, a machine brain.

The night nurse comes out to me.

"He needs to be changed and washed," she says. He's turned into a baby again. How I hate them, these nurses. They act as if they're doing you a favor. In any case your child is going to die, it's only a matter of days, so what's the point. The younger ones, especially the unqualified ones, insolent and lazy, don't even take the trouble to pretend. You say, "Come quickly, the infusion's not working." And she says, "In a minute." They're afraid of the daytime head nurse and they smile and pretend to ingratiate themselves with her. But at night it's anarchy.

A scream suddenly splits the silence, a scream on one note. Is it my son, or hers? She lifts her face and looks at me. I run inside.

Editor's Note: *PROFESSOR LICHT*

The next entry is undated: a page torn out of an arithmetic exercise book. I insert it here because it seems to me a kind of summary, perhaps jotted down in haste when she bundled all the papers together, a kind of last word.

Today I asked myself why I write it all down in this diary, why it seems so important to do so. And it occurred to me that it is to preserve it, as a housewife preserves fruit and vegetables to make them keep for a long time. So do I try to preserve the moments, so they won't recede and be lost to me? With every loss we die a little. I do this also, perhaps, in an effort to understand, perhaps to gain a little distance.

But I haven't understood anything, the people I thought were close to me are no more comprehensible to me than the others. They seemed to be closer to me only because I loved them. But today it seems to me that it is almost impossible to know about another. We project our own needs, and he always eludes us. In writing, on paper, we may fix him, as in a photograph. But just as a photograph falsifies, because it fixes the person at a certain moment of his life, in a certain light, a certain setting, and it doesn't take into account his other moments, his other disguises, so, too, does writing.

This woman I wrote about in my diary, in my stories, is she really Henrietta? And this Elisheva, the heroine of this diary—is she really me, or only bits of me, a mere literary creation?

Nevertheless, it seems to me that the heroes of my life have something in common with each other and with me, which is the way in which we wove our romantic fantasies; which were nothing, in the end, but fixations. And this is the intention of romantic fantasies, too—to set up a landmark in eternity, outside the shifting, elusive flow of nature, and of the other. What the other wants is to elude us and take hold of us, at one and the same time. He wants to absorb and submerge us in his shifting self. And it is the same with me, with all of us. All the great loves of my life were unreal, were illusions.

PART
FIVE

Bread

From the posthumous papers of Yanis Stephanides.

YANIS

My homecoming was not an auspicious one. I cannot write, as Alcaeus wrote of his brother: You have come from the ends of the earth with a gold and ivory hilt on your sword.

True, the poem is addressed to his brother, but do the words not pertain also to the poet himself, who spent so many years in political exile?

Why, when I recall the circumstances of my return to my motherland, does this forgotten poet, Alcaeus of Mytilene, come to mind? What do these lines he wrote to his brother some two thousand and five hundred years ago have to do with me? Yet I think of him, not only because I was an exile like him, but because his brother's fate takes me back to the place of my own exile. When Alcaeus' brother was exiled from his home, he enlisted in the army of Nebuchadnezzar, King of Babylon, and took part in the fighting which led to the fall of Jerusalem. And, who knows, perhaps Alcaeus himself, on his way to Egypt, passed through the land of my exile?

When I think of Alcaeus and his brother, I cannot ignore the historical laws that bind the destinies of our lands in a harsh and bitter knot, lands lying on the shores of this sea which has been central to our lives from the beginning of time.

My homecoming was not auspicious, and I do not feel like a man who has come back to his home; I feel like a friendless exile. And, although I am now at home, I am a stranger here.

151

For I have come this far, a child who has become a man and whose life is nothing but a "bitter furrow in the sand, that will disappear." Indeed, soon I will vanish, leaving no trace. Only the sand will know that once there was a furrow, now vanished.

Once, in the municipal park in King George Street in Jerusalem—it was during the summer vacation—a mother and her little girl sat down near me. They spoke about the fall of the Temple to the Romans. Suddenly the little girl said: "Mummy, if I ever go to Italy, I'll take a gun with me." The mother asked in astonishment: "A gun? Why? What for?" And the little girl said: "To kill the wicked Romans."

A historian would laugh and say that it's no longer the same nation, that the Italians of today have no connection to the Romans of those times; and that, similarly, there is no connection between the ancient Greeks and my people today. But I deny this. There is a connection. The sea is the vital connection, the sea and the climate, and the colors of the sky and olive groves; the poorness of the soil and the scarcity of water. If the sea on the shores of Israel is polluted, surely it affects our seashores too. And thus, right at the beginning, I come to ecology, the subject which so preoccupies my Israeli friend, Elisheva.

My homecoming was not auspicious. Sick and disappointed, I returned in a troubled time. My father's enemies rule this country, and I am powerless to act against them. My father's friends are imprisoned, or exiled in foreign lands. Every day I hear of arrests, searches, tortures. The tyrants are trying to break my people, and our freedom is gone.

Yesterday, late at night, Slavos visited me in secret. He said that they had searched his house for hours, without a warrant. "They didn't find anything," he said, "but I know that they'll be back for me."

"Run," I said.

"Where will I run," he replied, "this is my country."

Slavos showed me letters smuggled out of jail, written on toilet paper: "My name is Photis Pravatas. On Christmas Eve, 1970, they took me by force and without an arrest warrant to the building of the General Security Police in Athens. I was kept in solitary confinement for twenty-two days, in a dank, dark cell in the cellars. I was taken to a room on the fourth floor of the same building, where they stripped me and threatened to tie me up. They struck me with their fists again and again, on my back, my stomach, my legs, my buttocks, my chest. They crushed my private parts. They dragged me about by the hair, threw me down and trampled on me, kicked me, and beat me with a heavy wooden club, muffling my screams with the plastic cover of a typewriter.

As a result of the blows to my wrists and knuckles and the backs of my hands, all the bones of both my hands were broken.''

I am copying out these letters, so Slavos can try to get them out of the country. The world must know. I know that this won't help much. Didn't the world know about the murder of the Jews? They knew and they didn't lift a finger. When we used to talk about it, Alexander and I, Alexander would always ask the unanswerable question: Why didn't the allies bomb Auschwitz? Well, why didn't they? Is there an answer to this question? Nevertheless, we may not despair. We must go on trying to arouse the conscience of the world.

"My name is Theodosius Spilliotis. When they arrested me they hit me on the head and threatened to throw me down the slopes of Mount Parnassus. They jammed a pistol against my temple and threatened to kill me. They beat me in one of their offices for hours. They smashed my head against the wall, rained blows on my chest, my stomach. Again and again they gave me electric shocks. They stuck their fingers into the sockets of my eyes, they pretended that they were going to strangle me, they crushed my testicles. They tied me to a bench and beat the soles of my feet with a thick iron pipe.'' (Turkish methods of torture: another proof of the historical connection between the nations living on the shores of the Mediterranean sea.)

"My name is Lycurgous Vlassas. Men from the General Security Police of Athens arrested me without a warrant. They took me to the Security Police building in Athens and beat me and gave me electric shocks. Then one of the policemen pushed me into the laundry room, where they tied me to a bench with my feet sticking out over the edge. Then they beat the soles of my feet with an iron pipe, throwing a jacket over my face to stifle my screams. Another officer took over, pummeling my stomach and threatening to torture my fiancée, who had been arrested the day before. After a long time, they made me stand up and ordered me to walk to cell number seven. My fiancée was in the next cell. She was destroyed by her fear and kept on moaning. They kept her there like that for a whole week.''

I expect more letters to arrive in the course of time, and there is no reason to be surprised by what is happening here and now. Most of the Nazi collaborators not only never were tried, but, on the contrary, became members of the government or were given important jobs in the top echelons of the army and the police after the war. It was only to be expected that the moment the King showed any signs of weakness, they would seize power. People blame the CIA for what happened. I have no doubt that they were party to the coup d'état. But they only took advantage of a situation that existed anyway.

Cowardice and fraternal hatred destroyed my country. You only have to look at the men in charge, such as General Kokolakou, one of my father's greatest enemies. In 1940 he was divested of his command for cowardice. During the occupation, when we were living in the mountains, we heard that he had turned up in Patras as commander of a security squad working for the Germans. This collaborator not only was not punished, but he was given an important job in Karamanlis' government, from which he later was fired for embezzlement. And who was Grivas, if not a man who was armed by the Germans and Italians to fight the freedom fighters? And Papadopolos? Filth.

All this is nothing new, and my country cannot boast of any particular distinction in this respect. In repressive societies, it's the monsters who rise to the top.

How would I have acted if I wasn't tied to a wheelchair? Would I have fought? Would I have been as courageous and resourceful as my father in his time? Or have I been corrupted by the good, easy life I've been living up till now? Perhaps that life has softened my soul, and weakened my proud heritage.

Elisheva believes that I am a born poet. She says that I have a natural talent for metaphor. When I think of my life running out, I compare it to the flour that escapes the cook's fingers. It should have made bread, black peasants' bread. That is how I would have liked my life to look, like black peasants' bread.

But Elisheva is mistaken. I have an amazing memory and I read a lot of poetry. Fragments of poems stick in my mind and later on, unconsciously, when I sit down to write, they find their way into my lines. Slavos once drew my attention to this when he read one of my essays. He said: You're a kleptomaniac, you know? I didn't know then, but today I do. But this doesn't stop me from continuing to write, continuing to construct metaphors that are only half mine.

I would have liked my life to be like black peasants' bread. Or a mixture of olive oil, rocks, pine resin, wine, and honey. That's what I would have liked. My life that is nothing more than a bitter furrow in the sand. I was an exile in a foreign land, and now I am a foreigner in my own country.

As is my habit lately, I am sitting in my wheelchair at the window of my house in Kefissia, looking at the street, organizing my notes, writing a little, making corrections, deleting, adding.

You can't see the sea from here, so yesterday I asked an estate agent to find me a little house in Phaleron, or in Glyfada, next to a little bay. I love the sea. A view of the sea from my window might shed some clarity on these notes of mine—the rough draft for a book I will never finish. A view of the sea would help me to seclude myself with memories of my forefathers, seafarers and peasants, and with my own memories—the memories of a scientist who, for reasons of conscience, abandoned science for poetry and philosophy.

When I reflect on my dwindling life I ask myself how I would have acted if I were a healthy man. I do not think that I would have joined the active struggle. I am not a coward, but this struggle seems to me ineffectual. A grenade here, a bomb there, and then if they catch you they crush your balls and whip the soles of your feet and you die slowly in a dark cell; and nobody knows and nobody cares. A nation whose peasants support corruption out of fear and ignorance must first be prepared for redemption. Unlike Socrates, I chose exile. Slavos doesn't agree. He is prepared to die for his principles. My father may not have agreed either. They are made of different stuff, simpler stuff. They grew up here, in this country, a country enclosed by mountains and roofed by low skies, a strangled land. Whereas I went away, I learned to know other things. If I learned anything from the Jews amongst whom I lived, I think I learned about diseases. Holocausts, oppression and persecution have consequences. The soul becomes a hothouse of germs. In many cases it is maimed. The Israelis regard themselves as strong and unbowed, they are proud of their freedom. But the truth is that they, too, bear in their souls the dangerous germs of degradation and terror. And in my brothers, my countrymen, I can see the same disease. Therefore, I say, the people must first be prepared for redemption.

My days go by passively, flour sifting through a sieve, I think a lot about my forefathers, and I understand that I myself am proof of the weakening life force, an example of the degeneration of the race.

The house is very quiet. It's raining and I'm listening to the rain. The hours drag by. I light a match for my pipe, see the little flame reflected in the windowpane, flickering, shrinking, slowly dying.

Dying people scream.

An acquaintance of mine, who loved his wife passionately and all his life, so they say, treated her with respect and indulged her every whim, became her deadly enemy when he fell ill with a fatal disease. All night long he sent her running around on meaningless errands, and by day he heaped abuse and curses on her head, and persecuted his children mercilessly. He made her life such a misery that in the end the poor woman killed herself.

Some of the people in the hospital ward, when I first fell ill about a year ago, treated their friends and relations in the same way.

People who are dying are exposed and reduced. The worse their sufferings, the more they are reduced. The dread of death haunts their every act and exposes their shame and wretchedness. This form of distress, unlike others, makes no compromises with conventional behavior or human demands.

When I recovered a little from my illness and was able to get about in a wheelchair, I began to grasp the amazing nature of the strange world into which I had been cast without any preparation.

At first my perceptions were dull and vague. I could think of nothing but myself, my illness and my ruin, and I was prepared to listen to others only if I was certain that they would listen to me when my turn came. You could call me a sophisticated man, but here I shed all my sophistication. Like all the other patients, I pestered the doctors and nurses without consideration, and without appreciating their patience and devotion. I was a sick man, who regarded himself as far more deserving than others of sympathy and understanding, even love. I never stopped feeling sorry for myself except when I read the newspapers, and I never allowed myself to be influenced by the false encouragement the doctors offered.

I knew that my time was short, and the thought of all the things that I had not been quick enough to do filled me with despondency. The philosophical essays I had been too lazy to compose, the stories I put off writing from day to day, believing I had all the time in the world; the poems I had not published.

With sorrow and self-pity I thought of how I had wasted my time and my life.

There is a basic human conceit which prevents us, in normal situations, from letting ourselves be seen as the miserable creatures we are. All our lives we are guided by this conceit, which forces us to behave like happy, successful people, even if we're not. In the hospital I saw this mechanism collapse, and I, too, driven by the ugly, tireless machine of self-pity, hardened myself to the world and my fellow human beings.

I even treated my friend Slavos rudely and impatiently. One day, sitting in the visitors' room in the hospital waiting for Slavos and looking at the crest of Mount Lycabettos that rises above my beloved and tormented city, and seething with powerful hatred and immeasurable love—an image from the past surfaced before me.

I was full of resentment against Slavos for his lateness, cursing and abusing him in my heart for not considering my feelings—the feelings of a dying man. He knew how I detest impunctuality, how impatient I am at being kept waiting. Bitterly I thought of the indifference of the healthy, and of the injustice at the heart of the life going on outside the hospital walls, streaming on, indifferent to the sufferings of those about to die.

And even as I cursed my friend, I saw my stern-faced father standing at the bedside of his dying friend Andreas, one of the greatest of our underground resistance fighters. After carrying out a dangerous sabotage operation, Andreas had been hit by a German grenade. Fatally wounded, he somehow succeeded in getting back to the arranged meeting place. His men ran back to cover up his bloodstains as best they could, and then carried Andreas to their hideout, where my father and I were waiting. And now, in my mind's eye, I saw Andreas lying on the improvised bed, dying.

I said to my father: "I'll go and fetch Dr. Platanos." "There is no need," he replied, "Andreas is dying. No doctor can help him now, and that would only endanger us." "No, father," I pleaded, "let me go. Andreas won't die. The doctor will cure him."

My father seized hold of my arm and, looking sternly into my eyes, said: "Be silent. His wounds are fatal. Only God can help him."

Andreas, whose eyes were closed, groaned, and my father forced his mouth open and poured some ouzo down his throat. I had never seen a dying man before, and the sight of Andreas' agonized face, the sound of his savage, inhuman grunts, terrified me. Then my father covered his mouth to stop him from betraying us.

After a while the groaning stopped. My father crossed Andreas' arms across his torn chest, ripped apart by the shrapnel. The comrades must be informed and burial arrangements made, he said quietly.

Then he turned to me and said, "Yanis, I want you to know that this is the right way for a man to die. Willing and proud. This is the first time you have witnessed a man's death, but I, who am older than you, have been present at many such scenes. The sight of a man dying without dignity is not a worthy one. Some men lose their pride in the face of death, and this is not right. A man should die in silent defiance, but without bitterness. Only thus can a human being prove to God that he despises His unjust laws."

Sitting in the hospital waiting room, opposite the peak of mount Lycabbetos rising like a protest from the heart of the city, my father's words echoed in my ears. And I thought of the terrible death of Ivan Ilyich, who screamed for three days without stopping.

My resentment toward Slavos ebbed, and I made up my mind that I would not be like the people with whom I had been shut up now for so many days, people consumed by panic and eaten up by bitterness. I resolved to cleave to life for however long or short a time it was granted me. Remembering my father's and grandfather's way of facing death, I was ashamed. Mine, unlike theirs, would not be a hero's death. Consequently, the demands on me would be far more severe.

To a certain extent, I am glad of this, since it gives me the chance to prove to myself that I am a worthy descendant of the Stephanides family, even though I was never a warrior, nor even a peasant or a sailor. Composure does not mean submission, and if I require drugs to attain it, it is because I am not privileged, as were my fathers, to die a hero's death.

I realized then that I wished to preserve my pride, in a world that is losing its honor; that I wanted to express a quiet contempt for the arbitrary biological laws to which we are forced to submit. This was the only way in which to rob death of the power it derives from distorting the human image and terrorizing the human heart.

But, for all my resolve, the distress and bitterness soon returned. I was like a jealous lover who knows his suspicions are groundless, but is nevertheless condemned to go on suffering the pangs of jealousy. When death draws near it becomes the center of the world, like a great love at the height of its power, until a man can think of nothing else.

Waiting for Slavos, I forced myself to be patient and forgiving. Again and again I tried to escape into the world, to contemplate with composure. But my bitterness kept returning, making everything sink back into chaos, and I felt a profound self-contempt. My thoughts kept returning to Andreas, and then, somehow, to Henrietta as a little girl in the war. Where had she taken refuge, what had she experienced, who had hidden her? But Henrietta had never spoken of these things.

Slavos arrived in the end, with a bottle of fine French cognac. I didn't ask the doctor's advice and drank with him. I drank a lot, and the alcohol warmed my blood and softened my bitterness, and I grew gay, even nonchalant.

From that day to this I have gone on drinking, and I am usually in a good mood and, at times, able to work. But the hours of sobriety are very hard to bear.

At this moment, I am in a special state of wakefulness, a wakefulness which is accompanied by a certain dulling of the senses which enables me to perceive the world in a different way. The ordinary, restricting laws of daily life have been suspended, and the cosmos is full of new and happier possibilities.

There are certain riddles to which I seek a solution. Like a ship grounded on the rocks, without a yesterday or a tomorrow, taking her leave of this wreck which is—herself. I want to understand the mistakes which spoiled my life and the lives of those close to me; I want to sort out chance from necessity in my friendships with Henrietta, with Alexander and Elisheva, in order to understand what they made me feel. I want to understand the roots from which my personality grew and the principles which shaped my life in this way and not another.

My forefathers were seafarers and peasants. Fierce, sturdy people, experienced in hardship and sacrifice. They were Greeks made in the mold of Odysseus—wily, adventurous, freedom-loving and patriotic.

Stratis Apostolides, my mother's grandfather, was a well-to-do peasant from Stylis, a little village not far from Lamia, a bleak and dusty little town that, like most Greek towns, climbs a hill towards an ancient acropolis, and where the desolate ruins of a Frankish castle still stand.

Every week, before market day in Lamia, Stratis would harness the horses to his cart, heavily laden with fruit and vegetables. In the small hours of the night, he would leave his village and set out on the dangerous journey to the town.

In those days the roads of Thessaly were beset by highwaymen, and Stratis encountered them more than once on his nocturnal journeys. My grandfather told me that Stratis was never afraid to set out alone. The story was told that once, in a deserted spot halfway between Stylis and Lamia, he was accosted by four armed robbers. Brandishing the one rifle they possessed, they halted the cart and ordered him to climb down. Stratis, a resourceful man, cracked his whip, and with one mighty sweep flicked the rifle out of the robber's hands, sent his companions flying, and sped galloping on his way.

Did my grandfather's father bequeath to me this resourcefulness, which sustained him all his life as a proud man, dreaded, looked up to, and perhaps also hated by the inhabitants of his village? Can it be called resourcefulness that I have remained a childless bachelor all my life? Was it resourceful to leave Israel, to abandon Henrietta, sacrificing her love, and to resign from my scientific work? To stop composing my philosophic essays, none of which I ever finished, to stop writing my rather bad poetry? To remain without employment these several years, to espouse a political ideal without being able to commit myself to the struggle for its realization, except from giving an occasional talk in private parlor meetings? Not now, of course; since my illness I have abandoned any kind of activity.

Nearly all my life, ever since I was a boy, I have dreamed of writing a great book in which my history and the history of my family would serve as a symbol and an omen of things to come, yet an outline and a few notes is all it came to. And now I shall never achieve the complete creation of any project or design. So, in this, too, I was not resourceful.

And now I ask myself if I behaved rightly to Alexander, who was for years my closest friend in a country that was not my country. Didn't I allow him to slide downhill, just as I did nothing to stop Henrietta from racing to meet her fate, which I should have foreseen?

Could I have arrested the course of fate? And when my father went out to do battle, did he succeed in arresting the course of fate? Look at what has become of my country. If my father was alive today, he would have been among the first to be thrown into jail.

Stratis' sons, my mother's uncles, fought in 1913 with Venizelos' forces in the north, taking part in the liberation of Ioannina and Salonika. One of them, who rose to the rank of officer, was among the commanders who supported the revolutionary government. Have I inherited their enterprise, those soldiers and rebels, their valor in the battle for a sacred cause, for the liberation of the motherland from a hated yoke? Stratis' grandsons, some of them, joined General Metaxas and forced the Italians past the Bulgarian border. Sixteen divisions against twenty-seven well-equipped Italian divisions. A fantastic victory.

One of these uncles later emigrated to France to become a junk dealer in Marseilles. Many of my mother's relatives became businessmen. The love of commerce has been part of the nature of my people, like other Mediterranean peoples, from the dawn of history. But even this spirit of enterprise, however worthless I, probably unjustly, consider it, was beyond my capacities; and I take no pride in that. In this, at least, I am a true son of my people: I hate arrogance, *hubris,* and I consider it the worst of attributes. It was *hubris,* more than all his madness, which led to Alexander's downfall.

It was to the home of this merchant in Marseilles that my mother brought me when she escaped, in an advanced state of pregnancy, from the enemy. She died giving birth to the child who had been sentenced to death by the war while he was still in her womb.

My relatives in Marseilles sent me to an uncle, a childless textile merchant in Jaffa. I was about fourteen when I arrived in the country which was then called Palestine, a serious boy, experienced beyond my years. My father had taught me to love freedom, to scorn death and the oppressors of my country, and to worship a Messiah called Lenin. Apart from these things I knew very little: during the war years I had not had much time for study, getting messages, food and arms to the guerrillas was a full-time occupation. When my father escaped to the mountains, my mother and I followed him there. Later, with the help of friends, we managed to flee the country.

In Jaffa, my uncle, the textile merchant, took over my education. Monks drummed the gospels into me and made sure that I passed his Majesty's matriculation examinations. Lenin did not interest my uncle in the least. I had escaped one country at war only to find myself in another. Although I was not involved, I could not help taking sides in a struggle for freedom, any struggle for freedom. When the situation became dangerous and my uncle and aunt debated the question of whether to stay or run away, I announced firmly that I had enough of running and had no intention of doing so again. So they left me behind to look after the family property and went to Cyprus to wait for the storm to blow over. Although I never said a word to him about this treachery, I never forgave him.

After they returned and got the business going again, the question of the resumption of my studies came up. My uncle wanted to send me to a university in England, but I refused to hear of it. Instead, I chose to stay and study Hebrew. I thought: I won't be the only student not fluent in the language. There are many other new immigrants who'll be in the same boat.

My uncle gritted his teeth and said nothing. He didn't understand. In fact, I don't understand either, to this very day, why I decided as I did. Could it have been simply an act of defiance, of rebellion against my uncle's wishes and ambitions for me?

I want to spend my last days sitting by the window, gazing at the sea from which my fathers earned their bread. Through the open window a breeze will blow from the sea and touch my face, plant a salty kiss on my lips. I shall sit by the window, all day, all night, within sight of the harsh rocks and the sea. I want to reflect upon my life, to go back to my childhood, lost somewhere among the gardens of Kefissia stretching out beyond this window; to let my thoughts wander through the little alleys in the vicinity of Kapnikareas Street and the streets leading from Syndagma Square and Omonia Square, to my father's little restaurant, and the Pireaus port, where the little boat in which we used to go out fishing on Sundays, instead of going to church like other people, lay anchored.

A long time has passed since we went down to the sea together. Once I was a child, and from that time I don't remember anything but broken bits of pictures. And because of my present straits my heart isn't really in it, this journey back to those days, and I repeatedly escape from it to the thoughts of the lives of others, or of my illness. And to escape from these latter thoughts, too, I submerge myself in the former; I think of those who are still living ordinary, everyday lives, bound to the laws of their base natures; or those who continue to exist in my heart alone.

Oh my Henrietta, with your noble soul and generous heart, with a constant smile on your gentle, white face—a face like the radiant full moon that sheds light on everything from the depths of an abundant grace, a benevolence that encompasses the whole world.

Will I find the strength, despite the illness which is leading me with sure, rapid steps to the expected end, to devote myself to writing my book—to organizing my notes and giving them form—an act which will weigh in the scales against all the failures from my lack of resourcefulness and daring, my laziness and self-love?

In my new house, the sea will shine outside my window. Day and night it will play its never-ending lament to me on the concertina of its waves and bring me dreams scented with basil and mint, lit by the starfish in its depths, and full of the rustling yellowing leaves of the plane tree.

Perhaps the sea will distract me, perhaps its many-sided, treacherous image will awaken and strengthen in me the dormant heritage which has decayed in a world that never gave it a chance to flourish. This longing for the sea reminds me of my father's stories about Captain Iorgis Stephanides, the poor fisherman from Khania in Crete, after whom he was named.

My father often told me about the heroic exploits of his grandfather, how in the 1898 revolt he had killed some two hundred Turks, how he had fallen into captivity, and, like my father, been executed after terrible torture. My father, although he earned his living from a little restaurant at the top of Kapnikareas Street, kept faith with the Stephanides family tradition, and every Sunday he went out in a fishing boat he had built with his own hands, to fish in the sea.

Whenever I reflect on the glorious—yes, glorious—history of my family, I am ashamed of my need for alcohol and drugs to help me escape from the fear of death and the pain. But it affords me lucidity, grants me moments when I am still capable of contemplating the past and the people with whom my lot was cast.

I am descended from a line of men who loved danger. But in me the life force has waned, a sign of the degeneration of the race. My people now tread the paths of their motherland with bowed heads and eyes fixed on the ground. They have submitted to their fate. Their king, a foreigner, has abandoned them to wicked men, and they do not rise up to fight. And I, an invalid no longer fit for anything, exemplify this downfall.

The height of bloom, apparently, is the beginning of decay. Or as one philosopher put it: "The height of sleep is the beginning of wakefulness"—or perhaps the opposite. And how does this fit in with the proposition that "the way up and the way down are one and the same"?

If this is indeed the case, then there is hope.

I lived my life in exile, cut off from my family traditions; and, unlike my forefathers, peasants and seafarers, I became a scientist and, in the end, a failed writer. The line declined, but nevertheless I feel that my life was saturated with that unique vitality so characteristic of our race. I console myself with the thought that the Greeks were always attracted to science, poetry, and philosophy, and I do not regard myself as a traitor, despite the fact that my best and best-loved friends were not Greeks.

I want to understand if the possibility of death can give access to a new vision. What Heraclitus said fascinates me, because it is open to so many interpretations. He said: If God had not created the golden honey, men would think that figs were sweeter. And indeed, I believe that what exists, if seen aright, is best, unless you imagine the honey which is sweeter than the figs which are your lot.

But the honey, even if we know of it, is rare and hard to come by, whereas to enjoy the figs all you have to do is stretch out your hand. It seems to me that in preferring the figs I prove myself to be a true Greek. And this is the real difference between me and Alexander. He was never satisfied with the figs.

I am satisfied that, in spite of everything, my life was as it should be, even if I never brought all my beginnings to a conclusion. I am happy that I never exchanged this climate for another, and that, although I was an exile, I was never tempted to wander far from this sea, which sustained my forefathers, all my life long. I think it was not in my power, or in the power of any man, to prevent Henrietta from meeting her fate. I did everything in my power to restrain Alexander, and that he abandoned his scientific pursuits and settled in a remote kibbutz is proof of this. In sum, I am content. This evening Slavos will come with the notary. Everything is provided for and I am not afraid.

I think a lot about Henrietta. Alexander wrote to me that she did not give up the ghost immediately, that she died in his arms and her lovely face was gone. There is something symbolic in the way she died: her ruined face, and the pouring rain. To give it meaning, the destruction of beauty should be violent and cruel. When I close my eyes I can hear Alexander whispering to her, and the howls of the desert animals in the night. A hyena watches and waits. The wadis swell. Water pours down the rocks.

I know the desert well. I know its sporadic, elusive sounds, and how it presents the unexpected, suddenly, to our eyes. During my vacations I used to go hiking in the southern Negev with Alexander, who accompanied me at first with resentment and suspicion, and later on with enthusiasm. Alexander, with the flat chin too big for his face, his straight, black hair, which keeps falling into his eyes, and which he flicks back with a quick, nervous toss of his head. His myopic eyes, which open wide whenever he is moved or excited, whenever he speaks of his dreams, mesmerized by his insane delusions.

In those days, when we were both working as doctoral candidates in the scientific institute, I still believed that these strenuous hikes, with the wild, desolate landscape and the blazing sun stripping a man of everything but the sensation of his own exhausted body, might heal his sick and storm-tossed spirit.

At first Alexander objected to our hiking the desert. He preferred the north, saying that the south reminded him of the Nevada and gangsters. I dismissed his repeated objections as illogical. I preferred the harsh climate, and my deeper purpose was to exhaust him to the point of collapse. What have you to do with the Nevada desert? I asked him impatiently, and he would shrug his shoulders and smile enigmatically.

I too loved the north of the country, but the vegetation in those olive-clad hills, the thorny great burnet, crab apple, and rush broom, those landscapes of oak and pine and plane forests, aroused in me unbearable longings. The desert, on the other hand, lies outside the borders of civilization. Its primordial desolation holds for me a powerful attraction. Sometimes it seemed to me that my ancient pagan inheritance was revived in the desert. I was capable of shouting my head off at the moon, running naked, and leaping about like a demented goat.

Soon Alexander grew accustomed to the desert and learned to love it. In one little place where we spent a night or two, where the inhabitants lived a solitary, heroic existence on the borders of the red-rocked mountains whose veins of iron ore streaked the earth with rust, he was later to live out his exile.

I remember what he said to me on one of those nights, before we went to sleep, in a little hut next to a cowshed: "Perhaps I'll come to live here one day. The place pleases me. . . . One might live here a simple, monastic life, like the Essenes in the Judaean desert. You must have heard of them, some people say they were the first Christians. Their clear, precise rules of life—I feel drawn to them. That's how everyone should live, frugally and with fortitude. This is a place where there is no latitude for passions; a rational place. Yes, one day I'll come here. A person could plant Chinese gardens here. I'm grateful to you for teaching me to love the desert. . . ."

That was the first time I heard him talk about the Chinese gardens.

We would make for mountains eroded by wind and rain, quarried with magnificent pillars and walk in the footprints of hyenas. God had cast big boulders in disarray over the land, and broken slabs of white granite, smooth and gleaming in the sun like marble. At the entrances to the caves gaping in the red sandstone lay the lean white bones of animals, which Alexander looted for his zoological collection. We would climb the steep rocks in the tracks of the tender-footed deer with their tangled antlers, and sometimes, when we reached a summit, we would be greeted by the sight of the sea.

We tramped through wadi beds, over the pure crystals of sand, glittering in the sunlight like gold, discovering ancient inscriptions and drawings which holy men had engraved on their way to holy places. From the depths we would look up to the heights, and from the heights down to the depths, walking for hours on end and sleeping wherever the fancy took us.

At night we listened to the screaming wind, the calls of night birds seeking their prey, the groaning of stray camels, or sometimes the sounds of caravans of smugglers stealing across the borders. Sometimes a fire flickered in the distance, and the smell of dung was borne towards us on the chill, dry air.

How well I know those places—treacherous as a woman, many-sided as silver-maned Proteus. I can pinpoint in my imagination the very place where the accident happened. But the place is not important. . . .

Henrietta was a woman dominated by curiosity. Anything out of the ordinary attracted her attention, and she longed to understand the demons that drive people to do unusual things. It seems to me that she was fascinated by Alexander's eccentricities. On the other hand, she was also the kind of person who would submit to fate without a struggle. She always accepted her circumstances. Otherwise she would surely have married me. Perhaps she regarded Alexander as a destiny to be followed blindly, I don't know. . . . But this is the only explanation I can find. I believe she never loved him. He attracted her, yes, her overpowering curiosity was aroused. She wanted to solve his riddle. And since he wanted her, she surrendered to him, with her ingrained submissiveness.

Could I have helped to alter her fate if I had not returned to Greece? I think not. Henrietta's was a doomed and innocent beauty, bound to perish. God was jealous.

I have time on my hands, but I am not bored.

My time is full now in a way hitherto unknown to me.

Mostly I sit by the window overlooking the street. I contemplate the passersby and the plants in the garden.

Each day when he passes, the postman nods to me in greeting. Occasionally he brings a letter or postcard, from Elisheva, or from my uncle who still lives in Jaffa, from people far away. On fine days women push prams up the street, and gardeners hurry to their work in the gardens of my wealthy neighbors, their tools on their shoulders. Their complaints do not reach me here. In the morn-

ings, maids pile bedclothes on the window sills and verandah railings, beat carpets noisily and make the dust fly. At night, lives of
love and hate are conducted behind drawn curtains. On the surface,
there is not much difference between life here and the life I knew in
Israel.

Last year, as Elisheva asked, I planted a magnolia tree in my
garden in memory of the days we spent together in Italy. I doubt
that I will live to see it bloom. In Rome, too, at the end of our first
trip, years ago, the magnolia trees of the Villa Borghese had not
come into flower, and I know only their cone-like fruit.

We spent two months in Italy, restlessly wandering from place
to place and waiting in vain for love to flower.

I met Elisheva in Rome; I went there after Henrietta joined
Alexander in his desert exile. A lonely man and woman in a foreign
country, we were happy to see each other; a man and woman bear-
ing a weight of shared memories, private miseries, seeking to escape
from ourselves. I tried to take care of her, but I wasn't very successful. I had problems of my own.

Despite her nervous depression, and frequent tears, despite
these difficulties, our first days of discovery were surprisingly
happy. I enjoyed her full, supple body, the pleasure of her sad
embraces. I think it was above all her sadness that I loved. She was
like an exquisite narcissus that had been thoughtlessly trampled, a
crushed narcissus which, nevertheless, had preserved its fragrance
and the whiteness of its petals. How can I explain my desire to
touch her wounds? It was there, and only there, on the edge of suffering, that we met. As the days passed, we began to grow impatient, and our lovemaking, hasty and careless, became a joyless
habit. When the time came for her to depart, both of us felt a certain relief.

"Our journey was a kind of hell," Elisheva said to me in part-
ing, "but I don't want to talk about it. But these months, in
Rome, in Florence, in Venice—we loved each other, didn't we?. . .

"In my sleep I embraced my red-headed Pierre and mourned
my child; and you thought about Henrietta all the time. Nevertheless it's hard to say good-bye. Will we ever meet again? I don't
think so."

♦

Most of the time, gazing from my window, I let my thoughts drift and carry me. Sometimes, not often, I write, without pressure, with composure. I know my book will never be written, this is all I will ever write. Consequently I must choose to write only what is truly important.

For many years I have lived far from my friends, but, in one way or another, they have always accompanied me. They bound me to them, and tried to save themselves with my help. But my life after I left Henrietta was one of exile and desolation, and this none of them, except Elisheva, knew. I never told her, but in Venice, when I took her to church on the anniversary of Henrietta's death, she understood.

Perhaps my life would not have been very different if Henrietta had married me long ago, as I wished her to do; or it may be that my love was nothing but fantasy and illusion. Nevertheless, as long as I live Henrietta will be the woman I hunger for, the woman I want to kill. I didn't mean to write that. . . . Naturally, I resent her rejection of me. But to the point of doing murder?

The bond between us was almost dream-like, and dreams hold all possibilities: even love's consummation in the absolute possession of death.

I wrote to ask Elisheva to come to me here. Today, when the notary arrives, I'll arrange to will her my money; and this house which Slavos loves, which my father built for my mother with his own hands, I'll leave to him. When I'm dead, Elisheva will be able to realize her dreams of traveling. Perhaps she'll go to Mexico. . . . But I don't think that anything will really change for her.

I seek out the mistakes in my friends' lives, lacking time to discover my own. But their mistakes, of course, are my mistakes, too. We all fail in love, in loyalty, in honor. And perhaps this whole business of mistakes and failures is a misconception from the start. Perhaps the ancient concept of the rule of *Moira*, her absolute power over all the gods, holds a truer perception of the human condition. Sometimes it seems to me that the ancients were wiser than we are, closer to the roots of life. The belief in the absolute power of fate gave people a strength and vitality greater than ours. And perhaps it is precisely this belief which could set us free.

No, my money won't make Elisheva any happier, she isn't made for it. None of my friends is made for happiness. They're complex, restless people, children of a sick nation, a nation haunted by anxieties. In this sense we are similar. For hundreds of years we Greeks haven't known how to hold up our heads, and to this day we still don't know how.

I haven't much sorrow left and very little room for love. I doubt whether a dying man can say anything which will be acceptable to his fellows.

Every day I try and fail to renew my connections with the world. I think of all that we miss through our ignorance, impatience, and destructive, profitless lusts. And when it all comes to an end, what a wretched affair the whole business seems. Only one thought can still flood my heart with fleeting warmth. Oh Henrietta, how lovely you were.

Now, to conjure up her radiant countenance, I need the help of a photograph. As for Alexander, he's no more than a blur, whose voice, for all our talks once, I can no longer hear.

I can imagine the feel of Henrietta's flesh, which I never touched. Even now, in face of death, I envy Alexander, who never deserved her, for having won her. And I understand clearly now that love is the only thing of value in life, no matter what it costs. Love, any love.

Henrietta and I never believed Elisheva's stories. Henrietta used to say, she's got a highly developed imagination, don't take any notice. There's no need to take everything she says seriously.

When she spoke about the man she loved, there was an unusual gentleness in her tone. Perhaps she was the captive of her own imagination, but when she spoke of this man, and how, in their chance meetings, he smelled of expensive soap, with his hair still damp from the shower, and bursting with gaiety, we would listen avidly and incredulously.

We never saw the man, nor did we know his name.

Pierre Bezuhov she used to call him, and she liked to tell us amusing stories about him. ''My Pierre Bezuhov,'' she would say, ''looks like a bear, too. He's tall and strong, but more of a teddy bear, really, than a real bear. But they're similar—exuberant, emotional, reckless and irresponsible."

She didn't mention him in the letter she left when she tried to kill herself. Even in this letter, so bleak and desperate, there was a characteristic note of realism even in her most fantastic stories. I still have that letter. When we returned from the hospital, Henrietta and I, confused and upset, and Henrietta went to the kitchen to make tea, I searched Elisheva's room. I was looking for a clue, something to help us understand. She had seemed so gay when we left her earlier. And as we were saying good-bye she said, smiling as if it were a joke, My Pierre has left me and I am very sad. I'm so sad that I don't feel the least desire to go on living.

And when we left, right at the door, she said: Good-bye, we won't see each other again.

But she said these dark words in an affected and playful manner. This was nothing new, she was always acting, pretending to be joking. You could never tell if she meant what she said. It wasn't the first time that she'd declared, with just such a mischievous smile, that she was sad. So we didn't take any notice.

Henrietta would scold her when she acted like that: "Aren't you ashamed of your childishness? Life isn't a joke, you know."

Henrietta had no sense of humor. This, I think, was her only fault.

In her room, on her desk covered with sketches and notes, I found the letter.

I didn't show it to Henrietta, I don't know why. Even today I don't know why I hid it in my pocket. The letter was obscure. . . .

How Elisheva has changed since then. She is no longer flirtatious, she's stopped pretending. During the course of time something sharp and resolute has gathered around her mouth, her once full cheeks are sunken and deep, frown marks score her brow. These things, I think, betoken bitterness rather than age.

I no longer remember exactly what the letter said. How could she bring herself to this act of despair, which I myself sometimes consider, without being able to bring myself to it, although the pain is sometimes unbearable.

I wheel myself to the bureau, in one of those drawers I have kept that letter, among other letters, and albums and manuscripts.

There it is, at the bottom of a cardboard box which once contained sweets, among other letters from Elisheva. I read it again, after not touching it for years, but it adds nothing to my understanding.

The riddle with which the other confronts us fills us with anxiety because we are not capable of standing in the place where he stands, we can have only the vaguest idea of what he feels. It seems to us that if we touch him, his skin will betray his secrets, but this is not so. We cannot die his death, suffer his sickness, love with his love. What did Elisheva use to say? That we are windowless fortresses. Sometimes, from a hard blow, the stone may crack. But that's all.

This is what she wrote:

> I no longer have the strength to cope with your demands. It seems to me that they are exaggerated and even insane. This all-embracing and exclusive loyalty which you demand from me is beyond my powers, and makes me feel useless. The world has lost its flavor, there is no joy from experiences you refuse to share, whether by your own fault or not. If you were capable of giving, perhaps my world would fill up again. But you are capable of nothing but looting and despoiling, and I am bereft.
>
> True, love is not something to be bargained over, and I know very well that by making demands I demean and contradict my love. But it is because I have become so small and poor that I say these things.
>
> So in my own poorness of spirit, and in awareness of your impotence, I hereby declare the annulment of our one-sided pact.
>
> You are going away. Therefore, I, too, shall go.
>
> I am setting my soul free. Farewell. You are not to blame, since it is through my own fault that I go to the place where I am going.

I still don't understand. True, Henrietta and I were critical of her. Henrietta was offended by Elisheva's reserve, and her false jocularity, at times. What devil possesses her? Henrietta would say. And why is she so hostile, sometimes she treats me like an enemy. . . .

Was she ill, I ask myself. Okay, she loved someone, loved him very much. But is that sufficient reason?. . .

Now I pity Elisheva, now when the fear of death has opened my eyes.

When we met in Rome, acquaintances, old friends perhaps, I said to her: "Let's travel together, I hate traveling alone." She said: "I don't mind, but I'm afraid."

"Afraid of what," I asked, "we're grown-ups." And she said: "I'm afraid of intimacy. What will happen if I fall in love with you?" I mocked her: "And what will happen if I fall in love with you? Nothing will happen. It'll be fun." And she said: "Love involves suffering. I haven't the strength for it."

As if I didn't know that love involves suffering. Or perhaps I really didn't know?

The lives of my friends, my own life, which once seemed to me so clear and transparent, show hidden contradictions now. Had I been gifted with true wisdom, perhaps I would have been able to foresee Alexander's end the day we met.

We sat at the same table in the little oriental restaurant at the bottom of Jaffa Street in Jerusalem. I usually frequented a restaurant near my room, but that day, a summer's day near the close of the academic year, I was held up at the library, and this place was close by. It was cheap, too, and they served certain dishes that reminded me of the food my father served in his restaurant at the top of Kapnikareas Street.

The place was packed. One of the tables was occupied by a young man I had sometimes seen in the faculty laboratories. I asked him if I could join him, and he readily agreed.

"We're in the same classes," he said.

"Physics and mathematics?"

"Physics and chemistry."

I can remember what I ordered: an economical meal of rice with peas, vegetable salad, black bread, and watermelon.

Suddenly the young man asked: "Are you Greek?"

"Yes, that's right."

"Your Hebrew's very good. Are you a real Greek? A Christian, I mean?" he asked.

"Yes, but I'm not religious, I don't consider myself a Christian. But I was baptized, of course."

"You intrigue me," he said. "My name's Alexander. . . . How did you land up in Israel? You're probably the only Greek student at our university."

"You could be right, but there are plenty of Greeks in Israel—in Jaffa, Jerusalem, and Haifa. The Greek Orthodox Church has a lot of property in Jerusalem. We're a nation of merchants, and merchants are wanderers. Like you Jews."

To change the subject, and because of his accent, I asked if he were from England.

"New York," he said brusquely. He too, it seemed, had no desire to talk about past history.

We finished our meal and started to walk to our five o'clock class. Alexander said suddenly, "You interest me."

There was something odd about him. His frank and brusque way of speaking made me want to laugh. But he was arrogant, too.

"The professors hate me," he said, "because there are some things I know more about than they do. I ask a lot of questions and it gets on their nerves. But I'll be a professor by the time I'm twenty-four—if nobody stops me. The academics over here are a jealous lot, and they do their best to prevent the best men from getting ahead. In America it's different."

I knew that he was highly regarded by the faculty, but the students, envious of his gifts, often mocked him.

"If you think it's easier in America, why don't you go back there?" I asked, with some irritation.

"I can't. There are certain difficulties. . . ."

I didn't press him, I had been taught not to ply strangers with questions. But I didn't mind his questions, it was his boasting I found objectionable. In the course of time, I grew accustomed to that, too. . . .

By the time we had reached the lecture hall, we agreed to go to a movie together that evening. Thus began our friendship, whose wretched consequences I was too shortsighted to foresee.

Soon Alexander, who was short of cash, moved in to share my room. Together we dreamed of the great futures awaiting us in our field of space science. Alexander really was capable of great things, whereas my own abilities were mediocre. Even if I had stuck to my profession, I don't think I would have gone far. But Alexander was convinced that I was an original thinker, destined for a brilliant career. At the time I thought that his affection for me colored his view. Now I realize that his grasp on reality was pretty tenuous, he believed what he wanted to believe.

Perhaps it was my disappointment in my own abilities that led me, in the end, to give up science, rather than ideological reasons, or my friend's madness, as I used to think . . . .

At first everything went smoothly between us. But then Alexander began to dream about building rockets. He studied intensively, constructed models, and began to apply for funds to set up a laboratory in which to conduct experiments. His detailed and precise designs for producing low-cost rockets seemed, as far as I could tell, quite sound. He claimed that with a well-equipped laboratory everything was possible, and I helped him in his work as much as I could.

But Alexander was impatient and the indifference of the authorities plunged him into despair. Perhaps the project itself was beginning to bore him. He was never a practical person, he was interested only in theories. And one day, sitting at his desk and going through the file he had prepared to show the experts, he suddenly got up and said: "I'm fed up with this stuff, Yanis. I've had it."

His expression as he said this was strange and rather frightening. I had never seen him like this before.

"Take it easy, Alexander," I said carefully, "you must be patient. You know how long these things take."

Alexander did not reply. He stared at me with wide-open sightless eyes and I don't think he heard a word I said. For a while he stood before his desk, breathing heavily. The way he was breathing reminded me of how the underground fighter, Andreas, my father's friend, gasped for breath when he was dying. Then he suddenly banged his fist on the desk, grabbed hold of the file, and flung it onto the floor, stamping on it as savagely as a wild horse trying to throw its rider. In a terrible rage he kicked and trampled the papers, running around the room like a demented creature, tearing the scattered pages to shreds. There won't be any rockets! he shouted. If they don't want rockets they won't have them! In the end I had to throw a pot full of water in his face. His work was ruined beyond repair.

Later on he began to say that the authorities had stolen his ideas, and I prayed silently that he wouldn't get any new ones. The price seemed to me too heavy.

Alexander is so different from me, a man who has no need of other people. I was a kind of nurse to him, but he could have done without my company, or so it seems to me. Perhaps it is precisely this solitude of his which draws people to him and uses their need to enslave them and incorporate them into himself. Thus he turned me into his lieutenant, but never took my advice or requests into consideration. Alexander was unwittingly cruel to those who loved him, and when we lived together in Jerusalem I was always forced to serve him. I did so willingly, because I admired him, and now I think that I was also afraid of him.

We pooled our money and shared expenses. Alexander was an absentminded person who didn't know how to take care of his own needs. He would forget to eat and wash and cut his hair. He was an only child, spoiled by his mother, who looked after him for as long as she lived. When he came to live with me, I took over this troublesome task, and, as I say, I bore it willingly. Nature seems to have intended me for a protector, and taking care of Alexander, whom I came to love, gave me satisfaction and joy. I was older than he, this eccentric and hot-tempered person, for whom I became a dutiful father. . . .

After the destruction of his rocket papers, Alexander no longer spoke to me of his plans and projects. For a few months he went on working quietly and without fuss, and his old boastfulness seemed to have subsided.

I won't annoy my professors anymore, he said, you'll see. From now on I'll be a good little boy. Although he said this sort of thing often, I was not completely reassured, and gradually grew more suspicious. He became increasingly haggard, hardly ate, and in contrast to his previous habits, began washing compulsively. There was a new look in his eye—austere, detached, painful—somewhat frightening. He grew remote and withdrawn from me.

One day, when I was studying for my final exams, he turned to me and said: "Listen, Yanis, don't you think that too many people in the world die violent deaths? Not from old age or illness, but from violence. People can become easily addicted to murder. Think about it. You're supposed to be a Marxist, aren't you, a person who dreams of a better world. Have you ever asked yourself how many people have died as a result of the crimes of Al Capone and his gang?"

"You see too many gangster movies for your own good," I answered lightly.

Alexander never missed any of the gangster movies that were shown in town, and he could sit through even inferior movies of this genre two or three times.

"It's got nothing to do with gangster movies! You're just like my professors. . . . I'm talking hard facts. If we take into account all the wars and revolutions and fights and road accidents and brutal murders, it adds up to millions and millions of people. Look, nowadays everybody's busy planning murder, improving weapons of destruction. Even I was dragged in, with my rocket design. But nobody thinks about creating life. It's all wrong. Human nature has been distorted in our era. The ancients told tales of people who went down to the underworld to resurrect their dead and loved ones: Anath, Orpheus, Gilgamesh, Ezekiel, who spoke of the resurrection of the dead. Today, anyone who talked of such things would be considered insane. People have resigned themselves to death. It's against human nature."

Alexander always sounded logical, never mind how improbable the things he said.

"All right," I said mockingly, "so what do you suggest? Are you going to invent a cure for death?"

"Why not?" he said, staring at me coldly. "I'm going to begin right now. There has to be a solution, a formula. In the end everything comes down to formulae. Life is a formula, too, nothing more than a formula. I'll find a formula of life, we'll do it together. . . ."

As he made this wild and passionate speech, Alexander's big, black eyes, which usually narrowed because of his poor sight, were wide open and glittering. Trying to quiet him with reason, I said: "But Alexander, such things are out of your field. They're matters for biologists. You don't know enough."

"Nonsense! I know everything I need to know. Over the past few months I've been reading up on all the literature those dumb biologists have to spend five years at university studying. I'm telling you, you don't need more than a few months."

"Alexander," I said, as gently as I could, "biology requires laboratory work, not just books. . . ."

I remembered the thick volumes he had been bringing home lately from the library, and the intensity with which he had poured over them. It has never occurred to me to wonder what he was up to. I had been pleased, after the destruction of his papers, that he was occupied and quiet again. I thought he had grown out of his nonsense, that the business with the rockets had taught him a lesson. Suddenly I felt responsible for him. He seemed to me like a small child, a child who liked playing with revolvers and fireworks, who had to be protected from his dangerous games.

Alexander answered me contemptuously: "Do you think I'm stupid, or what? Of course you need laboratories for doing experiments. But not for arriving at formulae. Formulae come from pure thought."

"Your idea is impossible," I said helplessly.

"Impossible?" He was hurt and indignant. "Don't you believe in me, in Alexander?"

"I can't believe in this idea," I said.

"In other words, you're not with me?"

"I can't be, not in this, Alexander. I'm a physicist, not a biologist."

"Fine. I'll work alone. I thought you'd want to share in the glory. I only asked you out of friendship. But I don't need your help."

In the following days, Alexander stopped talking to me. From my classmates I heard that he had been given permission to work in the biology lab. Some of them wanted to know what he was up to, but I kept my mouth shut. Later on, after we reached a kind of reconciliation, he tried to tell me about his work, but I refused to listen. The whole thing seemed fantastic to me. At the same time, I feared for Alexander's sanity. I believed that if I was firm enough in my opposition, he might reconsider this crazy project. It was clear to me that he would keep trying to confide in me, that he needed me, although he would never admit it. And this gave me grounds to hope that a firm stand on my part might help.

And so I waited, and Alexander went on doing whatever he was doing, and I knew nothing about it. After a time he began to complain about the hostile actions of his rivals, and he designed special locks for his desk. I couldn't help admiring his ingenuity, and for a moment—but only a moment—I was tempted to believe that even his wild project might succeed, such was the force of his personality. . . . These locks of his seemed to me to have excellent commercial possibilities, and I tried to persuade him to take out a patent and try to sell the idea to a manufacturer. But Alexander was secretive; even such things he resisted sharing with anyone, and he regarded me suspiciously when I made the suggestion. And my refusal to collaborate with him, rather than bringing him to his senses, seemed to have only hardened his determination.

At this time, Henrietta had already fallen in love with him. I knew about it, although they tried to hide it from me. My anxiety about Alexander's deteriorating condition was growing. And now there was another person to think of.

Is that really the way things were? Or did I unconsciously encourage him in his impossible project, in the hope that it would distract him from Henrietta? Even today, facing death, I'm not sure of the truth. But I know that I loved them both and I suffered the agonies of hell.

I well remember the first time Henrietta visited me in Jerusalem. She was in her second year of studies at the Technion, and had come to Jerusalem to look for a rare book in the National Library. I prepared a Greek lunch in honor of her visit.

Had I guessed that Henrietta too, would fall under my dangerous friend's spell—cool and rational woman as she was—I would have done everything in my power to prevent their meeting. But perhaps it was destined, and I was cast as fate's dumb servant. . . .

I think she fell in love with him that same day. Alexander ate very little, excited by the presence in our wretched room of such a beautiful young woman. We had never entertained a girl there before; Alexander never had any girlfriends, and he hardly saw anyone but me. He was not an easy man to befriend, so lonely, reserved, and shy, and he shrank from strangers. Sometimes he reluctantly accompanied me to parties, but it wasn't a success. He couldn't dance, and he would sit alone in a corner, obviously bored.

But Henrietta's presence seemed to intoxicate him, and he talked without stopping. The way that he spoke seemed to cast a spell over Henrietta. I noticed at once that she was bewitched. His low, soft voice, together with his powerful inner conviction, masked the confusion and lack of logic in his speech. His words that filled my heart with anxiety, his vehement personality, filled and dominated the little room, and I felt crushed to insignificance. And the way that Henrietta hung on his every word, even when he was lost in a passionate exposition of his crazy project, aroused in me a terrible, blinding jealousy.

"Just imagine," he said, his gaze fixed on her intently, "if it were possible to discover a hormone capable of destroying everything base and irrational in human nature. The emotions definitely depend on the structure of the brain, on chemical formulae, perhaps on a flawed nervous system which leads people to murder and bloodshed. Violence is ugly—I hate it! We must find a hormone to eliminate it from our instincts. Perhaps a certain nerve center in the brain should be put out of action. I'm working on this now, looking for a way.

"If only we could destroy the human lust for power, destroy jealousy and love, we could save the world forever. These emotions do us nothing but harm. . . . I'm interested in order and discipline, and for this political solutions are useless. Look at communism. This noble idea only succeeded in inflaming passions more than ever before. Fine ideas and rotten results—that's what all ideologies amount to. No, the solution is biological. We have to improve the human stock, as with cattle and poultry. Don't worry, I'm not talking about any kind of master race, it's them I'm fighting against. I'm talking about the improvement of the race from exactly the opposite point of view. Too many people have died and are dying violent deaths. There is too much cruelty in the world, too much competition, too many passions. . . ."

In the evening, when I accompanied Henrietta to the bus, she said: "Your friend frightens me. . . ."

I asked myself if this fear was at the root of the attraction she clearly felt. But I said nothing.

Today, when I think about that afternoon, I hear again Alexander's voice filling the room with its low notes and odd gentleness, rare in a masculine voice. It astonishes me that he never went to see Henrietta in Haifa, not even once. He never courted her. It was she who came to us, at first rarely, and more often later. Why didn't he court her? Why didn't he visit her in Haifa? Was it his shyness, especially with women; or was he simply indifferent?

Henrietta must have suffered greatly on Alexander's account. She never spoke about it to me, doubtless because of my jealousy. I traveled up to Haifa whenever I could, to try to persuade her against this dangerous involvement. But she wouldn't listen, and Elisheva sided with her, too. We behaved with appalling stupidity, all of us, including Elisheva and me; we share the guilt for her death. And yet something did happen later, I don't know what it was, to separate Henrietta from Alexander for a while.

Eventually, Elisheva left the Technion. After her suicide attempt she continued her studies for a month or two, and then she disappeared. "Why did she leave?" I asked Henrietta, "what happened?" "She just got fed up," she answered, but I had the impression that she was being evasive.

Later on, a year afterwards, Elisheva went to Vienna to study landscape architecture. When she returned, I was no longer in the country. After Elisheva left Haifa, Henrietta's visits to Jerusalem grew less frequent, I don't know why. I never really understood their relationship, because neither Alexander nor Henrietta confided in me, and I never questioned them. But I was glad that it seemed to be coming to an end. . . .

Alexander was not a person who gave of himself. He didn't know how to love. In his wild, fantastic inner world there was no room for anyone else. What he demanded from others was unqualified admiration. I don't think he wanted love.

When I saw her to the bus that evening, Henrietta said: "I read somewhere once that people with very long limbs and with prominent chins are either geniuses or simpletons. Alexander's a genius, isn't he?''

"I don't know," I said irritably, "but he has a lot of crazy ideas in that big head of his, and they'll lead him to his ruin in the end."

"You're so intolerant, Yanis. You won't consider any ideas that deviate from your Marxist theories."

"Tolerance? What the hell has it got to do with tolerance?" I said bitterly. "Didn't you hear what he said? Hormones to regulate the activity of the mind! Don't you realize the man's insane?"

But nothing I could say, then or later, could alter the sympathy that had begun to take root in her heart.

Perhaps Elisheva will go to Mexico after I die. She'll sail from New York, as Hart Crane did, and perhaps she'll read his poems to one of the passengers. She read one of his poems to us once, a poem about the need to learn to love; about the beauty radiating from a man who finds he can give himself again, after wasting the best years of his life. As for me, my best years were wasted long ago, and I am incapable of giving anything to anyone; while Henrietta clings to life, in the face of death. Thanks to her I perceive the world's beauty, which only a few know how to touch. And the most beautiful thing in the world is the person you love.

Elisheva used to talk about Hart Crane as if he were someone she knew intimately. She dreamed about the clear, green Caribbean, with its swarming shoals of brilliantly colored fish, and she liked to tell us about the cruel warfare which was waged there.

I prefer the Mediterranean, its blue light in summer, and the keening of the fishermen's wives in the winter storms. Everyone needs a motherland. Henrietta came as a child to the Mediterranean from a northern land where she had known hunger and cold. Alexander, Henrietta, and Elisheva weren't rootless even if they wandered to Israel from other places.

But we Greeks are different. We love life, but we don't devour it. We eat without haste; we drink our wine slowly and deliberately; we dance and sing, with a stirring of the senses, to music made of the mountains, of goats' bells, and waves breaking against rocks.

Alexander, like the great king after whom he was named, wanted to take the place of God on earth and save men from suffering. But Plato did not speak of suffering, he spoke of justice and truth. It was the Jew, Jesus, who spoke of suffering. And Elisheva, the wanderer, knows how to face death. Theirs is a people haunted by death. We Greeks are haunted by freedom.

Elisheva told me about the last day of Hart Crane's life. Perhaps what she said was invented, but as she spoke of the fate of this complicated and solitary man, it seemed to me she was envious. It was only later that I realized it was not Hart Crane's last day of which she really was speaking. . . .

Hart Crane, she said, spent his last evening in Mexico in the port of Vera Cruz. He was bored and sad and wandered into a movie theater, perhaps to find a lover for the night. He watched this crude, silent movie about the revolution, full of blood and guns, and traitors hung from tall trees, and a dashing Pancho Villa. The audience wept. Hart asked himself why he should return to New York. Why not stay and weep with the Mexicans over the revolution, drink tequila, and look for boys. . . .

The lights went up in the crowded hall, its floor littered with crumbs and paper wrappings, and the crowd began to push their way to the door. As Hart followed, he saw people coming in for the second show. (Is the door leading out not the same as the one leading in, as Heraclitus might say.)

The poet returned to his hotel before the sun set. It was near the harbor, in a sordid neighborhood, which filled up at night with prostitutes and their pimps, cardsharps and gamblers. Cockfights were held there. It was a place where you could be casually stabbed in the back for a few dollars. An old Indian fortuneteller was sitting outside the hotel, and he sat down on a low stool, facing her, and held out his hand. His palm was pale and smooth as a child's, the hand of a man who had never done manual work. His father, a wealthy man, had taken care of his needs for most of his life. Now, with a smile on his lips, and thinking of the elegant cinematic exit he was planning, he listened to the words of the fortuneteller. She spoke of his forthcoming marriage. She predicted that he would have two sons and a daughter, and a long life. She saw some serious illnesses and many family quarrels on the palm of his hand.

Yo quiero saber la verdad he said to her, with a gentle smile. But the wrinkled Indian woman with her shriveled paps looked at him blankly and said no more. He placed a few coins in her hand and went up to his room.

That night his back pained him severely. As a child he had fallen from a horse and injured his spine. From then on he suffered recurrent bouts of pain, for which he took aspirins, lots of aspirins. The doctors had recommended a dry climate. And he did, indeed, feel better in Mexico City with its high altitude and thin air. But at night the oppressed and plundered Maya people would come to disturb his sleep. All night long he would hear their weeping and lamentations, and the rats scrabbling in the rubbish bins, and the secret grumbling of the mighty volcanoes of this sad and desperate land growled in his dreams.

Now, in the seaport of Vera Cruz, his pains returned. He had a bottle of anise in his bag and he began drinking it, at first in small, economical sips, and afterwards in reckless gulps. Slightly drunk, he went out again to prowl the dockside streets. The bars were still open, and dark women with red flowers in their hair offered him favors. He drank a lot of tequila, watched a revolting cockfight and, escaping the clutches of an unattractive boy, returned at last to his hotel, where he fell into a dead sleep, untroubled now by desolate wailing and volcanic growls. . . .

At dawn, when he boarded the dirty old steamer, the *Orizaba*, she was already sounding her siren and the deck was crowded with passengers. The rough crew were contemptuous, but Hart Crane hardly noticed.

Two days later he went up on deck. He had left no letters. His *salida* was not to be an elegant one, after all. Like most people, he loved no one, and hated himself. . . .

What did he think about then? Perhaps he thought of nothing. Perhaps he was quiet and full of dread, perhaps ashamed. Perhaps he remembered his grandmother's letters in the attic, so old that they melted to the touch like snow in the sun.

The poet threw off his coat before he jumped. His body was crushed against the side of the ship and sank fathoms deep, never to rise again.

His belongings were sent to his parents' home, in Alabama.

◆

The injection is wearing off and the pain is starting again.
Elisheva is disintegrating, I am disintegrating, Alexander. . .everything is disintegrating all the time, dust of the earth. Time mocks us
ceaselessly, and time itself is perhaps an illusion. Everything flows
and you cannot step twice into the same river.

The sweet-box is still in my hand, and I restore Elisheva's letter
to its place. There is Henrietta's photograph—not a good one—
Henrietta as a young girl, which she gave to me the summer that we
met. In her white, childish face her eyes are wide and surprised
under the masses of black hair. I stroke with my finger the thick
black hair, the soft shining skin; then I close my eyes and bring the
picture to my lips. It smells of celluloid. In vain I try to feel the texture of her skin, imagining it as it was that distant, happy summer,
exposed, half-naked to the early morning sun on the lonely beach.

One day—one of the days of the long summer vacation, in the
chill air of early morning, after a swim in the sea whose waters still
held yesterday's warmth—strolling down Jerusalem Avenue in
Jaffa, with my wet bathing trunks rolled up under my arm, I met
Henrietta. In those days I used to go for a swim at the Bat-Yam
beach and make my way back on foot to my uncle's house in Jaffa,
where I was staying then. I wanted to be strong and fit, and
devoted a lot of time then to swimming and walking, as well as boxing and running.

At that time, Jaffa was full of new immigrants and the first floor
of my uncle's house, where an Arab family formerly had lived, was
occupied now by a Mrs. Feuerstein and her three daughters,
refugees from Hungary who had come from an immigrant transit
camp.

As I strolled along the avenue, thinking of nothing in particular, I was stopped by a tall girl in a white dress, the most beautiful
girl I had ever seen, with black hair and a northern complexion,
transparent and angelic.

"Excuse me," she said, "perhaps you can help me."

"Yes, of course," I replied, enthralled.

She held out a crumpled piece of paper with an address. "I've
been looking for ages, and nobody seems to know where this is.

Everyone sends me in a different direction," she said with a tired smile.

She set down with a sigh, the heavy suitcase she was holding, and I thought to myself, I'll carry it for her to wherever she wants to go.

The crumpled note, to my astonishment, bore my uncle's address, written in a wavering scrawl that I recognized as Mrs. Feuerstein's. I could already see us in my imagination as friends and lovers.

"She's a relative of mine, who's invited me to stay for the summer vacation, but I've never visited her here before," the girl explained. "Do you know her?"

"Of course, we're neighbors! We live in the same building, and now you'll be my neighbor, too." Mrs. Feuerstein had often invited me in for a cup of coffee, and she always talked about the war, the new regime, and communism—about which we argued violently. "Mrs. Feuerstein makes her living sewing curtains, she buys the fabric for her sewing work from my uncle's shop."

"Yes," said the girl shyly, "that's why she invited me to stay— she needs help with her sewing jobs. In the Home. . . ." She suddenly fell silent.

She protested at first when I picked up the heavy suitcase, and her blushes made her even more beautiful. We walked in silence and I sensed a certain sadness in her. I said: "Look, Mrs. Feuerstein's a good woman. I'm sure she won't make you work too hard. You'll be able to come for a swim in the sea every morning."

"I'm afraid not. I must work to earn money, so I can continue my studies." And again she fell silent.

"You can swim early in the morning. We'll go together, I'll take you. I know a wonderful beach." I spoke with an almost childish excitement, trying to cheer her up.

"We'll see," she said.

I had not known many girls. The Arab girls in the neighborhood had nothing to do with boys; and I had no contact with Jewish girls, either. My acquaintance was limited to my uncle's friends, who were narrow-minded and conservative. From time to time my uncle expressed his concern that I'd probably marry a Jewish girl. And, indeed, I felt so attracted to this girl, whose name

I didn't even know, that I could have proposed marriage to her on the spot.

The streets were very busy at that hour of the morning, full of heavily laden trucks stopping at the sides of the road to deliver their goods. Once I had to grab hold of her arm, to help her avoid a car that suddenly sped out in front of us, and that touch lingered in my palm for a long time.

Mrs. Feuerstein, a kind-hearted woman, encouraged Henrietta to accept my invitations, and so we went often together to swim. I took her to a nearly deserted beach where, alone among the yellow sand dunes and almost naked in the morning sun, we swam and then lay in the lap of the warm, damp sand. I yearned for her perfect body, almost suffocating with desire. "I love you, Henrietta," I would say over and over again, and she would laugh evasively and reply: "Nonsense! I'm a Jewess and one day soon you'll go back to your country and find a Greek bride."

Elisheva loved Henrietta, but she confessed that she envied her, too. Once she said to me: Envy and love are supposed to be mutually exclusive. When we envy someone, isn't that a kind of ill-wishing? But I loved Henrietta, even though I envied her. She was so beautiful, so serene, so secretive. I wish I knew more about her last hours. . . .

I'm waiting for Slavos and the notary. My housekeeper baked a cake for the occasion, before retiring to her room. The house is very quiet. It's raining, and I can hear the wind agitating the branches of the trees, the rain rushing down the gutters: the intervals of silence and the thrashing of the branches in the wind.

A little car has stopped across the road, its parking lights like red eyes staring at the falling rain. The winter days grow short, and already, at six o'clock, darkness descends. I light my pipe, and the little flame flickers in the window, trembling and slowly dying.

Before I fell ill I used to go out in the early evening to the little square, and as I sat in the shade of the plane tree, near the fountain and the laurels, your image would hide among the shadows. Now you wander through my sleepless nights, blood on your lips, and the gold of lost summers in your coal-black hair. Your body was fragrant as hyacinths. You wander through the shores of the bay, a wandering ghost, and the riddle of my life. I am not sad. I see you in the window. Your face, a little blurred, looks back.

I will face death as a man who has lived rightly should face it. If I was a real Greek, an Orthodox Greek, I would cherish hopes now of seeking my love in the other world. But I do not regret my loss of faith. Heaven, hell, a life different from the life we know, and meetings after death—such things are meaningless.

The rainwater collects in runnels and flows down to the sea. I think of Henrietta's last journey in the rain. Alexander would not tell me about it, although I begged him in my letters. Elisheva, too, knows no more than a few details.

They were driving through the desert, in the rare and dangerous rain. Such journeys are very risky. The wadis overflow unexpectedly and with unimaginable force. They flood the roads and sweep away everything in their path.

In her last letter Henrietta said:

Alexander has been hurt. The car he was driving hit a mine and his head was injured. When he returns from the hospital and is completely recovered, I shall tell him what I have decided. Our marriage hasn't worked out. This is the saddest letter I've ever written. It took me a little too long, didn't it, to see that you were right. It's a cruel thing to discover that you've made a mistake like this.

It's too complicated to write about. It isn't really clear even to me. I don't know how I came to fall in love with him, and if I really did. Perhaps the whole thing was only an illusion. Perhaps if I'd been born here, like Elisheva, and my parents had not met such a hard fate, I would have gone with you. But the war dominated all the subsequent choices of my life. Sometimes it seems to me that we are not free to choose at all, that everything is predetermined. At any rate, I was not free. Marriage to a non-Jew would have been a betrayal of my parents. Living parents can be betrayed or rebelled against, but it's impossible to betray dead ones, as you are well aware.

Nonetheless, this doesn't explain why I went with Alexander. I still don't know. Perhaps because he's a sick man, and I thought that I was capable of curing him. I was naive. I acted blindly. You always claimed that I was a rational woman, but you were wrong. I don't plan, I usually act on

impulse. And now things have gotten worse and it's very
hard. I don't know what to do. But I can't stay with Alexander, I can't. . . ."

I can see him with his head wrapped in a rakish bandage,
Henrietta sitting next to him, laughing. She always laughed when
she was worried. Alexander must have been offended by her
laughter. He hates not to be taken seriously, and he can't laugh at
himself. Why wasn't he more careful? He drove like a madman—
there was evidence of that and he didn't deny it.

The darkness is full of ceaseless, flickering vibrations. A pity I
can't open the window to smell the rain. It's too cold; and,
anyway, I can't reach the handle. The trees are black in the
incomplete dark and light breaking from the windows of the
houses across the street stirs in the wind-ruffled puddles. "All
things flow. . . ."

Did the doctors, bank managers, government officials—wealthy,
successful people, some of whom were here during the war—take a
stand? Do they now? Is there indignation in their hearts, or are they
indifferent? Do they attach any importance to freedom, to pride?

One defeat after the other, each more humiliating than the last.
And intrigues and hatred between brothers, between neighbors.
Do they go to church on Sundays? Do they dream of a different
future? Do they think about the past? Does the defeat of 1922, the
defeat of 1940, the defeat after the war, the defeat of 1967—do all
these defeats weigh heavily on them? Where do they turn for consolation?

There is only one law, that of change. Our fate is the same as the
fate of the silt at the bottom of a wadi. Rotting leaves and debris.
We delude ourselves that we are in control. Henrietta was right
when she said that everything is predetermined. It's all fate. Har-
mony and disharmony come into being of themselves, by virtue of
ananke, the law of constraint and necessity.

I am ready. I feel no regret. I do not go to my death beaten and
humiliated. I am a Greek.

♦

Henrietta, too, heard the splashing of water, water coming from
the mountains, overflowing the wadi, flooding the flat, desolate

plains.

Henrietta heard it as I hear it now, on the other side of a pane of glass. As she always did in times of crisis, at that time too, beyond the sound of the flooding water, she must have heard the sound of soldiers' boots tramping at night over her cellar hiding place. They were filthy, unshaven men, and she heard them marching from a cold, distant land. Perhaps, too, when Alexander spoke to her of his formula, his Chinese gardens, she listened with growing dread to the marching boots. . . .

"Slow down!" she must have shouted at him in the roar of the wadi, "Please, slow down!"

She wouldn't listen when I warned her against him. She said I was jealous.

"Slow down a little!"

"It's all right," he may have answered, it would be like him: "I've got my formula, don't forget."

The ascending stream and the descending stream: everything flows.

Henrietta never spoke about the death of her parents. She couldn't remember. One day they went away and never came back. But she remembered the Russians, and her fear: They loved gold. They would take anything, but gold they loved best.

On that last night she must have laughed. As Elisheva laughed the day we left her early in the afternoon, to see a movie. I had never seen her so gay, chattering without pause, and her cheeks burning. I thought that she was feverish.

"Hart is like heart," she said. "The Spanish say *mi corazón*. They know everything, the Spanish, they know where it hurts. I have two hearts today. How can you get rid of your heart? Even if you've got two, it's impossible. . . ."

When we returned, she was asleep and she didn't wake up even when we made a noise. Usually she slept lightly. Henrietta was worried.

"Elisheva, we're back. Don't pretend," she said. Nothing. . . .

Henrietta bent over her. "She really is asleep. But how can she be?"

Then she saw the little packet on the bedside table.

"Look," she said "the packet's empty. There were a lot of sleeping pills left."

Elisheva didn't know we would be back so soon. Perhaps she thought that we would seek the seclusion of the park to make love. I longed for it, but it never happened.... And that day, too, Henrietta insisted on hurrying home.

I didn't stay the night; Henrietta wouldn't let me. When I phoned a couple of days later, she told me that Elisheva had returned from the hospital, packed her things, and left: She didn't say where she was going. It was impossible to talk to her. She told me not to worry, that she would get in touch in a week or so.

I did not see Elisheva again until four years later when we met in Rome. Her face was no longer as I remembered it.

At the end of that year Alexander left, too. I remember him sprawled on his bed in our room, looking more somber than usual.

"What's wrong?" I asked.

"I'm leaving," he said quietly, almost in a whisper.

"Where are you going?" I asked in astonishment.

"Away from here. They're after me. They keep after me all the time.... Pentothal...hypnosis...thieves and robbers. There's nothing more for me to do here. I'm leaving."

"Pentothal—what on earth are you talking about?"

"Never mind. There's nothing more for me to do here. I'm going. I'm taking Henrietta with me."

"Where to? America?"

I thought that he would go back there one day. He had spoken often of the great opportunities for scientists there.

"Do you remember that place in the desert? That little kibbutz where we once spent the night?"

"Yes, of course I remember."

"That's where we're going. I told you I would one day, didn't I, that I liked their way of life...."

"And what makes you think they'll have you, or that Henrietta will go there with you?"

"They've agreed. I wrote to them. And she agrees too, she'll join me at the end of the academic year."

The next morning his things were packed. I went to Haifa to talk to Henrietta, to try to dissuade her. But she was adamant.

"I can't go on living here," she said to him that last night, before they set off for the theater.

And he replied: "The desert is the only place suitable for Chinese gardens."

I believe that Henrietta knew she was going to her death, that beyond the roaring of the floodwaters she heard the sound of jackboots. She was ready. Slow down a little! she must have cried. For God's sake, slow down!

She parted from her parents a second time, she watched them leave. She felt once more the taste of their farewell kisses. The child she was must have believed that they would return from their trip after a few days.

The truth is that I don't know much about Henrietta. She was reserved and she didn't talk much; a quiet woman. Our conversations were inhibited and halting and touched no depths. All I know about Henrietta is that I loved her.

A woman whose body has never given you joy remains a stranger. How can you know a woman if you have never awakened together to greet a new day? How can you imagine her sweetness, if you have never watched her as she sleeps, her calm face, framed in long, tangled hair. Henrietta evaded my love. She very rarely spoke about herself. She was attentive to others and thirsty for knowledge. She wanted me to talk to her about my studies, about science. I don't know why she chose to study architecture. Perhaps it was out of a passion for order and beauty. But her mind was analytical. She would have done well as a scientist.

As I spoke to her of these things, all the while gazing at her hungrily, she would listen intently, avid to learn. And I would gaze at her white hands, discovering the blue veins beneath the transparent skin. Her fingers were long and firm, her palms were soft.

When I tried, from time to time, to speak to her of my love, her face would become distant and expressionless, as if a door had closed. Sometimes this caution led me to suspect that she consented to our friendship simply from politeness. But when, occasionally, she dropped her guard, it was clear that this was not so; that her reserve stemmed from the fear of a commitment deeper than friendship.

Her last letter, in which for the first time she spoke the truth, confirmed this. How strong she must have been to behave with such restraint.

Oh, my beautiful Henrietta, even now as I stand at the gates of hell, afraid and in pain, I still long to hold you in my arms, to cup your lovely face in my hands. I remember how, once, you gave in to my entreaties and went dancing with me in a dark, crowded nightclub. And when we danced, I treated you, big as you were, like a china doll. My hands still remember the touch of your skin that filled me with longing, the scent of your hair as it casually brushed my face, and I close my eyes voluptuously.

She only let me kiss her once. It was just before I was to sail for Greece. I spent my last night in the country which had become my second motherland in Elisheva's room; she had disappeared a few months earlier.

It was early in the morning. We had breakfasted and were preparing to leave. While she was locking the door I was seized by a sudden panic and, without thinking, and taking her hand in mine, I told her not to come with me to the ship, that it would be painful for me to say good-bye there, in all the noise and commotion. Henrietta understood. She embraced me and kissed me, and for a moment we were like any other pair of lovers. But only for a moment. And then she tore herself from my arms saying: Go now. Don't forget to write to me.

Thus I parted from her, so that I would be able to go on thinking of her as she was then in all the days to come.

I will spend my last days with Elisheva. She'll have Slavos' company if she needs it. My housekeeper will take care of our needs, and she will be able to devote herself entirely to me. We will live together in the new house in Phaleron or Glyfada, on the rocky shores where white seagulls and blue-backed kingfishers swoop down to fish. In the morning I shall watch from the window as she goes barefoot to the beach to gather seaweed and shells and swim in the cold waves. I believe that it will not be too onerous for her. On fine days I shall ask her to take me out for a walk and we shall speak about our friends and lovers; perhaps I shall ask a few questions, perhaps she will be able to provide a few answers.

As the drug wears off, the bitterness and the pain slowly return. I ring the bell for my nurse, and she comes, a squat, starched woman dressed in white. The syringe is in her hand and she inserts the needle into my thigh.

The doorbell rings and the notary enters, white-faced. Slavos has been arrested. Ritsos has been exiled to Leros, a sick man who will die there. Soon it will be my turn, he says. They won't touch you. You don't count anymore.

I give him my will, but we need two witnesses. Never mind, I say, no one will contest it.

Slavos, my friend, is taken. . . .

What else shall I write about? About the time we spent in the beautiful towns of Italy, about my suffering country, about the hatred of brothers, about my longings for the country I left behind some years ago. About the fate of our poets, the cruelty of the colonels, about the days and nights I spent with my father in the mountains. About the sea? About the fact that things have to happen as they have to happen, thus and not otherwise.

Now everything is alien, remote, and far away, fragmented like the high, thin clouds of summer, and my days run out.

One of these days I shall go out when evening falls to sit in a tavern with Elisheva. I'll watch as the glass jar of the *espresso* machine empties a little more with each cup of coffee, as a man's life is used up and empties.

The café swarms with secrets, people coming and going, the lines of anger and sorrow written on their faces. They speak of simple things—the difficulties of bringing up children, of earning a living, and quarrels. . . . The *bazouki* player sings a lament about birds freezing on fences of iron and stone, about the snow falling in sad, distant towns. He sings about a fish caught in a net, with a pearl in his heart. He sings of dying slowly, and of the refusal to die. The window panes are steamy and the air is full of cigarette smoke. People's faces are flushed with the heat. Whenever the door opens a gust of stinging cold bursts into the room.

Like a fisherman I spread my net to catch a fish in whose heart was embedded a shining pearl. But now, as the tavern buzzes with meaningless chatter, I ask myself if this simple human coin is not itself that pearl. . . . This, and the scent of anise, and the gleaming black Kalamata olives, and the clouds of tobacco smoke, and the aromatic spices. And, I see, past the warm steam that hangs in the air, blue veins twining in transparent skin, pale thighs, gleaming breasts, black eyes that gaze at me from the spell-binding, lunar radiance of a beloved face.

The rain falls with a sound as monotonous as the ticking of a clock. I feel better now, and I make myself more comfortable in my chair. Not far from here, at the bottom of the hill, the wind and sea assault the rocks. In the night, a seagull's flight leaves no shadow on the water.

As the poet, Elytis, said:

> *I have brought my life this far*
> *White summation, black total*
> *A few trees and a few*
> *Wet pebbles*
> *Light fingers to caress a forehead*
> *What forehead*
> *Anticipations wept all night and are no more*
> *There is no one*
> *That a free footstep might be heard*
> *That a voice may dawn refreshed . . .*
> *I have brought my life this far*
> *Bitter gash in the sand that will vanish . . . .*

EPILOGUE

LICHT

My work on the task imposed on me by Miss Green lasted a number of months, during the course of which certain changes took place in me. When I began, I was on the brink of despair, and saw in this labor a possibility of rehabilitation. At the start, the distress and suffering of the protagonists evoked in me a profound sympathy. Now that I am done, this pain, which I believed would never diminish, has grown less acute: the wound has become a scar. I can begin to contemplate taking up my life again, throwing myself once more into the fray.

I confess that the people whose stories are unfolded here now inspire in me no more than a mild repugnance. What puts me off most is the excess of emotion. And now I find it hard to understand how I could have been seduced by their fantasies of love.

I'm prepared to forgive Elisheva. A woman is a woman, after all, and woolly thinking, sentimentality, and irrational behavior are to be expected of the "fairer sex." But I cannot extend the same tolerance towards Yanis. He repels me. What a superfluity of "love"! What exaggeration! I don't understand it, and I don't want to understand it. I absolutely reject this inflated emotionality. In my opinion, it's nothing but a fiction, the exaggeration of a feverish brain.

The further I proceeded with the work, the more it bored me. If at the beginning I was tempted by the idea of meeting Elisheva

199

again; further reading of what she wrote soon cured me of any such desire, and I now feel quite indifferent to her fate.

Nevertheless, I fulfilled my task, although sometimes I felt like throwing the whole lot into the rubbish bin and saying, let them go to hell, let them stew in their own juice, what have I to do with them? And, indeed, what have I to do with them? But I fulfilled my promise despite, and perhaps because of, the fact that it cost me an effort to do so. It wasn't a promise, really, but a sense of obligation, a feeling of responsibility because Elisheva had borne our child. And now that the work is finished, I feel a profound relief.

Dealing with Yanis' unfinished little book caused me real distress. His interests were foreign to me, his talk of love made no sense to me; I was alienated by his romanticism. How could a twentieth-century man, a scientist, indulge in such stuff? I grew thoroughly sick of Yanis and his inflated and bombastic prose. In short, I had to mobilize all my resources to cope with this part of the book.

Yanis' renunciation and his passivity are beyond my comprehension. It seems to me that if I had ever loved a woman like that, I would have struggled desperately to win her. On the other hand, when I try to be objective, I ask myself if this renunciation is not in some way inherent in the man's character. In other words: Yanis was violently deprived of the most significant love in his life, the love for his father and mother, and his feelings for his uncle in Jaffa could certainly not have provided a substitute. As he saw it, his father was a model of manliness and heroism, whereas his uncle was nothing but a wretched bourgeois coward. As for the love of a mother, that is something for which there is no substitute, and a person deprived may be condemned to fail in all his future loves. So it may be that he was foredoomed to love a woman with whom he would never be able to consummate his love.

I have made an effort to understand what, exactly, he saw in Henrietta. When all is said and done, she was quite a simple girl; good-looking, but not particularly attractive, for her beauty was cold. She had intelligence, but basically she was uninteresting. I, at any rate, did not discover any great depths in her, and our brief flirtation stemmed, essentially, from mutual boredom. In other words, it was a trivial affair, embarked upon for no better reason than convenience, propinquity. That's how I saw it, anyway.

Of all of them, the one I like best is Alexander, and I understand perfectly why Henrietta was attracted to him. Eccentric, certainly. But a man of rare originality. I would say, a fascinating man.

To return to the matter of love. . . . This is something that I know about from books, and it seems to me that books are the best place for it. Life doesn't need it. If all it offers is crumbs of happiness along with great suffering, then it's superfluous. And besides, when all is said and done, the problems of little people and their loves are not particularly interesting.

I'm relieved to have concluded this project at last, but at the same time I would not like anyone to think that I am ungrateful. I am certainly grateful to Elisheva for providing me with something to do in a difficult period of my life. Working on this book rehabilitated me, as I said to my friend I.A., and I only regret that my initial enthusiasm didn't last long. Besides, I must admit that I derived a certain additional benefit from the work. And I learned from it something of the utmost importance about myself and about people in general. I realized, beyond the shadow of a doubt, that the most important thing as far as I am concerned is clarity of thought, detached from the confusion of emotions.

Let me put it like this: there are some people, like Yanis, and I imagine that they are the majority, who are unable to apply logic to their feelings. When he was under the influence of his emotions, his intelligence was suspended. In my opinion this is deplorable. It seems to me that a true scientist is able to bring his powers of analysis to bear on every situation. This applies to Alexander, too, of course. (Naturally, I have no such expectations of Elisheva, since she is wholly ruled by her emotions.) I hope that I fall into the category of people whose emotions are ruled by reason. It seems to me that people of this kind realize themselves more fully.

Another thing I would like to draw attention to here is the great difficulty I encountered in the construction of this book. From the outset I was confronted by the question of how to construct a rational edifice from these fragments. I believe that I did quite well under the circumstances. At any rate, nobody can accuse me of lack of effort.

Tomorrow I'll give the manuscript to I.A. to see what he makes of it. One thing that bothers me a little is that, at first, I intruded myself and my thoughts into this book. It happened that, at the beginning, I felt a certain need for confession, perhaps for self-examination. During the course of time, however, this need left me. Quite soon, I felt a stubborn resistance to soul-searching overtake me. At that point, a number of ideas, subjects for large-scale, really serious studies presented themselves to me. To be obliged to postpone all that for the sake of this book, filled me with impatience.

As I have said, I regarded my undertaking of this project as the payment of debt. There are five projects waiting for me and I'm impatient to get started on them. For example, there's the question of narcissism as it relates to Orpheus' descent to the underworld. An absolutely fascinating subject. And then I intend to explore the influence of existentialism on contemporary art. I have more ideas than I can handle, all of which fill me with enthusiasm. As I labored on this onerous task, I came almost to hate Elisheva for imposing it on me.

Fortunately for her, at about the time I was ready to give up on it, I.A. returned from Columbia University and persuaded me to finish the work on the book. I value his judgment, so I took his advice. I.A. regards my specialty, art history, as inferior to his, which is philosophy; he has never regarded my work very highly. It was precisely for this reason that I decided to show him that I could complete this task successfully.

Shortly after I received the letter and parcel from Elisheva, I traveled to Tel Aviv in order to meet Alexander. I had no intention of telling him what I was doing, but I wanted to see what really he was like. I frequented the *Kassit* café for days on end, until one evening he showed up. He's a tall, lanky man with straight, black hair, and I immediately recognized the peculiar toss of the head which Elisheva described so well, and from the first I had no doubt that he was the man I was looking for. But when I looked into his eyes, I suddenly lost my courage and decided not to immediately engage him in conversation, as I had planned. I thought, I'll wait, I'll follow him. I want to see what he does, whom he meets.

He sat there alone for a while, drinking Coca-Cola. Soon a woman joined him, Carmela perhaps, who was rather attractive, provocative. I experienced a sudden impulse to try to pick her up. There was something fitting, if sinister, in my making such a move, a sort of closing of the circle of destiny that bound the persons of this book, as Elisheva saw it, with myself. But, although they may believe in this king of inevitability and fatal connection, I do not. Some behavior patterns may be predestined by our early experience; the rest is chance.

Anyway, the woman didn't really attract me. On looking at her more closely, I saw an aging spinster in heat, arch and ingratiating. How could Elisheva, who was so delicate and shy, so reserved, have chosen her for a friend?

When Alexander, or the man I thought was Alexander, left, I followed him. He turned in the direction of the sea: Gordon Street, Ben-Yehuda Street, Yarkon Street. . . . I went on following his leisurely progress for a long time. Then, at the entrance to Independence Park he stopped as if waiting for someone. I concealed myself in the shade of a fence across the road, waiting too. At last I began to feel uneasy, even, for some reason, afraid. . . . As I stood there, undecided whether to stay or go, a youth, almost a boy, approached the man of whose identity I was no longer sure. After they had exchanged a few words, they walked into the park together. Should I follow? I was paralyzed by uncertainty. Maybe the man was not Alexander, after all. And this doubt as to one man's identity seemed to open the floodgate to all my dormant doubts about the whole matter. In the whole story, what's true and what's false, I asked myself. Maybe Elisheva invented it all: her love for me, Yanis' love for Henrietta, Alexander's madness, Henrietta's death. . . . Maybe it was all—all of it—no more than a figment of her disordered imagination. . . .

Suddenly a memory assailed me: Elisheva on the mountaintop, at the edge of the young forest, in a white summer dress, her fair curls swept by the mountain wind, soundless tears streaming down her flushed cheeks. And for a moment, no more, my heart was torn by terrible longings. But only for a second; and then the image vanished. In vain I tried to hang onto it, to bring it back, to feel once more the tenderness of her young woman's love.

And then I said to myself, No, this man is not Alexander. What would I have asked of him anyway? Alexander had interested me because I coveted his brilliance, but such a thing is not transferable, it can't be had for the asking. So what was I doing, lurking in these shadows, making myself ridiculous?

I am a man lacking in polish, detestably coarse, like my father, my brother. But maybe that's not true, and, anyway, I don't want to think about it, about what I am or am not. The one thing of importance is my work and what I hope to achieve by it. And no meeting with Alexander could contribute to this aim.

And so I turned away. In Ben-Yehuda Street I took a number four bus to the Central Bus Station, and from there I caught another bus home.

In any case, I'm glad that I was able to finish this exhausting task. I can say to myself with confidence, Licht, you're a responsible human being—and get on with my real work at last. First thing tomorrow morning, I'll begin my research on *Narcissus and Orpheus's Descent to the Underworld*, determined that with this work I will make my mark on the world.

About the Author

Ruth Almog, born in Petah Tikva, Israel, to an Orthodox family of German descent, has taught literature and philosophy and is the author of novels, short stories, and children's books. Since 1967 she has been a regular contributor to the literary section of *Ha'aretz,* Israel's leading newspaper. She has won prizes for her children's literature and was also awarded the Brenner Prize for her novel *Roots of Light.*

THE RED CRANE LITERATURE SERIES

Dancing to Pay the Light Bill:
Essays on New Mexico and the Southwest by Jim Sagel

Death in the Rain, a novel by Ruth Almog

The Death of Bernadette Lefthand, a novel by Ron Querry

Stay Awhile: A New Mexico Sojourn, essays by Toby Smith

This Dancing Ground of Sky: The Selected Poetry of
Peggy Pond Church by Peggy Pond Church

Working in the Dark: Reflections of a Poet of the Barrio,
writings by Jimmy Santiago Baca